# Praise for The Masked Owl

"Extraordinary...Once again, the authors color-fully integrate authentic archaeological and anthropological details with a captivating story replete with romance, intrigue, mayhem, and a nail-biting climax."

— Library Journal

"It is fascinating to see how much like us these early tribesmen, and that the more things change, the more they stay the same."

— Romantic Times

I0564441

# The Masked Owl

# Also by W. Michael Gear and Kathleen O'Neal Gear

*Big Horn Legacy*

*Dark Inheritance*

*The Foundation*

*Fracture Event*

*Long Ride Home*

*The Mourning War*

*Raising Abel*

*Rebel Hearts Anthology*

*Sand in the Wind*

*Thin Moon and Cold Mist*


Black Falcon Nation Series

Flight of the Hawk Series

The Moundville Duology

Saga of a Mountain Sage Series

The Wyoming Chronicles

The Anasazi Mysteries

The Peacemaker's Tales

# The Masked Owl

## The Earliest Americans
### Book 2

**W. Michael Gear**

**Kathleen O'Neal Gear**

WOLFPACK
PUBLISHING
— EST 2013 —

*With special thanks to the Chamberlin Inn in Cody, Wyoming, for providing us a refuge every time we need a quiet, beautiful place to discuss the plot and characters of our next literary project.*

# Acknowledgments

This book was inspired by Dennis Labatt during our visits to the Poverty Point site. Every North American archaeological site should have such a dedicated and enthusiastic supervisor. We would like to thank Robert Connolly, Lisa Wright, Linda York, and Kay Corley for their assistance during our visits and for their cooperation in providing Poverty Point Objects—cooking clays —for our ongoing research in prehistoric starch, phytolith, and pollen analysis at Poverty Point.

We would especially like to acknowledge the work of Dr. Jon L. Gibson, who has dedicated so much of his life to the interpretation of Poverty Point's archaeology.

Once more, we would like to thank our longtime friend and colleague, Dr. Linda Scott Cummings, for her endless enthusiasm and pioneering ethnobotanical research. Working with us, she has recovered the first starches, pollens, and phytoliths from Poverty Point cooking clays. Now, when we say they were cooking foods like yellow lotus and little barley in the earth ovens, we can prove it. Thanks, Linda.

# Nonfiction Foreword

Ask any American to name the oldest city in the United States and he might tell you St. Augustine, Florida (A. D. 1565). Among an enlightened few, the name Old Oraibi (A. D. 1240), in the Hopi Mesas, might pop up. But, with apologies to both of these places, we wish to point out that North America's oldest city was not located in Florida—or even in the Southwest—nor was it built around St. Louis, or in the fertile valleys of Ohio. Rather, to find it, you must journey to north-eastern Louisiana, just outside of the small town of Epps. There, under the superb management of the state of Louisiana, you can still walk the stunning earthworks of Poverty Point, North America's first true city.

While earthen mound construction begins over six thousand years ago in North America, Poverty Point was inhabited between 3,750 and 3,350 years before present. From radiocarbon dates, most of Poverty Point's incredible earthworks were created during the last century of occupation. At its height, a permanent population of several thousand people lived on Poverty

Point's curving ridges. They traded for goods as far north as Wisconsin and Ohio. Materials were imported to Poverty Point across nearly fifteen hundred miles of Archaic wilderness.

The site itself is huge. From Lower Jackson Mound on the south to Motley Mound on the north is a little over five miles. The main earthworks cover more than four hundred acres and may contain as much as *one million cubic yards* of earth that was dug out of the ground and packed on human backs to build this leviathan. In sheer size, it would remain unmatched for another fifteen hundred years.

We agree with Jon Gibson that Poverty Point is a grand-scale projection of the human mind onto the landscape. Its form was not accidental or random, but a reflection of a shared vision of their physical as well as spiritual world, their kinship systems, and creation mythology.

A note on kinship: Non-Western societies organize their social structure in many different ways. What we see reflected in Poverty Point's architecture suggests two moieties, or social divisions, that contain three clans each. We have utilized a matrilineal matrilocal kinship system since that was present throughout the south.

Our reconstruction of prehistoric cosmology in *People of the Owl* must remain tentative, but we have looked for constants in South and Central Eastern Woodland mythology and oral tradition. We discarded elements that reflect later Mississippian—*People of the River*—agricultural traits. What is left is a shared tripartite belief in the surface of the earth, the sky above, and the underworld.

We have used real places as a setting for the story.

Poverty Point is Sun Town. The Panther's Bones is set at the Caney Mounds (site 16CT5) in Catahoula County. When Saw Back is exiled, it is to the Jaketown site in Mississippi. Twin Circles references the Clairborae Site near the mouth of the Pearl River in southern Mississippi. While we did not extensively explore distant Poverty Point settlements in *People of the Owl,* sites containing Poverty Point's distinctive artifacts have been found as far away as the Florida Gulf Coast.

So, what explains this spectacular thirty-five-hundred-year-old cultural fluorescence? These people were hunter-gatherers. Intensive corn agriculture wouldn't catch on for another two thousand years. The answer seems to lie in the richness of the Lower Mississippi Valley and its yearly floods. The people at Poverty Point ate everything that walked, crawled, swam, burrowed, and grew in their benevolent food-rich environment. In short, the Lower Mississippi Valley provided the surplus in resources that allowed remarkable cultural achievements.

In the coming years, we hope to learn a great deal more. As of this writing, one-half of one percent of the site has been excavated. In our own research with Linda Scott Cummings on Poverty Point Objects—PPOs—or cooking clays, we have recovered the first starches, phytoliths, and pollen residue from the food they cooked in their earth ovens thirty-five hundred years ago. As more research is tackled, our view of this complex site is going to change substantially. It will be important research. We believe that Poverty Point was to North America what the Fertile Crescent was to Europe: *the place that generated and disseminated cultural concepts that would influence subsequent cultures across the eastern woodlands.*

Information on the site is as close as your computer: povertypoint@crt.la.us. Jon Gibson's excellent read, *The Ancient Mounds of Poverty Point,* is available from the University Press of Florida. For an overview of the whole of North American archaeology, we recommend Brian Fagan's *Ancient North America* published by Thames and Hudson. At the end of *People of the Owl* you will find a selected bibliography. Finally, we urge you to visit the Poverty Point State Commemorative Area in person. Until you experience the wonder of it yourself, you will never fully understand the magic.

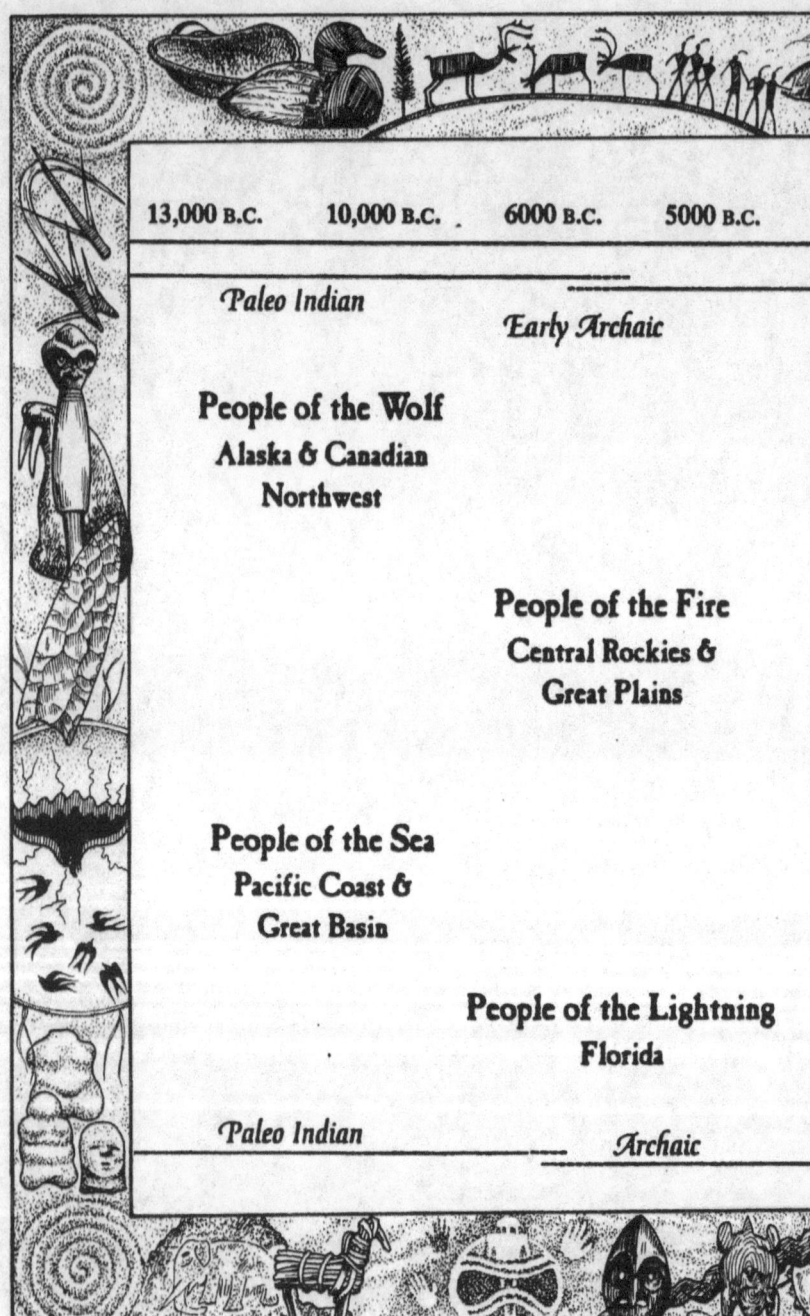

| 13,000 B.C. | 10,000 B.C. | 6000 B.C. | 5000 B.C. |

Paleo Indian

Early Archaic

**People of the Wolf**
Alaska & Canadian
Northwest

**People of the Fire**
Central Rockies &
Great Plains

**People of the Sea**
Pacific Coast &
Great Basin

**People of the Lightning**
Florida

Paleo Indian

Archaic

| 0 B.C. | 1500 B.C. | 100 A.D. | 800 A.D. | 1000 A.D. | 1300 A.D. |
|--------|-----------|----------|----------|-----------|-----------|

*Archaic*    *Woodland*         *Mississippian*

**People of the Earth**
Northern Plains
& Basins

**People of the Mist**
Chesapeake Bay

**People of the River**
Mississippi Valley

**People of the Masks**
Ontario &
Upstate New York

**People of the Lakes**
East Central Woodlands
& Great Lakes

**People of the Owl**
Lower Mississippi
Valley

**People of the Silence**
Southwest Anasazi

*Basketmaker*     *Pueblo*

S

W

E

NORTH

to Ground Cherry Camp

Dying Sun Mound

Raised Causeway

Rattlesnake Clan

Eagle Clan

Snapping Turtle Clan

Southern Moiety

Pine Drops House

Men's House

Morning Lake

Turtle's Back

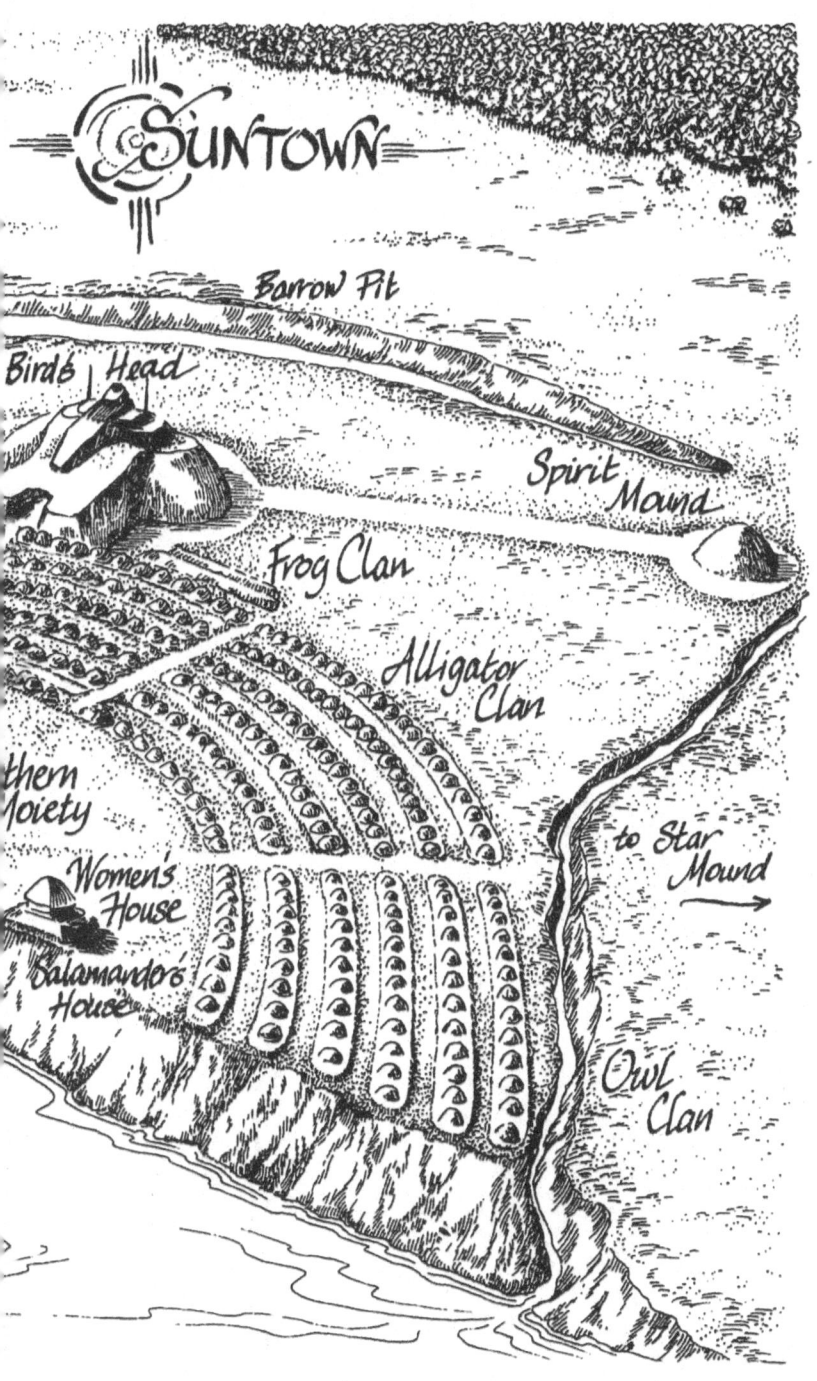

SUNTOWN

Barrow Pit

Birds Head

Spirit Mound

Frog Clan

Alligator Clan

thern Moiety

to Star Mound

Women's House

Salamander's House

Owl Clan

# The Masked Owl

The Masked Owl

# Chapter One

P ine Drop lay on her side, the hard pole of the bed frame under her hips. She could feel the heat from White Bird's body. Her own skin remained damp from the joining that had consummated their marriage. Careful not to wake him, she eased off the bed, squatted, and wiped herself with a handful of dried hanging moss.

She turned, studying the face of her new husband in the half-light cast through the doorway. The stranger slept on her bedding, his muscular left leg raised and braced against the mud-daubed wall. The right arm lay beside him, his left across his damp chest. His lungs filled and emptied with a slow regularity, and the dancing of his eyes under smooth lids reflected obscured dreams.

*How could this have happened?* She ran a calloused hand down her face, then glanced at Night Rain, where she, too, dozed on the bed adjoining Pine Drop's. Her sister rested on her back, her young breasts flat, a length of cloth covering her hips. She couldn't be sure if Night Rain slept, or just had feigned it during the time Pine Drop had been coupling with White Bird.

White Bird? Her husband? Who was this man? Two days ago she had been a young widow, heartbroken, her souls aching with grief. Today she was married —she and her sister. Together. It might have been a tornado that had uprooted her life.

Just now she had lain with a stranger. In defense she had closed her eyes when he mounted her, wrapped herself in the past, filled her imagination with Blue Feather. In her fantasy, it was Blue Feather who moved inside her. It was Blue Feather who brought her to ecstasy. As waves of pleasure rolled through her hips, she had tightened her arms around him—not this strange new man.

Time seemed to ebb and flow like stretched cattail dough in Pine Drop's memory. Through the whirl of events, she had glimpses: Blue Feather's body, hot and bright with fever, his eyes, racked by pain, losing focus as she held his hand. In those last moments, he'd gasped for shallow breaths and his souls loosened for the last time. Had it been she who had set fire to the house she had shared for those few moons with Blue Feather? Had it been right on this very spot that she had burned their dwelling down to a ring of charred cinders? She glanced at the tamped ash-laden soil before the doorway. Blue Feather's bones had been there, a tied bundle of them stacked atop a pile of white ash, oak, and hickory wood. He had been of the Alligator Clan. Members of his lineage had come afterward, picking through the bits of charcoal and ash to retrieve the broken and spalled slivers of fire-whitened bone.

*Now I am married again. To a man of the Owl Clan, of all things.* The hollow ache in her loins for Blue Feather had barely subsided. How could Mud Stalker and Back Scratch think this stranger could fill that place she had shared with Blue Feather?

"Is he asleep?" Night Rain whispered cautiously.

"Yes." Pine Drop glanced at her sister, seeing one eye peering at her.

"Snakes! Is that what it was all about?" She lowered her arm and swung into a sitting position. "Not like I imagined." She glanced down, her hair falling around her in a tangled black mass. "Not like it sounded when he lay with you."

"I wasn't with him," Pine Drop mouthed words, glancing uneasily at the sleeping man. At the question in her sister's eyes, Pine Drop soundlessly said, "Blue Feather."

"Oh," Night Rain mouthed in return.

Pine Drop reached for her kirtle and gestured. Night Rain dressed silently and followed as Pine Drop ducked out the door. The house was new, built on the ruins of her old structure. It had been on this spot that Blue Feather's dead body had been processed before the ritual cleansing. Now nothing remained of him except his Dream Soul. Had it been prowling around the house, watching this new man as he slid his manhood into her? Had Blue Feather known that she was dreaming of him, that she had willed White Bird's hard member to be his?

Night Rain turned her young face up toward the cloudy sky. A faint misty rain was falling. It speckled the young woman's hair in silver drops. "Remember how we used to talk when we were little? How we

3

swore that one day we would have a household together, that we would marry the same great warrior? That we would live on that way forever? Now, here it is, and it's not like I ever thought it would be."

"No."

"Will I ever enjoy coupling with a man?"

"Perhaps, with time." Pine Drop reached out and placed an arm around her sister's shoulder. "Did he hurt you?"

"No." Pine Drop felt Night Rain's shrug. "It just wasn't what I thought, that's all. I expected lightning, and joy, and some great experience like riding on clouds."

"And instead?"

"It was uncomfortable. He's..."

"Big."

"Yes." She glanced sideways at Pine Drop. "I thought it would feel more like a finger."

"I'm sorry."

Night Rain shrugged. "Do you think I'm going to get pregnant?"

"Eventually."

"You didn't. I mean with Blue Feather. And you were married for almost six moons before..."

"Yes, well, sometimes it doesn't happen right off in first moons you spend as a woman." She tried to keep the regret out of her voice.

"We have done our duty to our lineage and to our clan." Night Rain smiled sadly. "We are the grand-daughters of the Clan Elder. That is all that matters."

How could she say it with such simple faith? "That doesn't mean that we must like it. What has possessed the Elder and the Speaker? We have always been adversaries of Owl Clan, especially that haughty Wing Heart. She acts so superior to everyone else. Did I ever tell you about the time she kicked me out of her path? I was little then, maybe four winters old. She treated me like dirt."

"Now we are married to her son." Night Rain's eyes were on the long lines of houses that surrounded them. Cattails were waving green fronds above the dark water in the borrow ditches that separated the house ridges. "I wanted to marry Saw Back, of the Alligator Clan."

"Well, you had better forget him—and hope that White Bird remains alive," Pine Drop cautioned. "At least he is a Speaker, young though he is. He has war honors that will transfer to our children and clan. He has prestige and status, and from the looks of things, it will only grow greater."

"That is supposed to reassure us?" Night Rain asked hollowly.

"Yes, because the alternative is that if anything happens to White Bird, we go to that witless Mud Puppy! Think about that the next time our husband crawls on top of you and parts your legs."

Night Rain chewed her lip thoughtfully. "What could Grandmother have been thinking? I don't understand this new alliance with Owl Clan. It makes no sense."

Pine Drop sighed, looked furtively back at the doorway to make sure that White Bird hadn't awakened, and whispered, "We are to learn what we can about Wing Heart and help our clan gain ascendancy, silly gosling! The Speaker didn't talk the Elder into marrying us to White Bird to make us happy. We are here to serve the clan, and that, Little Sister, is what we will do."

Night Rain nodded. "I understand, Sister. When it comes to the clan I will do my duty."

# The Serpent

*My old teacher once told me,*
*When you are running, just run.*
*When you are walking, just walk.*
*When you are standing, just stand.*
*But never ever wobble.*
*That's when the Sky Beings see you.*

Thick patches of black cloud came sliding up from the gulf, accompanied by low rolling thunder. The moon after equinox was a time for storms. Wing Heart glanced up at rain-swollen heavens as she wondered whether to take down her loom and move it, and the half-finished fabric, into the shelter of her house. Faint teasings of a southerly breeze toyed with her hair and the fine strands of glossy hemp that she played through the warp, knotting the strands on certain threads to create a pattern before pressing it tight with her fine-toothed deer-scapula comb.

As she glanced up at the sky again, she noticed White Bird coming across the plaza, his sack of goosefoot *seeds hanging from one hand, a use-hardened digging stick from the other. Hazel Fire stepped out from the Men's House, crossing to intercept him. Across the distance she could see the two men wave in greeting, Hazel Fire breaking into a trot to catch his friend.*

*A satisfied smile crossed Wing Heart's lips. Her son was married, fresh from his first night in his wives' house. He was the talk of Sun Town, the culmination of years of her hopes and ambitions. His name was on everyone's lips—which meant her name was close behind, followed, of course, by that of Owl Clan.*

*Wing Heart filled her lungs, her breast fit to burst with an ecstasy she could scarcely contain. Had it been but two weeks past that she had been wallowing in misery, sure that her noble son was dead, and her only heir was the simple Mud Puppy?*

*"Hello, Wing Heart," Moccasin Leaf greeted as she stepped around the house wall. She carried a wicker basket in which lay several bass, their mouths gaping, dead eyes staring up at the dark clouds as though in last hope for water.*

*"Moccasin Leaf." Wing Heart nodded. "Good day to you."*

*Gray-haired Moccasin Leaf had lived nearly four tens of winters. She had a wrinkled round face with a jaw that sucked up squat against her nose, the teeth being long gone. Aged and frail, her dark eyes had lost none of the quick wit that had so long bedeviled Wing Heart and her lineage. The old woman wore a light brown kirtle today, the shape of an owl woven into the material. She lowered herself, grunting, and placed the wicker basket with the fish on the ground beside Wing Heart.*

"I have come to make amends." Moccasin Leaf worked her wide shallow mouth and placed her hands on her withered thighs. "You were right, I was wrong. White Bird has returned, and in the space of days, proven his worth not only to the clan, but to the moiety and our people. No one has been voted into the Council at such a young age. He will be twice the man his uncle was." She paused, looking out to where White Bird had stopped a dart's cast to the south. He and Hazel Fire were involved in some sort of passionate discussion.

"I was just lucky," Wing Heart conceded. "It could very easily have gone the other way. He might have been killed upriver." She paused. "Had he been, I would have declared Half Thorn to be the Speaker."

"As well he should have been," Moccasin Leaf muttered, her eyes on White Bird as he gestured a passionate negation in his conversation with the Wolf Trader. "No matter, the good of the clan has been served. I just came by to tell you that I will support you, and your son. So will the rest of my lineage."

"Half Thorn bears no ill will?"

Moccasin Leaf snorted through her short nose. "What do you think? Leadership of the clan has rested in your lineage for three generations. You have only sons for heirs, and one was missing while the other...well...Half Thorn was already addressing the Council in his dreams. People in the other lineages had begun to accord him a greater authority. Now that is gone. Of course he is upset, but it will pass." She gave Wing Heart a sharp look. "It would help if he were consulted on certain matters important to the clan. Especially given the youth of the current Speaker."

The old woman left the hint dangling like bait. Wing

*Heart considered. On the one hand, she had the authority and prestige right now simply to squash her old rival the same way she would a carrion beetle. Perhaps, in another time, she would have. Something stayed her. Am I grown maudlin? Softened by Cloud Heron's death? Or simply careless in the afterglow of victory?*

"Very well, Moccasin Leaf, I accept your offer of support. The Speaker and I shall be calling on Half Thorn. We look forward to sharing his knowledge and expertise." *As if he had any.*

She smiled at Moccasin Leaf the way a sister would at the resolution of a petty argument. It was a small price to pay for clan unity. What she and White Bird would spend in time and irritation for the short term would be countered by increased goodwill and the long-term ability to expose Half Thorn for the fool that he was. The man had been too long a fisherman and hunter in the swamp. He had no idea about the complexities of inter-clan politics or the layers of deception that leaders like Stone Talon, Mud Stalker, and Deep Hunter resorted to. Half Thorn took everyone at their word, thinking in his naivety that they said what they meant and meant what they said. The idea that a circuitously implied promise might be easily ignored or offered deceitfully had never found even a casual resting place in the man's souls. Even Mud Puppy was smarter than that, or at least, she hoped so.

"Very good." Moccasin Leaf sighed, slapping her thin thighs. "Then we understand each other." She looked out at White Bird, who was gesturing with the digging stick, indicating the sack of goosefoot seeds he held. Resignation lay in the old woman's eyes. "You have a great Power in your lineage. It is as if your blood has *been blessed by the Sky Beings. To stand against you is to be like a forest in the path of a hurricane. In the end, only broken trunks and litter are left."*

Wing Heart waited long enough to be politic, then said, "I have given my life to the betterment of my clan. Under my lineage's leadership, Owl Clan has risen above the others. All people look to us. All of our lineages, not just mine." Thunder boomed across the sky, and the southern breeze stiffened. "If White Bird succeeds, we all succeed."

Moccasin Leaf tucked a strand of gray hair back where the wind had worried it loose. "Indeed. What you say is true. But know this, Elder: Some of us worry about the risks you take to maintain your prestige. It is said that Water Petal will take your place when you follow your brother to the Spirit World. And if she carries a female child, or bears one in the future, that your lineage will be assured the leadership onward forever."

"That is a matter for the future, Moccasin Leaf. In the time you talk about, neither you nor I will be in a position to influence who is Elder or Speaker. That is for our grandchildren and their grandchildren."

"True. But know this as well: Many are disturbed that in marrying White Bird to the Snapping Turtles you also committed Mud Puppy. You may indeed have found a new ally and blunted other clans' ambitions, but many within our clan think that including Mud Puppy in the bargain went too far."

She smiled. "Mud Stalker insisted. Understand, Moccasin Leaf, in all dealings with the clans, there is an element of risk. Just as you, coming here today, gambled that I, being in a position of strength, would accept your offer of support and fish"—she gestured at the drying bass—"*rather than turn you down cold. And it worked out to our mutual benefit. The Speaker and I will do our best to ensure your lineage's position while you support us.*" Lightning flashed across the sky, followed several seconds later by thunder.

Moccasin Leaf still watched White Bird. The Wolf Trader had turned, looking somewhat upset as he stalked off for the Men's House again. White Bird resumed his course toward the clan grounds, face rigid in anger, the sack of seeds clutched in his strong hand.

The old woman said, "So, what would Mud Stalker gain by placing Mud Puppy in line for the Speaker's position? Why would he insist upon that? He has to know that it would be the decision of Owl Clan to approve him as Speaker. Snapping Turtle Clan cannot tell us who our Speaker must be."

"Exactly. He and his allies are working on many levels," she said thoughtfully, fully aware of her own complicity in the deal. "He has always been a crafty one Moccasin Leaf, and finding himself beaten, he has done the best thing he could."

"Which is what? Hope that White Bird dies mysteriously and that he can place Mud Puppy on the Council to humiliate us?"

"That is how it is supposed to look on the surface, but as you and I both know, it wouldn't be the thing to gamble on. No, what appears to be an act of desperation is but the covering to conceal the fact that he is buying time. More than that, he has gained a great deal of prestige, moving to block Rattlesnake and Eagle Clans from strengthening their position with us. Our crafty Mud Stalker now has more room to maneuver, the ability to broker different deals with the clans depending on how the future plays out." She nodded, half to herself. "It was a smart move, daring and rapid, given the sudden turn of events. Our clans come out ahead, the others lose."

"Then he is a very dangerous man." Moccasin Leaf seemed to have forgotten their antagonistic relationship for the moment.

"Yes, very," Wing Heart agreed.

"What is he doing?" Moccasin Leaf indicated White Bird. The young man had stopped at the edge of the borrow ditch, laying his sack down before vigorously punching the digging stick into the damp brown soil. He used his chest, pressing down to drive the stick deep, and then levering the soil to break it.

"He has some idea about those goosefoot seeds. Have you seen them? Larger than the ones we collect around here. White Bird thinks that by growing them, we can tap the plant's Power. That these larger seeds will be produced here."

"Looks like a lot of hard work." Moccasin Leaf shook her head. "Why go to all that effort when the plants grow wild everywhere. For all the work he's going to have to put into it, he could just wait and collect the wild seeds with half the effort. And not only that, when you go around and collect the wild seeds, you find other things: turtles, rabbits, squash, hickory nuts. It looks like foolishness to me."

Wing Heart bit her lip, aware of the darkening clouds. Black stringers of rain could be seen where they whisked down from the closing storm bank in the south. "It may well be. He saw it work among the Wolf Traders to the north and wants to try it here, that's all. He just wishes to see."

"I had better get home," Moccasin Leaf mused, her eyes on the storm front with its flashing lightning.

"Would you help me move my loom inside first?" Wing Heart asked, standing.

The old woman took the other end of the loom. "That boy of yours, I should say, the Speaker, he's going to get wet planting all those seeds of his. From the look on his face, he's determined."

"That is what makes a good Speaker," Wing Heart agreed, casting a glance over her shoulder. White Bird's body bent and swayed as he continued driving the sharp stick into the dirt, breaking the grassy sod, turning the soil. The expression on his face hadn't changed, as if it were a matter of honor that he plant his seeds.

The notion that it was a little silly lodged in Wing Heart's souls, but then young people acted on whims on occasion, Snakes knew, she had as a young woman.

Together, she and Moccasin Leaf maneuvered the loom into the shelter of the house and propped it against the wall beside the doorway. In the shadow of the storm, the interior was dark, inky.

"Thank you for your help," Wing Heart began. A sudden white flash lit the interior, rendering the beds, pots, and fire pit in brilliant contrast to the sharp black shadows. A split heartbeat later, a bang! fit to deafen exploded outside. The closeness of the lightning bolt left Wing Heart breathless, half-scared out of her wits.

She glanced at Moccasin Leaf, seeing the old woman's shadowy form, panting, her hand to her heart. "Close one," she gasped.

"Good thing we weren't outside," Moccasin Leaf agreed. "It might have scared the souls out of our bodies."

Wing Heart led the way out into the open. The first

*large drops of rain came pattering down. She could see people ducking out of houses or peering out from under ramadas. They were owl-eyed, wary, postures half-crouched. Some stared, eyes locked, a look of horror on their faces.*

*Wing Heart turned, following their gazes. Her thoughts stumbled, unable to fathom what she was seeing. A faint blue streamer of smoke rose from the lump, rapidly tugged away by the gusty wind. The shape confused her for a moment. A human body didn't smoke like that—it shouldn't be lying so stiff and...and...her souls froze. She couldn't move, couldn't think. The word no echoed hollowly inside her as if she were but an infinite emptiness.*

*"Snakes take us," Moccasin Leaf whispered as she stared through the increasing rain at White Bird's smoldering body. The digging stick had splintered, and yellow flames flickered on the seed sack beside the body. The rain came in a pounding rush to extinguish it.*

# Chapter Two

The village called the Panther's Bones lay on a low, flat-topped terrace that rose above the surrounding backwater swamp. Six individual mounds, some of them three times a man's height, overlooked the swamp. The seventh, a single conical mound, guarded the western edge of the village, a lone sentinel against the Land of the Dead and the dangerous souls that hid beyond the horizon. A prominent rise guarded the north, the symbolic place of darkness and cold.

A strong man, skilled with the atlatl, could cast a dart from east to west. It would take him two long casts to span the distance between the Bird Mound at the southern edge of the site and the northern prominence. Within that area, several clans of the Swamp Panthers had built their homes: domelike structures with thatched roofs atop low wattle-and-daub walls.

Jaguar Hide's people lived in a land of plenty. The pine-covered uplands to the west provided them with stone for tools, as well as pinesap to be mixed with bear grease to keep hordes of stinging and biting insects at bay. At the foot of the piney hills lay Water Eagle Lake, a dependable body of water that refilled annually when the spring floods inundated the land. His people wanted for nothing, except, perhaps in bad years like this one, for a little dry land. Relatives had come seeking shelter among clansmen and kin, bringing with them larders of smoked catfish, oven-baked duck, seasoned deer, raccoon, and opossum. Housing was so critical that cane-framed lean-to shelters had been attached to house walls and quickly roofed with palmetto and grass fronds. Under the high bank, row upon row of canoes had been drawn up onto the mud. When they weren't fighting among themselves, or squealing in play, a roiling tribe of children and flea-infested dogs was pestering people, snatching morsels of food, and generally being a nuisance.

Jaguar Hide sat in front of his house and watched the last of the storm fading into the northern horizon. Sunlight slanted through the treetops, sparkling in wet leaves. Blue fingers of smoke rose from damp fires in the open, or through the gap between the rafter poles and supporting walls. He could smell fish broiling in the earth ovens. Two women were taking turns pounding cattail roots in a wooden mortar. The rhythmic *thump-thump* of the tall pestles might have been the heartbeat of the village.

He glanced at the dark doorway behind him when he heard his niece stir on the bedding within. How many times had he waited thus? How many times had one of his relatives or friends lain in misery as their bodies or souls struggled to recover from some wound inflicted by the Sun People?

He tried to remember any single turning of the seasons when his people hadn't been mourning some injury. One by one, a seemingly endless litany of faces passed through his souls' memory. So much pain, so much tragedy. All of his life he had tried to harm them, pay them back. His raids, the constant warfare, had done nothing. Sting them too hard, and they struck back, violently, their greater numbers blunting any advantage the Swamp Panthers had in their endless swamps.

*If only there was a way to really hurt them!*

He heard Anhinga as she flopped on her bed, then groaned. She might have been a grub the way she clung to the darkness inside the house.

"It's a beautiful evening. Why don't you come out and help me eat some of this fish? It is smoked and seasoned with freshly picked mint leaves."

No answer.

"Are you going to lie around in there like a mushroom? Just feeding on the dark?"

Still no answer.

He grunted to himself, knowing full well what her trouble was. His knees cracked as he rose and ducked through the small doorway into the dim interior. She lay on her side, knees up, arms tucked against her breasts. He could see the scabs on her smooth young flesh. Like the old man he was, he settled himself on the bed's pole frame and reached out to stroke her hair. "No one is blaming you, Anhinga. The other clans understand war. They understand that when young men go on raids, sometimes they don't come back."

Her body tensed under his touch, a suffering sound caught in her throat.

"If I could have just one wish, I would have you talk to me again." He gently patted her head. "I would have you tell me what you are carrying between your souls. I would not care what you said, if only you would talk again."

He lost count of his heartbeats as he carefully stroked her long black hair. He had washed it for her, and during the process, she hadn't said a word, enduring, expression vacant as if carved of wood. Her eyes had been fastened on something far away, some terrible memory.

She whispered hollowly, "I want to kill them, all of them. I will dedicate my life to it. I swear."

"Ah, you are set to lead another war party?"

"No," came the weak reply.

"How will you do this thing, then?"

"Go alone." She swallowed hard. "Just me. I'll hunt them one by one, find them alone out in the swamp and kill them until they kill me."

He grunted noncommittally. "Are you sure that you don't want to stay here, live with me, help to keep your silly brother from pitching us headfirst into lunacy?"

She turned then, staring at him for the first time with impassioned eyes. "They *killed* me, Uncle! Not my body. My souls. I am not the young woman you knew. I am someone, *something* else. When I close my eyes, I see them, ripping pieces out of my friends, slinging their intestines around in the air. I see them throw a human liver into the air to watch it spatter when it hits the ground. I watch them urinate into Mist Finger's eye sockets over and over and over again. Those things fill my souls. Knowing that, do you really think I can just step out of here, marry some young man, and be the woman I once was?"

He pursed his lips, allowing the sting in her words to chill his souls. "No, Niece. Of all people, I understand." He paused, waiting, knowing that she was watching him, trying to read his pensive expression.

"But you don't agree with me," she said bitterly.

"I agree with your goal, yes."

"But?"

"I don't think you will accomplish much." He cast her a sidelong look. An old, often discarded plan surfacing between his souls. *Is she the one? Could she do it?*

"Why is that, Uncle?"

"Because in the end you may kill one or two, maybe even three or four before they find you and kill you. It has been tried before. Your actions are those of a mosquito. You draw only a little blood before they swat you and go on about their business."

He could see the hardening in her eyes, the distrust mingled with suspicion that he knew something she didn't. "What other way is there?"

*If you tell her, if she accepts, you will be condemning her to death.* The memory of the endless faces came back to haunt him, as if all those long-dead eyes were watching, waiting. Hatred stirred like a serpent in his breast.

She was expecting him to try and talk her out of it, so his answer caught her by surprise. "I don't know if you are strong enough, dedicated enough. I have waited, planned, and hoped, but until now no one has impressed me with their dedication to our people. None of the other clans would have permitted it, not with the risk to their young woman."

"What risk?"

"The risk entailed in truly harming our enemy. Oh, I don't mean killing some stray fisherman, or some woman out digging for ground potatoes. I mean striking into the heart of one of their clans. Wounding their pride, soul, and spirit."

"How would this be done?"

*Is her life worth it? And even if she succeeds, will it make a difference in the end?* He ignored her, allowing an expression of satisfaction to change the lines in his face as he imagined the consternation among the Sun People.

"Uncle?"

He drew a breath, letting her stew, then asked, "What was the name of the one who captured you?"

"White Bird."

"Yes, of the Owl Clan. He has just been made Speaker. I've heard that that foul beast Mud Stalker has offered two of his clan's women in marriage. Indeed, quite a name the young White Bird is making for himself."

"How do you know that?" Anhinga was up on one elbow, watching him now, a dark gleam in her eyes.

"Traders passing along the White Mud River have talked to some of our people who were out casting nets. Word gets around, and White Bird, it seems, is the source of a great many words." He smiled happily. "Owl Clan. He is the son of Elder Wing Heart. Quite a woman, that one. A most worthy adversary."

"How would you strike her?"

"In a way she would never suspect. Through cunning, patience, and misdirection." Yes, she had taken the bait the way a catfish snapped up a minnow.

"What would I have to do?"

"The hardest thing that any hunter must do, wait. Bide your time while opportunities pass before you. You would have to control your hatred, bury it deep like a coal in an ash pit. You would have to accept the man you hate the most, smile into his eyes, open your body to him. But, most difficult of all, you must earn his trust." He slapped his hands on his thighs. "And, that, I fear, is beyond you. Injured though you are at this moment, I don't know if you have the true dedication of the souls to really harm this White Bird and his clan."

"Then you do not know me very well, Uncle." She flashed him a defiant glance, hands knotted. "I Dream of seeing him bent down, in tears, blood running from wounds I have dealt him."

"It's a nice Dream." He shrugged. "But if you succeeded, they would kill you—kill you in a most unpleasant way. For that reason, I can't let you do this."

"I am already dead."

"Yes, for the moment. But if you stay here, I think you will heal in the end. Perhaps even smile again."

She looked away. "You don't know the things I saw." She swallowed hard. "Souls don't recover from that."

"I know what you saw." He shrugged. "I just don't know if you really hate him enough to go through with it in the end."

Her hand fastened on his arm, bruising in its intensity. "They took *everything* from me," she hissed. "My brother, my friends, my future. They made me an exile among my own people. I *hate*, Uncle. Deep down between my souls, the burning is there. Upon my honor, upon my souls, I *hate* like no one you've ever known."

"So you hate? Even the weak can hate. In the end it eats them like a liver fluke. From the inside. And ever so slowly." A pause. "If you want to *hurt* them for what they did to you, it would take something more. Something I'm not sure you have within you."

"What?"

"Strength." He was watching her eyes, searching for any hint of dismay or fear when he said, "If you would truly hurt him, go back. Marry him, Anhinga. Be his wife, earn his trust. And then, when the time is right, you may kill him and his mother, too."

Not even a flicker of doubt reflected when she said, "I can do that."

"Are you sure? Do you understand what I'm asking? You must deceive a man you are living with day and night. You must trick him into believing that you love him. Have you any idea how difficult that is?"

She was smiling now, eyes fixed on the distance in her souls. "Uncle, I am strong enough to do this thing. He will never know until it is too late. On the souls of my dead friends, I swear it."

The thing that horrified Mud Puppy the most was his brother's head. The lightning bolt had split the skull, popping it open like the husk surrounding a chinquapin seed. Both of White Bird's eyes protruded, pushed out from inside. No amount of pressing could return them to the sockets so the corpse just stared in a gray-filmed, crab-eyed amazement. The Serpent had managed to wipe the white foam from his lips and press the tongue back in. He had wound the head tight with a length of cord to keep the gaping mouth shut. A seared streak ran from under the jaw, along the side of the throat, across the right chest and stomach to follow the inside of the thigh down through the heel.

White Bird lay on his back, arms thrust out, legs stiff as logs. A faint gurgling could be heard from inside his gut. The way the firelight from the central hearth flickered over the smooth and tight skin teased Mud Puppy's imagination. Unwilling to dwell on the horrifying corpse, Mud Puppy kept staring up at the sooty rafters, searching in vain for any sight of his brother's souls. They should be hovering up there, twirling around in the haze of smoke, watching, exploring what it meant to be freshly dead and talking with all the other relatives who had preceded him. Mud Puppy saw nothing in the haze that reminded him of White Bird's souls.

The Serpent rocked on his heels, chanting the familiar Death Song that reassured the Dead that they were still cherished members of the lineage and clan. In the rear, Wing Heart was racked in sobs. She lay on her bed, cramped on her side, prostrate in a way that Mud Puppy had never seen before. Water Petal sat beside her, holding one hand, her face streaked by tears. Outside, voices could be heard periodically as kinspeople, friends, and well-wishers dropped by to leave gifts of food, or express their shock and grief at the young Speaker's sudden death.

*It can't be true!* The words kept repeating in a Dream-like resonance inside Mud Puppy's head. But all he had to do was look at the body an arm's length from his nose, and there was the terrible reality. White Bird was dead. In one instant he was alive, levering soil from the ground, and in the next, his blasted body lay straight-limbed in death.

Mud Puppy swallowed hard. *I told him not to plant the seeds.*

He could sense the Serpent's wary hesitance to work on White Bird. Yes, Power lay all over the body like a glittering spiderweb, shimmering and bright one moment, invisible the next. It radiated like heat from glowing cooking clays.

His mother broke into another violent fit of sobbing, her body writhing on the bedding. Water Petal tried to soothe her, failing miserably.

"My son," his mother's voice rose in a reedy wail.

"Shshsh!" Water Petal smoothed Wing Heart's damp hair. "He's gone, Elder. It just happened. It's no one's fault."

But Mud Puppy knew that it was.

"He's all I had left!" the Elder moaned, her voice breaking as she choked. *"All...I had...left!"*

The wound in Mud Puppy's breast lay open and jagged. He had loved White Bird, had admired him as the most marvelous of big brothers. It was all right that his mother cried. He wished he could, too, but instead he just sat there, empty-gutted, unable to do more than stare at the ruined body in disbelief.

The Serpent turned, his eyes intent, knowing, as he

studied Mud Puppy. That look by itself was more frightening than death.

The unbidden voice inside said, *You are the Speaker now!*

The Serpent smiled absently, as if he, too, had heard.

# Chapter Three

The fire burned hot and yellow, Mud Stalker adding branches anytime it seemed to slow. It was extravagant to burn a fire this hot and large, but it was a night to celebrate. To Mud Stalker's right sat Red Finger, to his left, on the sleeping bench, Elder Back Scratch hunched, a shawl around her age-bowed shoulders. Young Pine Drop and her sister, Night Rain, sat across from him, their backs to the door as they glanced uneasily back and forth. They looked, and no doubt felt, out of place. Alas, given the status of their birth, the frail innocence of youth had been pulled back to reveal their future in clan leadership and responsibility.

"You are thinking you should be with your husband's body," Mud Stalker said as he fixed them one by one. "Well, he's over in Wing Heart's house. Let them care for him. I've taken the liberty of having White Bird's possessions sent there, with the offer that we will support whatever decision Wing Heart makes about the treatment and disposal of the body."

"Let her burn her house down." Red Finger jerked his head in a nod. "We just built the one Pine Drop and Night Rain are living in." He smiled. "And, it seems that we have to begin the search for new husbands. It isn't often that fortune casts as wide a net for us as it has this day."

"They have a husband lined up," Back Scratch said in her thin and reedy voice.

Red Finger stopped short, a puzzled look on his face. "Who? Surely you're not thinking..." He couldn't finish.

Mud Stalker suffered a moment of sadness as Pine Drop's eyes fastened on his. Yes, she understood.

She cried, "You don't really mean for us to marry that *boy?*"

"What?" Night Rain chimed in. "You mean *Mud Puppy!*"

"That was the arrangement," Mud Stalker replied firmly. "Though we couldn't have guessed the rapidity with which the event might befall us."

"Why?" Red Finger demanded. "Tell me, what is the point of following through with this mad plan? Right here are two young women, in line to be Clan Elder. We could use them to create obligation with Deep Hunter or Cane Frog? Snakes, if you don't want to go there, if it has to be someone in Owl Clan, marry them into Moccasin Leaf's lineage. That would really cut the ground out from under Wing Heart."

"And strengthen another lineage in Owl Clan in the process," Mud Stalker reminded. "You are making the assumption that the enemy we know is worse than the one we don't."

"Mud Puppy is still a boy!" Pine Drop insisted. "Not just a boy—a *peculiar* one at that!"

"Do I have to?" Night Rain asked in a timid voice.

Mud Stalker steepled his hands, glanced at Back Scratch, and nodded. "Nieces, there is more at stake here than either of you knows. For three generations we have watched Owl Clan's authority and prestige grow. Wing Heart and her brother made a formidable team. Given the way young White Bird was developing, it made a great deal of sense to marry the two of you to him. It gave us a way of controlling him, using his talent for our advantage."

"Name a single advantage we would gain by marrying my two cousins, here, to that idiot, Mud Puppy!" Red Finger snorted, his jaw cocked.

"Cousin," Back Scratch said from her place on the bed, "we want Mud Puppy to become the new Speaker. The one thing we can count on for the future is that Wing Heart will do anything to maintain her position on the Council. To do that, she must remain the Owl Clan Elder. If Moccasin Leaf is able to remove her, she has many heirs. It will be a smooth transition. Imagine, if you will, that Wing Heart remains the Elder, and with our help, is able to name this half-wit, Mud Puppy, as Speaker. Now, put the two of them in the Council, say in a debate with Deep Hunter about the redistribution of disputed resources?"

Red Finger made a face. "That boy would be ludicrous."

"Exactly." Mud Stalker ran gentle fingers over the ridges of scar tissue on his forearm. "You see, Wing Heart made a bargain. We intend to honor it."

"At the price of our freedom," Pine Drop muttered, looking away angrily.

Mud Stalker raised an eyebrow. "Oh, come now. He's just a boy."

"I would rather have a man," Pine Drop retorted.

"There are plenty available," Back Scratch said reasonably. "It doesn't matter where you father a child. It still elongs to the clan. Just be discreet for the first year or so. After Wing Heart and the Owl Clan are broken down to size, a divorce will be an easy thing to negotiate. Better yet, it will add to Owl Clan's disgrace."

Pine Drop considered that. Night Rain looked horrified.

"In ten years, Pine Drop, when you finally become Clan Elder," Mud Stalker added, "it will be as the most prestigious Elder in the Council. Not, as it is now, with us in second place."

Night Rain might have been unconvinced, but Pine Drop nodded, saying, "Very well, but you're going to have to run that brat through the Men's House first. I'll not be made a laughingstock by taking a boy into my bed."

"That can be arranged." Red Finger seemed to have seen the logic. "And, who knows?" He fixed his eyes on Pine Drop. "He is young, and not very bright."

"That is supposed to make me feel better?" Pine Drop asked hesitantly.

"I was just thinking." Red Finger's pensive look did little to relieve her. "Could you make him love you? Pine Drop, do you and Night Rain see where I'm going with this? If you could seduce his souls as well as his body, he could grow dependent upon you. He might be induced to rely on your advice in matters of clan politics. It would take finesse and dedication on your part, but little Mud Puppy might just be young enough and dumb enough to grow into a real asset for us."

Pine Drop sat lost in thought, her expression one of distaste. "In other words, you want me to find a way to use him against his own clan."

"He's young, impressionable. You are older than he is, smarter. Handled correctly, an inexperienced boy can be twisted like a length of twine."

"Treat him well in your bed," Mud Stalker suggested. "The rushing of his loins might be your greatest ally."

Night Rain's silent expression tightened. She continued to sit with her hands in her lap, looking glum.

Back Scratch growled. "What's the matter with you young women? What makes you think that lying with a man has anything to do with your own pleasure? I know that a lot of these young people slip off and couple just because they *like* each other. It's a waste, that's what. Breeding is meant to be done for the benefit of the clan, not just so that you can feel pleasure burn through your hips." She smacked her lips in disgust, adding, "The only reason the Sky Beings made it feel good was to compensate for its being a person's duty, that's all."

Mud Stalker's eyebrow cocked as he studied his mother, but he said nothing.

Red Finger, however, blurted, "What is this, Back Scratch? Have the seasons dulled and blunted your memories? Have you completely forgotten all the trouble you caused as a young girl when you slipped away for three moons, supposedly to go Trade with the

Ring Villages on the coast? Wasn't the man's name Black Legs?"

"Yes," Mud Stalker nodded, remembering. "Black Legs."

Back Scratch scowled at him. "You weren't even born then."

"No, but the stories persisted for years. I was only a boy, but I recall the opposition to naming you Clan Elder. People still recalled your transgressions, and how you returned pregnant with my older brother." He ignored his mother's hiss of irritation as he looked at Pine Drop and Night Rain. "The Elder may have forgotten what it is like to be young, with your body bursting with desire for a certain man. She is, however, correct with regard to your duty to our clan. You will marry Mud Puppy, and as Cousin Red Finger points out, you must win him to us." He smiled. "Your elders understand the difficulties. We hope that you will understand the advantages to both yourselves and the clan in making this happen." He glanced back and forth, trying to read behind the young women's dark eyes. "If you must find relief in some other man's bed, come to me, and I will arrange it so that no one grows suspicious."

Pine Drop lowered her eyes. "Yes, Uncle."

He nodded to Red Finger and Back Scratch. "Now that that's settled, I suppose I had best make myself presentable and go deliver our sympathy and support to Wing Heart." As he rose, he turned his attention to the young women once more. "Remember, we are counting on you. That boy is the key to the Snapping Turtle Clan's future. With him, we can break Wing Heart and Owl Clan once and for all."

The afternoon sun sent shining bars of light through gaps in the milky white clouds as they drifted out of the southwest. Moist air hung heavily on the land, barely stirred by a lazy breeze. Moccasin Leaf helped Elder Wing Heart as they tackled the task of preparing a funeral feast. They were in the work area between the burned-out ruins of Speaker Cloud Heron's house and the Elder's now-abandoned structure.

Moccasin Leaf couldn't make up her mind about Wing Heart. The Clan Elder hunched over a soapstone bowl filled with sticky dough while Moccasin Leaf used a stick to prod at a heating fire burning beside the empty earth oven.

*Her son is dead.* That would affect anyone. *Dead so quickly after her brother.* But did that explain the woman's complete listlessness?

Moccasin Leaf jabbed pointedly at the cooking clays as she carefully studied Wing Heart from under lowered brows. Wing Heart looked as if a great hollow gaped between her souls. She might have been a husk, her spirit flown away like cottonwood down in the breeze. She worked mechanically, as if to do anything else was too painful.

Dough clung to Wing Heart's fingers, white and sticky. She continued kneading the mixture of little barley, cattail root, dried squash, and smilax root. Earlier that day she had used the pestle and mortar—a fire-hollowed tree stump—to pound the ingredients into mush. The mashed roots had been transferred to the soapstone bowl she now bent over. Adding water and white shooting star blossoms for seasoning, she had reached the right consistency.

Wing Heart hadn't spoken a word all day. Moccasin Leaf shot a glance at the shadowed doorway. *Her son is dead.*

*His bones are just there, on a rick of dry wood. Is this the end of her lineage at last?*

Wing Heart's automatic hands formed the final shape of the root-bread loaf.

"Is it ready?" Moccasin Leaf kept her voice light.

Wing Heart stared with empty eyes. She might not have heard.

Moccasin Leaf used a forked stick to stir the cooking clays. The size of green-husked walnuts, they glowed a dull red among the gray-white coals. A combination of shapes had been placed in the shallow-basined heating fire: Some were biconical, others square and pocked by round indentations made with cane ends. By mixing shapes and sizes of cooking clays, the earth oven's temperature and cooking time could be regulated and tailored to the kind of food being cooked.

"These clays are plenty hot." Moccasin Leaf waited for a reply that did not come. "Wrap your dough, Wing Heart."

The Clan Elder lifted a loaf of dough and placed it in the middle of a large green catalpa leaf. This she curled into a roll before picking up the next and woodenly continuing the process. It was eerie to watch her work that way.

Moccasin Leaf scooped a third of the cooking clays into the curve of a broken ceramic pot before dumping them into the excavated pit of the earth oven. Wing Heart knelt to one side as she finished wrapping the dough. The vacancy in her eyes never wavered as she went through the motions.

The oven had been dug arm-deep into the ground and about the length of a forearm across. Moccasin Leaf quickly placed the rolled loaves side by side in the pit, jerking her hands back after each one. "Hot in there."

Wing Heart remained mute.

"Good." Moccasin Leaf was ready with another scoop of coals, which she deposited around the sides of the loaf, retreating as the heat came boiling out of the pit. She scooped the last of the clays onto the piece of broken pot and sifted them over the loaf. "Cover it."

Wing Heart laid a flat section of bark over the hole and sat back, a slight frown on her face.

"Elder, it is plain that your souls are aching. Can I help you?"

Of course it was hard on Wing Heart. This was the second such feast she had prepared for in the last five days. Nor did she risk so much as a glance at her gloom-shrouded house, where White Bird's body, or at least his bones, lay. The dull vacancy in the woman's face sent a shiver up Moccasin Leaf's spine.

"Elder, since I came here, you haven't spoken a word. It might help if you talked about it. Sometimes words can free the grief from where it is lodged between the souls."

That morning the Serpent and Bobcat—their faces streaked with charcoal—had come by with their sharp chert knives. White Bird's flesh had been cleanly removed from the bones and carted off in baskets. By now it had been carried outside the protection of the ridges and laid out at Owl Clan's little hollow in the forest. There, crows, feral dogs, and other carrion eaters would dispose of it. Only the bones remained in the house for White Bird's Dream Soul to watch over.

Wing Heart closed her eyes, and a faint smile graced her lips.

"Are you seeing him, Elder?" Moccasin Leaf asked. "White Bird is alive, his eyes sparkling and brown. I see him that way, too."

Wing Heart said nothing.

Moccasin Leaf shook her head. She deserved some sort of a response. "What are those Snapping Turtle women bringing?"

Wing Heart just stared absently at the ring of blackened ash where her brother's house had once stood. By tomorrow night, her house, too, would be nothing more than that. A second ring of ash. Tomorrow, witnessed by the entire town, she would raise her torch to that roof and incinerate her son.

*Then what, Wing Heart? Where does the clan go from there?* Did she dare broach the subject? Wing Heart was obviously wounded, her natural craftiness blunted by grief.

"We need to talk."

Silence.

"Despite your grief, someone must attend to the business of replacing the Speaker."

Wing Heart gave her a dull glare.

Moccasin Leaf's gaze slid away. "Half Thorn is ready to represent the clan. He has been preparing for the role of Speaker for years. But for Mud Puppy's coming initiation, he would be here, ready to discuss matters with you."

Wing Heart's eyes seemed to lose focus.

Moccasin Leaf stiffened. "Wing Heart, it is time

that you began to place the needs of the clan above your own."

The Clan Elder's lips twitched.

"I think you are hurting, the loss of your brother and son, along with worry about your youngest, has clouded your abilities. It is with this in mind that I have come to offer my services. Perhaps you should take some time for yourself, allow your souls to heal before you resume your duties. You need not face the coming trials alone. We are ready to..." At the glittering intensity that suddenly burned in the older woman's eyes, her words went dry.

Wing Heart drew herself up, back stiff, clearly ready to lash out.

"Do not fight me over this, Elder," Moccasin Leaf crossed her arms. "You and your lineage have dominated this clan for three generations. You have done well for us."

Wing Heart's lips moved, her voice little more than an unintelligible mumble,

"Those days are over. You have no heir."

Wing Heart's glazed eyes wavered as she said, "The Speaker will deal with you. The Speaker..." The rest trailed away into babble.

"Give it up!" Moccasin Leaf stepped forward. "Half Thorn is the logical choice for the next Speaker. He has the age, maturity, and respect of the clan."

Wing Heart blinked, expression turning empty as she shook her head.

Moccasin Leaf smiled sourly. "Ah, I see. You will do anything to maintain your authority."

Her features sharpened as though she had just awakened.

"My concerns are for the best interests of the clan."

"She lies." Wing Heart worked her hands, stepping forward. "We must deal with her, Speaker. This is intolerable."

Moccasin Leaf watched, seeing Wing Heart's souls begin to fray, her control shredding. *Snakes! What is she thinking?*

"Yes, Cloud Heron, I agree. Let's wipe that arrogant face clean of that nasty smug look," Wing Heart muttered. She had balled her fists, back arching, and taken another step forward.

A sudden panic flushed Moccasin Leaf. She swallowed, retreating a step. Panic spurred her as she read Wing Heart's breaking rage in those glittering black eyes.

*Don't do this!* a pleading voice called from down in the hollowness in Moccasin Leaf's breast. She lifted placating hands. But Wing Heart wouldn't stop, the threshold had been breached. In one more step she would...

"Good evening," a pleasant male voice interrupted. Wing Heart stopped short, trembling. Moccasin Leaf spun to find Mud Stalker standing beside Water Petal's house. His mangled arm was cradled in his good left. A smirk bent his lips as his face reflected amusement.

"How long have you been standing there?" Moccasin Leaf demanded tartly to cover her fear-shaken relief.

"Long enough to decide it would be prudent to announce my presence. Bloodshed is always a nasty business. It upsets my stomach, and I'm expecting a delightful feast in honor of a newly made man later tonight." He stepped forward, greased skin gleaming in the fading evening light. "Elder, I have come to collect your son, Mud Puppy. We are ready for his initiation." He nodded at the bark-covered pit, where the first threads of steam carried the odor of baking. "That smells exquisite."

"The boy is up on the Bird's Head with the Serpent." Wing Heart waved absently at the distant mound. She seemed to half stumble as she dropped to a sitting position. Her back against the ramada pole, Wing Heart's expression slowly grew blank, as if when the rage leaked away, it took her souls with it.

Moccasin Leaf stared in fascination. *What is happening to her?*

Mud Stalker, too, seemed amazed at Wing Heart's behavior. Unwilling to be caught gawking, he glanced toward the high mound. "Good. I'm sure the Serpent has prepared him for the ordeal much better than I could."

"And what do *you* care for an Owl Clan boy's initiation?" Moccasin Leaf demanded. "What is he to you?"

Mud Stalker's eyes were half-lidded, his smile neutral and pleasant. "He is about to marry my cousins."

She couldn't stop the shocked look. "You mean to go through with that?"

He studied Wing Heart thoughtfully, then replied, "Oh, yes. Snapping Turtle Clan's alliance with Owl Clan is still solid and irrevocable. Which, if you will excuse me, brings up the matter of Half Thorn's appropriateness as a Speaker."

"You have no business meddling in our clan's decisions." Moccasin Leaf wagged her finger back and forth in chastisement.

"Of course not." Mud Stalker yawned, stifling it with his good hand. "But I do want you to understand that *should* Half Thorn be nominated to the Council as Speaker, his confirmation would be heatedly disputed." A grizzled eyebrow lifted. "It would be unpleasant for him, especially since I believe that Eagle, Rattlesnake, and Frog Clans will vote with me. As to Alligator Clan, well, perhaps, Moccasin Leaf, with the appropriate incentive, you might manage to sway them to your side. Have anything in mind? I'd be happy to mention it to Deep Hunter and Elder Colored Paint, just to see if they'd be receptive. Call it a personal favor to you."

Moccasin Leaf stood frozen. In horror, she shot a look at Wing Heart, but the Clan Elder seemed oblivious.

Saluting with a finger, Mud Stalker said, "Good evening, Elder, and to you, too, Moccasin Leaf. I shall be looking forward to sharing that loaf with you after Mud Puppy's initiation." With that he turned and strode off down the ridge, his course set for the Bird's Head.

"You and he *planned* this? Did you do this to humiliate me?" Moccasin Leaf was shaking, her face working.

Wing Heart's tumbling expressions were her only reaction. She should have been angered, should have lashed out at Mud Stalker for intruding on Owl Clan business. But she had done nothing! They had to have planned this whole performance. The silent grief, the vacant looks, they were all an act, a way of laying Moccasin Leaf and Half Thorn low.

"You are a foul woman, Wing Heart. I came here to help you. For the good of the clan."

"Witch, witch, you're a witch!" Wing Heart began

in a singsong voice, her head nodding in time. "Take a war club, break her head. Leave her body for the Dead. Witch, witch, you're a witch, throw her body in a ditch."

Cold fear traced its way down Moccasin Leaf's back as she stiffened her resolve. "I hope you know what you're doing. Because tonight you have made an enemy whom you will never vanquish." She stalked off, stiff-legged, in barely suppressed rage.

Wing Heart watched her go, then flinched as if touched by the whisper of wings in the still air above her. But when the old woman looked up, only the translucent skies of evening extended to infinity.

# Chapter Four

This was the event that boys most eagerly anticipated and desperately feared. Usually there was, who had time to prepare, but the initiation into manhood was being thrust on Mud Puppy at a moment's notice. He lay on his back on the split-cane matting beside the great fire in the Men's House.

Normally, he would have been excited to see the interior. Until this moment, it had been forbidden to him. Upon being led within, he had the briefest glance of the colorful masks that hung on the walls, the atlatls, darts, and smooth skulls. The latter, trophies of hard-fought battles, watched him with empty black eyes and grinning brown teeth.

All of the Speakers and lineage heads had come to the Men's House for his initiation. His only relative, Yellow Spider, sat just to his right, a sober concern in his eyes as Mud Puppy had undergone the ritual lashing with palmetto whips. They beat him to drive the child from his body. Then his smarting skin was splashed with salt water to begin the healing.

After that, he had been ordered to lie down on the floor, his head facing the West—symbolic of the fact that one day he, too, would die. The sharp cane cut into his raw back as the Serpent began the process of tattooing his chest. He closed his eyes against the pain. His jaw ached and knotted, and his teeth hurt as he clamped them against the stinging fire that prickled his chest.

*Don't be afraid. You cannot show fear. They can kill you if they think you are unworthy.* He hadn't wanted to do this. His heart had been thumping like a shrunken drumhead as the Serpent and Mud Stalker led him here. It had taken all of his courage to keep from breaking and running. But for the surprise of the moment, he would have.

Around him the irregular chanting of the men kept time with the clacking of rhythm sticks and thumping of a hide-covered drum. They were all here: the leaders of the clans, prominent men, and lineage leaders. They had dressed in their finery, brightly colored feathers in their hair, faces painted in red, white, blue, yellow, and black. Many had slathered alligator or bear grease on their skin, the mixture containing crushed honeysuckle, redbud, or other flowers to scent their bodies.

The last image before he'd squeezed his eyes closed was of the Serpent bending over him, blotting out the sight of the soot-grimed thatch roof. The copper needle in the old man's hand had gleamed in the firelight. A smile had split the Serpent's flat face as he stared affectionately down at Mud Puppy.

Again and again, the copper prick was twirled into

Mud Puppy's skin, only to be followed by the old man's blood-caked fingertips as he dipped them in charcoal and rubbed the black color into the wounds.

Mud Puppy would not receive the intricate pattern of dots his brother had been given. He had achieved no accolades in war or Trade. No one sang of his great deeds during the hunt. Instead, only a line of dots running down from the notch between his collarbones to the end of his breastbone and simple arches over each breast were being tattooed into his skin: the marks of manhood.

*"You must make no noise, no sound. You must not show the least sign of fear or pain. If you do, they will beat you with clubs and chase you out of the Men's House. You will live the rest of your life in shame. If you cry like a baby, they will be forced to kill you to cleanse the shame from inside the Men's House."* The Serpent's words echoed in his head. *"But you do not worry me, Mud Puppy. This is nothing compared to the terrors of that night on the Bird's Head. After Dancing with the mushroom and walking hand in hand with the spirits, this will pass like a dream."*

A whimper rose unbidden in his throat. He swallowed hard to stifle it before it could be heard. No, he must not allow them to see any trace of pain or fear. But how? The pricking needle, the rubbing fingers, the line of fire crossing his chest was growing worse. Panic curled and flexed under his ribs. Within heartbeats, he would be screaming his fear and pain.

*"Talk to me!"* the voice came echoing from deep in his souls.

"Masked Owl?" he asked, hardly aware that he'd

spoken aloud. The faintest break in the rhythmic chanting and clacking could be heard.

"Hush!" the Serpent muttered angrily.

The voice told him: *"Keep your eyes closed. Concentrate. I am here. Hovering above you, around you, my wings beating away the pain. Look with your souls. Do you see me?"*

Mud Puppy tried to see Masked Owl's familiar form, but a glowing blackness, a hovering dark shape, flew around him on midnight wings that traced rainbows through the air.

"Many Colored Crow?" Mud Puppy asked. "Is that you?"

"Hush!" the Serpent's voice chastised again.

*"Yes, I have come to watch you be made into a man. You are important to me, young friend. The future lies with you."* A pause. *"Your brother is here. He says you look like a splayed worm, wiggling and jiggling."*

At that, Mud Puppy laughed and spoke from his Dream, "That's like you, isn't it, White Bird? You always made me laugh when you teased me."

*"He says to tell you he misses you."*

"And I miss you, Brother."

*"He asks, Do you remember the time you greased the log bridge across the gully?"*

"We thought Yellow Spider was supposed to come home that way, but it was Uncle Cloud Heron who appeared on the trail. He started across, carrying a sack of poison sumac cuttings to make fish poison out of." His uncle had slipped, and plunged headfirst into the sticky black mud. The subsequent rash had deviled him for weeks. Mud Puppy chuckled out loud, remembering his uncle's mad roars as he and White Bird cowered in the modest concealment of a cane patch and hoped they wouldn't be discovered.

From somewhere in the distance he heard the Serpent make a shushing sound.

"And the worst thing was, we did it to him again, not a year later," Mud Puppy added silently, then burst into giggles.

"Quit that!" the Serpent's voice intruded.

Mud Puppy blinked his eyes open, the last of the giggles dying on his lips. He realized that the room was silent, that the pain in his chest was returning. The Serpent had a puzzled look on his face.

"I was talking to Many Colored Crow," Mud Puppy blurted. In panic he realized that the men lining the walls were staring at him with uneasy brown eyes. "Did I do something wrong?" He tried not to wince at the returning pain.

"No one laughs," the Serpent muttered. "It is supposed to be a test of courage. To be taken seriously."

"I'm sorry." Mud Puppy glanced around nervously. "Forgive me."

He nodded for the Serpent to go ahead, and couldn't help but hear the soft whispering as the chanting began again. The words didn't carry the conviction this time, and Mud Puppy could feel the difference in the air: uncertainty, hesitation. He screwed up his face to mask the renewed pain as the Serpent twisted the needle in the seemingly endless process of making him a man.

*Can't I do anything right?* When he opened his eyes again, it was to see Mud Stalker staring hard at him from one side, something dangerous and provocative behind his eyes.

*"Beware"* Many Colored Crow whispered to his souls. *"They will begin to fear you now."*

*Fear me?* The notion took him off guard. Since when had anyone feared Mud Puppy?

*"You laughed during your initiation,"* Many Colored Crow reminded. *"They will remember that. And the fact that you talked to me."*

A sudden fear ran through him.

*"From this night forward,"* Many Colored Crow whispered, *"you must live differently, Mud Puppy. Everything has changed. Hear my words: After tonight they will try to destroy you. Place your trust in your Spirit Helpers, in the animals, and in the plants. Look beyond the skin. See into the souls. You will not find allies in the usual places."*

"Masked Owl said—"

*"Has he promised you the One? Promised you the Dance? Are you just another of his playthings like your brother, White Bird? A thing to be broken and discarded if you disappoint him?"*

"What?"

*"Let me show you what Masked Owl has in mind for you."*

The vision came spinning out of the darkness behind his eyes. Death swirled around like a charcoal wind. The odor of putrefaction wafted past his nostrils, while coldness touched his skin. He could sense the huge black shape of a malignant bird hovering above, feel the cold strokes of the spirit bird's midnight wings.

Mud Puppy bolted into a sitting position, pointing up at the charred rafters. *"There!"*

"What?" The Serpent stumbled backward, clawed for balance, and craned his thin neck to peer up at the smoke-hazed ceiling of the Men's House. The clacking music died along with the chanting on everyone's lips. Heads craned, wide eyes fixed on the ceiling.

"A big black crow!" Mud Puppy blinked, his chest pulsing with agony. He could feel blood trickling down the sides of his ribs as he searched the ceiling. "Up there," he sputtered lamely. "Dark and...smelling of death."

In the deepening silence, only the crackle of logs in the fire could be heard.

"Yes, I feel him up there." The Serpent drew a wary breath, letting it out as a hiss. "Leave here!" He pointed a finger at the dark roof. "This place is not for you. This boy is not for you! Go back! Back to the darkness of the West and your lair of corruption."

Mud Puppy could feel the rising tension in the room. He was acutely aware of the stares going from him, to the ceiling, to the Serpent, and back to the ceiling again.

Mud Stalker broke the silence, hardly masking his impatience. "I don't see anything."

"You wouldn't," the Serpent replied softly, his eyes still fixed above.

Mud Puppy cocked his head. "Did you hear that?"

The Serpent frowned. "What?"

"Giant wings beating the air," Mud Puppy told him. "Like the whistling a crow makes when it takes off fast."

The Serpent nodded, as if this made perfect sense.

"What is going on here?" Mud Stalker demanded, stepping forward. "Is this the way a man is made?"

"It is tonight." The Serpent shot him a hot glance.

"Power is loose! It is shifting and curling, surrounding us—held back only by these four walls!" Silence filled the room. "Now, watch, you men. Study this boy! Your futures are borne upon his blood!"

The Serpent slipped a hand into the sack hanging from his waist thong and removed a sliver of milky gray chert. "This stone comes from the far north. There, the Earth Beings deposited their semen, and it hardened, became this stone." He straddled Mud Puppy's legs, pushed him flat again, and squatted. In two quick motions, the old man slashed a deep cross on the middle of Mud Puppy's breastbone over his heart. "With it, I mark you."

Mud Puppy's souls twisted, and his lungs jumped and pulled at the bottom of his throat. Tears silvered the edges of his vision.

The Serpent raised the bloody flake of stone for all to see, and cried, "Know all, that this man, whom I today name Salamander, is marked with two crossing lines. The cross on his chest reminds us of the four directions. It is the place where things come together, an intersection between Power and the world. From now on, when you see this man, you will think of things coming together, crossing."

"This isn't right," Clay Fat muttered from his clan seat along the south wall.

"No, it isn't," Deep Hunter agreed. "This boy isn't acting right."

The Serpent stalked forward, and his hard eyes challenged the Speakers. "It is *very* right. More right than you could know. What has happened here tonight isn't about you, or your scheming clans. This new man, this place where we live, is caught between warring Powers. I will tell you this thing once, knowing you will not understand or heed my warning. This man we have made tonight, Salamander, will have to fight for you all. He will have to do it alone, for most of you will betray him!"

Mud Puppy blinked against the tears and tried to understand the seemingly insane words the Serpent spoke. The slit skin oozed and pulsed in red—the flow of it down into his navel frightening and terrible. He barely registered the looks of uncertainty that passed from man to man, or comprehended how individuals were shifting warily, jaws working. The room roiled like water about to erupt into steam.

The Serpent pointed a gnarly blood-caked finger at Mud Puppy, and cried, "I give you Salamander, son of Wing Heart, of the Owl Clan! Nephew to the great Cloud Heron, brother to the late Speaker, White Bird. Greet him and praise him."

With that, the Serpent pitched the bloody flake into the fire and strode toward the doorway. He walked as though possessed of a terrible purpose, then his thin body vanished into the night beyond the Men's House.

*Salamander. I am now called Salamander. That is my man's name.*

Through the agony in his chest, Mud Puppy was aware of one or two muttered greetings. One by one, the men seemed to shuffle to their feet, easing away as if they were tendrils of smoke. He barely noticed, his blurring vision fixed on blood that had begun to mat and dry on his chest. The throbbing pain was growing worse, and he could do nothing about it but endure.

"I don't understand what happened here tonight," Mud Stalker said as he bent down and met Mud Puppy's gaze with hooded eyes. "But know that I am your friend, Salamander. Don't forget that. In the coming days you are going to be in need of a friend." He offered his good hand. "Come, let me help you up. Your mother and your late brother's wives have prepared a feast for you."

Yellow Spider appeared by his other elbow. "I don't know what you did, but it got everyone's attention." To Mud Stalker, he added, "I'll take his other arm. Let's get him home."

Salamander's souls screamed in agony, but no sound passed his lips as Mud Stalker and Yellow Spider pulled him upright.

The room seemed to sway, and through the pain, an urge to throw up coiled in Salamander's stomach. He fought it, struggling to keep his balance despite the weakness in his knees. Mud Stalker's firm hand stabilized him.

*"They will fear you now,"* Many Colored Crow's voice called through the haze of pain and blood, "...*and people always seek to destroy what they fear."*

Salamander lay on a cane mat in the midday shade behind Water Petal's house. The incisions on his chest burned and ached under the slathering of bear grease. Before rubbing it on, the Serpent had mixed it with a concoction of gumweed and pine resin. The latter, he said, promoted healing and kept the insects away.

W. Michael Gear & Kathleen O'Neal Gear

So many things were wheeling through his head. From where he lay, he could see the smoking remains of his house. Or, rather, his old house. It had been torched the evening before, in full ceremony, and White Bird's bones had been incinerated along with everything that had been Mud Puppy's. Not only had his few possessions gone up in fire, but so had an entire lifetime. Nothing remained the same.

He kept stumbling over the inevitability of that, eyes focused on the smoking rubble. It was then that Hazel Fire and Jackdaw came trotting along the edge of the embankment, turned onto the ridge, and approached. Their bodies were lithe and lean in the midday sun, muscles flexing and sliding as they trotted forward. Their hair had been pinned to one side as was the manner of their people, and they carried atlatls and darts in their right hands. As they caught sight of Salamander, both waved and turned in his direction.

Salamander managed a smile, but the pain that accompanied the subsequent wave brought a grimace to his face. His chest skin might have been pulled apart, given the way it felt.

"Greetings, Salamander," Hazel Fire called as he slowed and led Jackdaw into the cool shade. "It is our pleasure to greet you as a man."

"I am happy to receive you." Salamander smiled at them. "Could I get you something? There's water inside. I think some of the root bread is left." He gasped as he started to sit up.

Jackdaw waved him down. "Don't move, at least, not on our account." The Wolf Trader was frowning at the swollen scabs and pustulant tattoos. "We have come to bid you farewell."

"You are leaving?" Salamander asked. "I hope it's not because of White Bird. He wouldn't want you to go just because of what happened to him."

"It isn't just that," Hazel Fire said as he hunched down and leaned his back against the wall. "The water in the swamp is beginning to drop. People have been more than generous. We can't carry all that we've been given in Trade as it is."

"White Bird was our partner," Jackdaw added.

Hazel Fire gave Salamander a serious inspection. "He was more than that. He was married to my sister in my own village. That strengthens the tie between us. It is for that reason that we are leaving you all the goods we cannot carry. Some we have given to Yellow Spider. The rest are yours to dispose of as you will."

Salamander frowned. "This isn't necessary."

"You will need it," Jackdaw replied, squatting and resting his wrists on his knees. "You should hear the talk. People are saying all kinds of things about you, about your mother, and what Mud Stalker is planning."

"I don't want any part of it." Salamander looked away, a sadness in his breast.

"No, but it is being thrust upon you." Hazel Fire rubbed his back against the rough mud wattle, scratching between his shoulder blades. "We have learned a great many things while we have been here in your town. You were kind to us, Mud Puppy."

"Salamander," Jackdaw reminded. "They call him Salamander now."

"Your brother spoke to us of you." Hazel Fire studied the smoking ruins of Wing Heart's house. "But I don't think he understood who or what you are."

Salamander cocked an eyebrow as Hazel Fire pulled the little red owl from his pouch.

"This owl has brought me Dreams." He held it before his sober brown eyes, studying it thoughtfully. "I have thought about the day you talked to the alligator. You wear Power the way other men wear a cloak."

"I'm just me." But he wasn't sure he wanted to be himself any longer. Nothing led him to believe that things were going to get better. Many Colored Crow speaking to him at his initiation had frightened him. As of that moment, the Spirit World had taken on a threatening quality.

"Your people see you through slitted eyes." Hazel Fire turned the little polished owl in the light. "Sometimes it takes a stranger to look at a man with his eyes wide open. I speak for all of us when I tell you we are honored to know you."

"I had a Dream last night," Salamander said cautiously. "It concerned you."

"I would hear your Dream." Hazel Fire gave him a clear-eyed look.

"In it, I saw you reach the mouth of a great river that fed in from the east. High bluffs rise on that eastern bank. Raiders lie in wait there. They have a camp on a stone outcrop that overlooks the Father Water. From there, they can see who passes on the river."

"You saw this?" Jackdaw asked uneasily. "From the river?"

"No, I was riding on Masked Owl's wings. Circling high above. These raiders, they wear black stripes on their faces and do not honor the Power of Trade. In the Dream, you passed the mouth of that river at night and no harm came to you. Do you know this place?"

Hazel Fire nodded. "It sounds like the mouth of the Great Eastern River that feeds the Father Water. What if we were to pass during the day?"

"The raiders will sweep down on you. In loaded canoes, you will not be able to outrun them. On the open water, flooded as that place will be, you will make easy targets."

"Why do you tell us this thing?" Jackdaw asked, clearly uneasy.

"You are my friends." Salamander smiled. "You are good men. Kin to me through marriage. We are bound by the gift of that carved owl. I would have you return in safety to my brother's wife and his little daughter."

"You know that Lark had a girl?" Hazel Fire narrowed a skeptical eye.

"She has a birthmark, like a flower petal on her hip." He pointed to the fleshy swell of his own hip to mark the place. "If you pass that place I have told you of with great care, you may yet see that mark on my brother's daughter."

"I would dearly like to see that." Hazel Fire had turned his attention to the gleaming stone owl. "We will deliver those goods to your house, Mud Puppy."

"They call him Salamander now," Jackdaw reminded.

"Yes, yes." Hazel Fire shot Salamander a sidelong gaze as he raised the small carved owl in his fingers. "We live far away, my friend. I know not what I can ever do for you, but by the Power in this owl, I will do what I can to help you."

"I ask only for your Trade. That, and that you beware at the mouth of the Great Eastern River. They will be waiting for you there. It would pain my souls if they caught you."

"We hear your words, Salamander. And are warned." Hazel Fire gave him a wary scrutiny. "You are headed for great things, young friend."

He smiled sadly. "Greatness and tragedy seem to embrace like lovers."

# Chapter Five

Wreaths and streamers of rain cascaded from the low bank of afternoon clouds as Pine Drop, Night Rain, and Mud Stalker stood on the high embankment above the canoe landing. In silence they watched the Wolf Traders lean into their paddles, pushing their heavily laden canoes toward the channel that would take them east to the Father Water.

Yellow Spider accompanied them in his empty canoe, leading the way lest they get lost in the backswamps.

A number of people had come to wish the Traders off on their long journey homeward. The three Wolf canoes bulged with goods produced in Sun Town: woodwork, rope, netting, black drink, smoke-cured alligator meat, red snapper, black drum, smoked conch, and other delicacies from the gulf that were Traded through Sun Town via its extended clans.

"I wish it was Yellow Spider that we were going to marry," Night Rain whispered. "He's a handsome young man. He's been to the north and has prospects for a great future."

"That is precisely why Salamander is the one you must marry," Mud Stalker replied. "I could not have planned better myself. You should have seen the young fool. He had half the Men's House in a panic before his initiation was complete. Even the Serpent, who believes in the young fool, was driven away by the rantings."

"Your words don't inspire us with confidence," Pine Drop noted sourly.

"You don't need confidence," Mud Stalker added in a precise tone. "All you need is to think of your future, and the clan's."

"How long will we have to endure this?" Night Rain asked.

"Just until Owl Clan is discredited," Mud Stalker replied. "And, given the anger growing between Wing Heart and Moccasin Leaf, that may not be as long as I had originally thought."

"So when do we marry this half-wit?" Pine Drop had crossed her arms under her pointed breasts.

"Today, if you'd like." Mud Stalker turned to study his young kin. At the expression of dismay on their faces, he burst into laughter.

The forest rose tall and green. Interlocking branches heavy with the bright growth of spring leaves cast a perpetual gloom over the leaf-matted earth. Wraiths of mist, like ghost fingers, wove their way between moss-encrusted trunks whose thick girths were wrapped and wound with vines. Mushrooms poked colorful heads from the moldy soil and broke through the thick and spongy layer of leaf mat. Water dripped from above, pattering here and there. Occasional patches of heartleaf, mayapple, and native pipe lived in the gloom. Dead saplings, their battle for the light long lost, and rotting corpses of long-felled giants scattered the forest floor.

Salamander slipped silently through the trackless depths. The few sounds of his passing were immediately masked by the endless noises of the living forest. Birds sang in a melodic cacophony. The chirring of insects and the chattering of the squirrels fought in direct competition with the rustle of the highest leaves. Occasional discarded flower petals came drifting down from the gum, ash, and maple as new seeds were born in swelling green pods.

Salamander stepped carefully, his bare feet rising and falling with the grace of a cat's. He tightened his grip on his atlatl where it rested in his right hand. He wasn't particularly good with the weapon, but only a fool wandered the forest unarmed. The danger posed by the occasional black bear or cougar, though slight, was not to be discounted, but nothing could make a young man feel more like an idiot than to watch a deer, raccoon, or porcupine walk out, present a perfect target, then fade away into the forest. Meat was forever at a premium.

He slowed, bending his head back to stare up at the high canopy. Sunlight filtered through layers of green, speckles of light but mere pinpricks that glittered in the heights. The branches were interwoven with vines of honeysuckle, cross and trumpet vine, fox grape, and greenbrier until they resembled webs. Filling his lungs,

Salamander took in the scents of the forest, damp, sweet, and perfumed.

No one would find him here. Salamander allowed his souls to relax and enjoy the solitude of the forest. In the dense isolation of the endless trees, he had time to sort out the painful vortex of the last few weeks.

*Masked Owl and Many Colored Crow? I am caught between warring Powers.* The Serpent had as much as told him so when he incised that painful and deep cross in Salamander's chest. *Why did they choose me? What do they want of me? Why do they call on a mere boy?*

He still had trouble thinking of himself as a man. The name Salamander echoed oddly in his ears—but he still held hopes that one day the Earth Being might deign to become his Spirit Helper.

In the midst of horrific events, young Mud Puppy had been plucked from obscurity by both the forces of Power and the dealings of the clans, and in one fell swoop thrust from a boy's preoccupations into the role of an authoritative man. All this while Spirit Power loomed ever larger in his life.

Why, for instance, had he been given the vision of the Swamp Panther raid? Why had he been told to free the captive girl? Why had Mud Stalker insisted on becoming his mentor—and worse, remained intent on seeing him married to his brother's widows? The sensation was similar to being held by the wrists and spun around so fast that his feet had flown off the ground. He was being spun faster and faster until the world was a blur, and his arms were aching from the tug.

What if the Powers that held him suddenly let go? Would he fly off like a cast dart to land who knew where?

He swallowed hard, the fingers of his left hand prodding tenderly at the scabs on his chest. Where the wounds were swollen and inflamed, his touch produced yellow pus and a sting.

He took the faint trail down an embankment, crossed a sluggish creek, and climbed the other side. Figuring himself to be deep enough in the forest that no one would stumble upon him, he seated himself on a fallen beech tree, laid his weapons to one side, and removed a bit of red stone from his pouch. Using a chert flake, he began the laborious process of carving the round body of another of his endless line of owls.

A thought startled him. Why owls? He had been carving them ever since he had been a child. Had it been happenstance that he had settled on the form, or was there more to it? Something he knew down in his souls but had ignored on a higher level? He glanced up at the green canopy again.

*How long have you been talking to me in my Dreams, Masked Owl? Have I only now started to remember?*

No answer came to him, but he felt the short hairs on his neck prickling. Yes, he had been having Dreams, hadn't he? Dreams he couldn't quite remember during the waking moments.

Layers upon layers, deceit and guile, death and life, and him right in the middle of it—without a clue as to why, or what he was supposed to do. A sick feeling ate at his stomach. Was he, too, destined to be a pile of bones within a couple of weeks? Were his muscles, skin, and organs to be stripped away by the Serpent's sharp chert knife and carried out beyond the ridges for the scavengers?

He could imagine his bones: red, raw, and bloody, with bits of tissue clinging to them. In the shadowed depths of the hut, they looked dark where they rested on the broken branches and other lengths of firewood. The thought amused him that his lineage within Owl Clan was running out of houses to burn. Only Water Petal's remained, and she would need it when the baby came.

The whirring of the forest almost swallowed the knock of wood on wood. Salamander froze, his eyes searching the shadowed forest around him.

There, the faintest trace of movement! He barely caught a glimpse through the trees. Something moved on the trail he had just come up. With cautious hands he retrieved his atlatl and fingered a dart into the hook.

Bits of color and movement flickered between the boles, and then she stepped into the clear. Young, a newly made woman's kirtle swaying at her hips, she plodded steadily forward, eyes on the trail before her. A tumpline crossed her forehead, the thick straps leading to a heavy pack that centered on her hips just above the buttocks. She poked at the ground with a walking stick in her right hand, her left swinging in time to her gait. Long black hair had been braided and curled at the side of her head, held in place with a striking blue feather from a jay's tail. In the dim light, grease made her rounded breasts shine, the brown nipples conelike. Her pretty face expressed sadness and desperation.

"Spring Cypress?" Salamander asked softly.

She stopped short, eyes flashing this way and that until she discerned his form on the half-rotten log. "Mud Puppy?"

"It's Salamander now," he told her wearily. "They

made me a man." He indicated her kirtle. "And I see that you have just been released from the Women's House."

Her lips wiggled as if words were running in her head that she refused to say. In the end, looking wary, she asked, "What are you doing out here?"

"Escaping."

A weight might have lifted from her, relief rising to be mimicked in a smile. "You, too? I'm so glad to hear that." She swung the heavy pack down and walked over to him, her shining eyes on his. "We could go together. Anywhere. I thought I'd go north. Follow the White Mud River up into the mountains. I don't know what we'd do there, but I'm sure we could find a valley, someplace out of the way where the hunting was good and enough plants grew that we could feed ourselves."

Salamander blinked hard, trying to fathom what she was saying. "You mean, you're running away? Leaving Sun Town? For good?"

Her mouth hung open for a moment, the words forgotten, then she blurted, "You said you were escaping!"

"I am. But just for the day. I needed to get away! My chest hurts, my brother and uncle are dead, and everyone wants to marry me off to those horrible Snapping Turtle women."

A sudden fear brightened her eyes. "I just told you where I was going."

Salamander sighed and returned to his work on the little red owl. He had the head mostly right. The two triangular ears, the round eyes and pinched beak were visible. From the neck down, however, the wings and protruding belly were owl-like only if the viewer had a good imagination.

"You'll tell!" Spring Cypress looked crestfallen. "It means I have to go somewhere else."

"People are going to be very concerned about you. What about Clay Fat and Graywood Snake? They are your relatives. If you just up and disappear, they'll be worried sick."

The way her probing brown eyes were watching him made him nervous. "Mud Puppy?"

"Salamander."

"Salamander? Would you come with me?"

"Why?"

"They want me to marry Copperhead."

"He's a cruel old man!"

"I don't want to marry *anyone!* I wanted to marry White Bird. I loved him!" Her fists were knotted, her pretty face strained as tears edged her eyes.

"Tell them no."

"I *can't!* My uncle, Clay Fat, has made some kind of agreement with Mud Stalker. The Elder, my grandmother, has agreed." She shook her head, staring down at the damp carpet of fallen leaves under her small brown feet. "My life is ruined, Mu—Salamander. First the Snapping Turtle Clan took White Bird from me, then the lightning made it final."

"You're not the only one who lost him."

She sniffed and squared her shoulders as she looked at him. "I couldn't stand it the night he was married."

"I saw you paddle off in your canoe."

She nodded. "I went away, out into the swamp. I just wanted to be alone. I stayed away all night, but the cramps started at dawn, so I came back. Announced myself, and Aunt Turtle Mist took me straightaway to the Women's House until my moon passed. That's where they told me that I would marry Copperhead. Tonight."

Salamander shifted uneasily, wondering what to say, what to do to help her. Snakes, a young man, didn't just interfere with another clan's internal affairs. Worse, when he looked up at her, something deep in his souls was terribly aware of her slim body and the way her woman's kirtle hung slightly askew below the indent of her navel. Even when he looked away, the eyes of his souls retraced her thin waist and shapely stomach. The curve of her firm breasts gleamed in the light.

"I'll do anything if you'll go with me." Her words were spoken softly, and he could sense her presence as she stepped to him. The faint odor of her carried on the warm moist air. His heart began to quicken.

"What?" He looked right up into her large brown eyes. He might have been paralyzed, pinned in place by the mixture of longing and desperation there.

"Anything." Her fingers were plucking at the knots that held her kirtle in place, and before Salamander could understand, the pale fabric loosened and slipped down the round curve of her hips. "I'm a woman, now. You are a man."

He caught the falling of his jaw in time to keep from gaping like an idiot, his gaze stopped short on the black triangle of her pubic hair. It glistened, cupped in that Y of soft brown flesh. He found himself unaccountably short of breath.

She began gently stroking the sides of his face, her fingertips dancing lightly on his skin. Had anything ever stoked such a fire within him before? Dreamlike, she bent until her face was but a handbreadth from his. His souls were falling into her, drawn into that brown magical stare. Tremors ran down his arms and legs.

"Lie with me, Salamander." She was pulling him down onto the folds of the kirtle. An excitement, half fear, half anticipation, had begun to pound with each beat of his heart. He shivered as her strong fingers pulled the restraining breechcloth away from his hardened penis. A gasp escaped his lips as she wrapped her fingers around his tingling shaft.

She was drawing him onto her as she lay back on the crumpled kirtle and the cushion of leaf mat. A flood of energy bore him along.

He would never know whether it was the sting in his abused chest or the pain deep within her eyes that stopped him. He winced as he pulled back and shook his head. "No."

She propped herself on her elbows, staring at him like he'd just lost every wit in his body. "What do you mean, no? Do you know how many men would give anything to lie with me?"

Salamander scrambled backward, awkwardly shoving his throbbing penis behind his breechcloth. "It's not that. I mean, you're beautiful."

Her expression collapsed, soft sobs causing her breasts to heave in a way that completely unsettled Salamander. "Then you'll tell on me?"

"No." In defeat, he rose and walked in an aimless circle, shaking out his arms and hands the way a runner did when he needed to shed excess energy. "Go on, run away. I'll tell no one where you're going."

"Why?" Even wounded, she remained suspicious.

"Because I wish I could go with you."

"Then why don't you?" she demanded. "That way, I wouldn't have to go alone."

He closed his eyes, a terrible longing growing inside him. "I can't."

"Why?"

He looked at her, still achingly aware of her gorgeous body, so young and bursting with charms. She had been forever beyond him, the woman his brother would marry. "I cannot explain it. I just can't go with you, that's all."

"Afraid?" She cocked her head, those glistening dark eyes trying to read behind his souls.

He shrugged. "Maybe. Yes, that's it." But he dare not tell just what he was afraid of. "And besides, you don't want me, Spring Cypress. Not really."

"Then why am I lying here on my back?" She spread her hands in frustration and sat up, irritation replaced with exhaustion. "I would have taken you, Mud—Salamander. I've never lain with a man before."

"You're not thinking well."

"And you are? They say that you giggled and saw things during your initiation. They say you're a half-wit. Given what just happened here, I'm not so sure they aren't right."

"You didn't want me just now."

"Then what did I want?" She was glaring at him.

"A dream, Spring Cypress. You were desperate for a dream. The trouble is, dreams don't come that easy."

She was frowning at him the way she might if his words made no sense to her. "So, what? Are you going back to tell Uncle Clay Fat that I'm running?"

He shook his head, an unexplained sadness rising to replace the desire his manhood had pumped through his body. "No. I'm giving you this." He bent down and picked up the partially carved owl from the moss-spotted log. "I wasn't finished with it yet, but you can tell what it is."

She took the stone figure and held it between thumb and forefinger as she inspected it. "An owl," she noted. "Yes, I can see that. What is it for?"

"For you." He tried to shrug off the confusion that clouded his ability to think. "Unfinished. Just like you are." He waved. "Go on, Spring Cypress. If anyone asks —which they won't—I'll tell them I haven't seen you since the night my brother was married."

She stood, reached down, and whipped her kirtle up with a fluid motion. He watched as she wrapped it about her hips and cinched the cords that held it in place. With slender hands, she rearranged her hair, flicking bits of leaf from the glossy black braid before repinning it with the blue jay feather. "You're a strange one, Mud Puppy."

"Salamander."

A smile bent her full lips. "Salamander. Odd that they'd name you that."

"People underestimate salamanders."

She considered that as she walked back and picked up her pack. Before slinging it onto her back and fixing the tump line, she placed the little red owl carving into a pocket. "I've heard that some salamanders can change their colors."

"I've heard that, too."

She smiled wearily at him. "Good luck with your colors, Salamander. I thank you for this thing you're going to do for me. If you ever need me, I'll be in the mountains up in the northwest. When you find your way, come looking for me."

"I will."

He watched as she recovered her stick and started off again. She never turned, never looked back, just walked onward until her form was hidden by the endless trees.

"Watch over her, Masked Owl." He fought the terrible desire to pick up his weapons and run after her.

*Maybe I just don't have that kind of courage.*

# The Serpent

Courage?

    Why is it that humans think bravery is either leaping into a fight or running away from everything that comforts them? The most courageous act a human being can perform is to truly love another person.

There are those who would have us believe that love is easy, that it comes childlike from our hearts and floods out as effortlessly as rain falls from the fingers of the Sky Beings.

That is just foolishness.

Love is standing guard all the time. It is becoming a world to yourself for another's sake, and learning to share its most intimate corners. There is nothing more courageous than that. And nothing more achingly beautiful.

But I am an old man. I have failed at truly loving another person so many times that I know the misery of cowardice.

This boy is just about to find out.

# Chapter Six

Pine Drop watched the gentle rainfall and tried not to think about what was happening. People stood in a ring just across the borrow pit from her house. Most wore flat bark hats that shed the rain. In her damp hands, she held the offerings of food and turned toward Salamander. His gaze was fixed on the people as though they were a writhing den of water moccasins instead of his kin and hers. A swamp rabbit caught in a snare might look like that. Panic bulged behind his round brown eyes as he took the wooden platter from her hands. He raised the plate that carried the first meal he would eat as a married man. "By accepting this meal...I tie my life...with that of Pine Drop...and...and..."

"Night Rain," Pine Drop growled.

"Night Rain," he agreed, "daughters of Sweet Root, who is the daughter of...of the great Clan Elder, Back Scratch. My clan is now their clan, their clan is now mine. I accept these women..."—he seemed to pause forever—"...as my wives, to share with equally, to comfort and care for."

In the now-familiar ritual, Pine Drop and Night Rain held their hands demurely before their kirtles, and cried out in unison, "We accept this man, Salamander, of the Owl Clan, as our husband. In doing this, we bind ourselves to him and to his clan. Let it be known among all people that we are married."

"Let it be known!" Mud Stalker called from his place. He carried a war club for the occasion, and Pine Drop wasn't sure if it was for ceremony or to whack Salamander should he suddenly bolt from the proceedings.

"Let it be known!" Wing Heart mumbled absently from her place on the east. The Clan Elder's eyes were oddly glazed, her expression remote, as if lost in other memories.

Something about her sent a shiver down Pine Drop's spine.

Salamander's cousin, Water Petal, stood to Wing Heart's right. The woman looked worried, her stare darting back and forth between Salamander and Wing Heart. She had worn a small hat against the rain. It barely shielded her face, let alone her protruding pregnant belly, which was now rain-streaked over her kirtle. The woman's time was close, her belly button protruding.

*How long until I look like that?* Pine Drop glanced sidelong at Salamander and used all of her will to keep from showing her disgust. Not only was he scrawny, but he still looked like the foolish boy he had been but a week ago. *Him? Sharing my bed? After the likes of Blue*

*Feather—and even his brother? Never!* But she knew it was a lie.

"Let it be known!" the gathered people shouted. This time there was no smiling and slapping each other on the back. Despite the promise of food, people seemed to slip away like stringers of mist.

Wing Heart, her face still a mask, simply strode off, heading northward across the clan grounds for her own territory. To Pine Drop's surprise, it was the cousin, Water Petal, who leaned over to Salamander, and said, "If you need to talk, Cousin, come see me." And with that she gave him a sympathetic pat and started after Wing Heart, her gait more of a waddle to compensate for that enormous belly.

Pine Drop shot her uncle a hard look, but his expression urged caution in return.

"Come," Pine Drop said, as the last of the observers turned for their own dry homes or the protection of rama-das. "That food is getting soaked."

"Let it," Night Rain muttered, sharing her unease as her glance stole back and forth between Pine Drop and Mud Stalker. Salamander stood as if roots had grown out of his feet. She took the tray from his hands and ducked into the house she had shared with White Bird for only one night. Now the form of his little brother darkened the doorway. A moment later Night Rain ducked in and made irritated sounds as she wrung the water from her hair. "You'd think we could have waited until the sun came out."

"Uncle wanted this done," Pine Drop retorted as she seated herself behind the fire and dropped two pieces of wood into it. As the flames rose and cast yellow light over the interior, she studied her new husband. He was standing like a bulge on a pot, hands nervously twisting above his breechcloth.

"Sit." Pine Drop pointed to her right. "You, too, Night Rain. Come sit here beside me."

Night Rain at least did as she was told. Salamander seemed not to have heard, his eyes fixed on the fire. She caught his horrified look as he shot a glimpse at the pole beds behind her.

"Will you sit, *Husband!*" she chided, and slapped the floor to her right. "We have things to discuss."

He swallowed hard and lowered himself the way he might if a nest of red ants were near.

"What things?" he asked.

She could see his pulse jumping at the base of his thin neck. The oddly cut cross on his chest looked infected, swollen and angry.

"First, there are rules to be followed in this household." She took the tray from behind her and handed it to him. "Eat. Or do you want to mock the marriage ritual the way you mock everything else?"

"I don't mock everything."

"Oh?" she arched a brow, aware that Night Rain was watching silently, her lips twitching. "You didn't giggle during your initiation?"

"What happens in the Men's House is not to be spoken of to women." He looked sullen.

"Don't be a fool." She reached back for a buffalo-horn spoon and used it to scoop up some of the mashed squash. This she handed to Night Rain, indicating that she eat. "I suppose that men never hear the gossip from the Women's House, either."

Salamander said nothing, but did manage to at least plop a soggy bit of cattail-root bread into his mouth.

"As to the rules," Pine Drop continued, "they are as follows: First, you will not speak of the things that happen inside this house. Second, what you hear of Snapping Turtle Clan dealings are not to be shared with your relatives from Owl Clan. Third, neither I nor my sister will be made into fools. Do you understand?"

He shook his head, looking clearly uncomfortable.

"People are already talking out there." She gestured with her hand toward Sun Town. "Night Rain and I are laughingstocks. They are saying, 'Married to that half-wit, can you imagine?' Well, I won't have that. My sister and I will not be singled out for their pity or their ridicule."

Salamander swallowed his bit of bread.

"When you are asked about our marriage, you will simply answer that things are fine, do you understand?"

He nodded again.

"I want to remind you that you married into Snapping Turtle Clan. You have come here, to our territory, to live in *our* house. While you are here you will obey my instructions, is that clear? If not, well, it won't be a pleasant thing. Do you understand?"

What was it about his innocent face? He looked like a child with his hand caught in the stewpot. "Well, can you speak, except to spout nonsense?"

He nodded again.

Pine Drop rolled her eyes and glanced at Night Rain. Her sister looked absolutely miserable.

"One last rule, Salamander." She gave him a hard squint. "I understand that you have obligations to your clan. I don't expect you to sit around here, lazy as a bead on a necklace. Go off and do what you need to do. We would appreciate it if you could bring back some fish, game, or roots on occasion. It would make things look normal here. But you come home every night, do you understand?"

He frowned at her, obviously confused.

Snakes! Did she have to sound everything out for him? "One of us will always be here. So you come home. We would not like to find out that you were slipping off and spending the night at some other woman's house." She steepled her fingers and smiled. "Like I said, we will not be humiliated by you, so hear this, and remember it: If we find out that you've been slipping your hard little worm into some other woman, we'll use a serrated stone knife to cut it off. Are we understood?"

He gulped and nodded, looking as if he'd grown gills.

She sighed in resignation then. "Very well, Night Rain, hand me that cloth. Those wounds on his chest are oozing, and I will not have him dripping all over my breasts while we finish this marriage business."

At his increasing panic, she added, "You can carry out that part of your obligations, can't you?"

He was looking longingly at the door. Sweat, or was it old raindrops, beaded on his forehead.

The air was hot and muggy, one of those early-summer days when the sun burns down out of a white-hot cloudless sky. Heat rolled across the grassy plaza to the east of the Council ramada where Salamander stood next to his mother. He didn't want to be here, listening to Mud Stalker singing his praises to the Council. He wished he were far away, deep in the swamp, floating with the alligators.

He stared thoughtfully out past the crowded people beyond the Council House. They had come to watch his appointment as Speaker for Owl Clan. The crowd was huge, many of them from distant camps who had come for the solstice ceremonies and heard the amazing news that a mere boy was being made Speaker for the influential Owl Clan. They hadn't come out of respect for him or his clan. They were here for the spectacle.

By turning his head he could catch occasional glimpses of the ball game practice through the press of spectators. The Northern Moiety team practiced pitching in their half of the plaza.

On the last day of the solstice ceremonies, after the masked processions, the Dances, and feasts, the ritual game would be played. To win, one side had to score four goals. A deerskin ball was flipped or batted back and forth between the players by means of a long stick, flattened on one end. The object was to fling the ball across the borrow pit and onto the first ridge of the opposing moiety.

The stakes were high. Clans, lineages, and families bet huge piles of food and possessions against the outcome. Losing could leave entire clans destitute. It was such a loss that had first led Frog Clan into their slow spiral of decay. During the last two years the Southern Moiety had achieved victory, and given the looks of the Northern team's practice, it would happen again this year.

The games were the culmination of the annual summer solstice ceremony, which in turn was one of the most important observances of the year. People came from all of the dispersed camps as far away as the gulf coast. They brought canoe loads of food and locally manufactured goods to be wagered on the great ball game. It was a time of gift giving, fulfilling obligations, feasting, and socializing. Marriages were brokered between widely scattered clanspeople, and news was dispensed.

Salamander thought of the influx of people who came to solstice like a wave that washed into Sun Town, swirled around in the ceremonies, then washed back out again, renewed and revitalized. It not only reminded the People who they were, but invigorated them with the knowledge that Sun Town was indeed the center of their world. So long as Sun Town remained, the People could return to their roots.

The crowd closed in, blocking his view of the players. The last glimpse had been of Yellow Spider sprinting up to battle with a young woman from Alligator Clan for possession of the ball. Across the distance Salamander thought he heard the clacking of their sticks as they struck and parried.

"Pay attention!" Water Petal hissed.

Salamander blinked, shook himself, and looked back to the open center of the Council House. There, under the brutal sun, Mud Stalker had his good hand raised. He was turning slowly, meeting the gaze of the Council members one by one as he looked at them.

Salamander followed his gaze around the circle, past Frog Clan, Alligator Clan, into his own eyes, and then beyond the entrance to Snapping Turtle Clan, where Pine Drop and Night Rain sat behind old Back Scratch, looking both hot and embarrassed. Then

Thunder Tail from Eagle Clan and Clay Fat from Rattlesnake Clan rounded out the circle.

"We face an unusual circumstance," Mud Stalker stated matter-of-factly. "Young Salamander has my confidence. He is, after all, brother to the dead Speaker, White Bird. Nephew to Cloud Heron. He is the son of Clan Elder Wing Heart."

Salamander glanced up, but his mother, standing a step to his left, was staring off into the high distance. The slight frown on her forehead made Salamander follow her gaze up past the open roof and into the white sky. The only thing he could see were two far-off vultures wheeling around in circles in the hot air.

"I am happy to cast my vote to acknowledge Speaker Salamander to this Council." Mud Stalker balled his upraised hand into a fist. To Salamander it looked more like the expression of victory than anything else.

As if in a blur, he heard the voices of the Clan Elders and Speakers calling out in favor.

"Nay!" came the strident cry.

Salamander started, following all eyes as they turned to Deep Hunter. The Alligator Clan Speaker stepped out with his sister, Colored Paint.

It was Colored Paint who said, "Alligator Clan believes that the Council would be better served by more mature leadership. We want it stated on this occasion, that although we are outvoted, we believe the acceptance of a mere boy does not serve the Council well."

Mud Stalker glanced at Wing Heart, clearly expecting some answer from the Council's leader. She might have been sculpted of mud, as aware as a cooking clay as she gazed vacant-eyed at the sky.

"Cousin?" Water Petal called from behind. "Clan Elder, do you have a response?"

Wing Heart might have been deaf, lost in her thoughts.

With a slightly perplexed look, Mud Stalker turned, glaring at Deep Hunter. "Well, it is obvious that Clan Elder Wing Heart considers your objection so ludicrous that she needn't even acknowledge it."

Chuckles broke out. Salamander felt his ears redden with embarrassment. Deep Hunter was right. He shouldn't even be here. Why was this happening? What was Mud Stalker's purpose in insisting on his following in White Bird's footsteps when Alligator Clan's objections seemed eminently logical?

With renewed interest, Salamander studied the people in the circle. *They are laughing!* The notion came to him as he studied the smug faces of Mud Stalker and Back Scratch. Clay Fat and Graywood Snake looked uncomfortable, as if caught doing something embarrassing. Thunder Tail's expression was wooden, while Cane Frog's blind face exhibited a grin, as if she, too, sensed some sort of victory.

"The objection of Alligator Clan is noted," Mud Stalker replied with satisfaction. "The vote, however, is clear." His voice rang in the hot air. "*Speaker* Salamander, of the Owl Clan! Step forward and meet your Council!"

Water Petal's sharp jab sent him unsteadily forward, half-tottering on his feet. Mortification seared his souls as he forced his feet to carry him into the open. His tongue knotted at the back of this throat, and he tried to keep his knees from trembling. As he looked up into Mud Stalker's gloating eyes, he couldn't find a single word to say.

"Speaker Salamander," Mud Stalker cried. "With your acceptance, this Council has finished its business. In honor of the occasion, will you do us the favor of dismissing the Council?"

Salamander froze for a moment, the only sensation that of his heart battering against his ribs. "Dismissed," he croaked.

Laughter broke out, adding to his misery. He shot a quick look over his shoulder, hearing Water Petal telling Wing Heart, "The Speaker dismissed the Council, Elder. It's over now. Salamander is now Speaker."

"Who?" Wing Heart asked faintly as she turned away.

Salamander didn't hear Water Petal's response.

"I feel like a fool," Salamander muttered.

"You did fine." Mud Stalker beamed down at him. "Just trust me, young man. I'll see you through this."

And then they came, each of the Elders and Speakers, each congratulating him. The hands, pats on the back, and smiling faces blurred as they crowded around him.

Only after the others stepped away did Deep Hunter and Colored Paint approach. Deep Hunter's face reeked of disgust as he leaned forward, voice low. "So, you are now Snapping Turtle Clan's tool? My old adversary planned that well, boy."

"I am Owl Clan," Salamander managed.

"Yes, well, we'll see, won't we?" Then Deep Hunter turned and stalked off, his muscular body betraying an unbending anger.

"We'll see," Colored Paint agreed, following her brother.

Thankful to be left alone, Salamander noticed that Mud Stalker seemed to be the center of attention as the remaining Council members wished him well.

*Is that the plan? I am supposed to do as Mud Stalker wishes? Is that why he insisted on me?*

The knowledge was sobering. Even more so when Mud Stalker turned to him, slapped him on the back, and said, "Come, Speaker Salamander. Your wives have made a great feast. We look forward to celebrating our good fortune!"

But when Salamander looked in Pine Drop and Night Rain's direction, they glared back at him as though he were some sort of carrion-eating bug.

*I could have gone with Spring Cypress. I should have.*

Mud Stalker's heavy hand propelled him forward toward his future.

# Chapter Seven

wo days after the solstice ceremonies, he had followed the Serpent to the house where Clan Elder Graywood Snake had lived. The oval-shaped house had been built on the first ridge, just to the left of the low causeway leading up to the Bird's Head.

Graywood Snake had died suddenly. One moment she was hobbling across the plaza, the next, she cried out and fell over. Her souls had fled before she hit the ground. That had been last night.

Heat filled the house, heavy like a weight, and more stagnant, if possible, than the muggy afternoon beyond the door. In such hot weather a corpse had to be processed quickly, for in hot air corruption was drawn quickly to feed on a corpse. Salamander wasn't sure why that was. Something about corruption's ability to scent death? The Serpent had never given him a straight answer as to the reasons—which led Salamander to suspect that the old man didn't really know.

Salamander squinted in the dim light, his hands

working with smooth strokes as he severed the thin muscles inside the old woman's thigh. He had to saw at the thick tendon that tied her thighbone to the mound of her pelvis. In the process, he tried not to touch the woman's deeply wrinkled vulva. It reminded him of a shriveled gourd husk, whiskered with mold. Worse, it reminded him of his wives'.

Beside him, the Serpent's raspy old voice rose and fell as he chanted the Death Song. The melody called to the Sky Beings and Earth Beings, asking them to come and see, to be witness to the passing of the great Elder's souls. Next he Sang to reassure Graywood Snake that she was being cared for in the manner of her people, that her corpse was being treated with the proper respect.

The thick tendon parted, and Salamander was able to roll the leg back to expose the ball joint to his sharp stone knife. The Serpent turned his attention to the skin still left around the woman's hips. With practiced strokes he peeled away the old woman's vulva and severed the tissues inside to leave an arched hump of bone, raw and bloody. The bowels, vagina, and bladder that had once been cradled within had already been removed when they excised her organs.

Outside the door, Salamander could hear soft weeping as Speaker Clay Fat and his sister, Turtle Mist, mourned the death of their Elder.

What had been Graywood Snake's leg came free in Salamander's hand. He set it carefully to the side, picking bits of tissue from his fingers and wiping them on the inside of the wicker basket that held the old woman's flesh and organs.

"You have become practiced at this." The Serpent

studied him with thoughtful eyes. His sagging face—like Salamander's—had been streaked with black charcoal stripes to appease the Dead. "You are already better than Bobcat. Have you given thought to following me?"

"No, Elder. That is Bobcat's place. He knows the songs. He did very well walking at your side for the summer solstice ceremonies."

"You could, you know. Follow in my footsteps, I mean."

"I have other responsibilities."

"You are no longer the child I once knew. You have aged in the last three moons since you were made a man and married."

"I have too much to worry about."

"Yes, I haven't heard a word from your Clan Elder at Council since you were accepted there." Then he resumed his chanting.

Salamander pinched his lips, frowning, his thoughts locked on Wing Heart's perplexing silence. She might have lost part of her souls, given the way she walked about, a listlessness in her eyes.

He picked up the Serpent's words and Sang in gentle accompaniment as he thought of his mother. He couldn't help but compare her to Graywood Snake. Unlike his mother, he had always liked Graywood Snake. Even after his near-unanimous nomination to the Council, she had treated him like a fellow rather than a jest, as the others had.

Salamander ran his blade down the inside of the leg, separating the thin skin. With careful strokes he severed the ligament and tendons in the round, peeling the muscle back from the bone. That done, he had placed the cool flesh in the basket and reverently severed the tendons at the kneecap, then folded the leg bones double. He laid them with the arm and leg bones that already rested on the rick of wood. Dry and seasoned, the pyre would burn hot and completely, in defiance of the moisture that hung in the summer air outside.

"I will miss you, Elder," Salamander said as he cleaned the last bits of tissue from his knife and ritually passed it over the smoking coals in the fire pit. Not that the house needed a fire, given the melting heat of the day, but the smoke was required, not only for purification of the tools, but to keep evil spirits out and away, and to assist Graywood Snake's souls in their passage from this life to the next.

Sweat beaded on Salamander's forehead as he Sang the final verses of the Death Song. Then he and the Serpent carefully placed the naked bones of her torso atop the pyre, propping them in the cradle of her limbs so that they wouldn't roll off.

"Rest well, old friend." The Serpent patted the rounded globe of her skull with blood-encrusted hands. "You have always been a light in my life. Your fond wit and smile brought happiness to many of my days. I will see you someday soon."

Salamander watched the old man's gentle motions as he caressed the bones. "Does it bother you?"

"Hmm?" The Serpent turned, gaze absent. The skin seemed to hang like a wet rag from the flat planes of his charcoal-smeared face.

"She was your friend." Salamander gestured toward the bones. "We have just cut her into pieces. It seems like a violation."

Salamander hated it when the old man gave him that look of irritated consideration. "Her souls have left the body, Salamander. I am overjoyed to be the one to help her during her passing. Put yourself in her place. If your souls were hanging here in the air"—he pointed at the smoke-filled ceiling—"would you want some rude stranger, or an old and dear friend, seeing to the care of your body?"

"I'm not sure."

"Ah, that's because you have not considered death, my young friend. The living lose themselves in the pain of the moment. They are completely absorbed by their own sense of loss. They never think about how fragile the souls of the freshly dead are. Imagine yourself as having just died: You are lost, grieving, your body refuses to respond to your orders as it did when you were alive. Your loved ones are all around you, crying, pulling their hair. You try to help them, to calm them, but they are deaf to your entreaties. You can only watch their pain, unable to soothe it. Meanwhile, all around you, spirits are gathering, calling to you, trying to get your attention. Old friends, long dead, are crowding close and demand to speak with you. Other spirits are circling, knowing you are vulnerable, easily attacked. You must guard against them, but you are so confused, worried, and scared like you have never been before." He shook his head. "I think dying is much more frightening than being born."

"You think they are linked?"

"Yes," the old man replied. He looked at the basket made of split cane. "Can you carry that?"

"If you can Sing. I'm still learning the words." Salamander stepped over, crouched, and shifted the basket onto his back. Graywood Snake had been old and frail, and she weighed almost nothing. He took the load and ducked out into the hot sunshine. Eyes slitted against the glare, he could see Clay Fat, his portly body streaked with perspiration, his round face stricken. Turtle Mist's features were drawn, her eyes sad.

*They will be all right, won't they? Not like Mother.* The aftereffects of death now scared him. His mother hadn't been the same since White Bird's death. Instead, she had turned into a walking husk, the seed that should have been within gone black and shriveled. He wondered if perhaps White Bird had been so frightened that he had clawed away part of Mother's souls as his own had been drawn into the realm of the Dead.

The basket leaked, and as he walked, Salamander felt wet drops of fluid spattering his legs. Their route took them southwest, proceeding through the gap that separated Rattlesnake Clan from Eagle Clan. One by one they passed the remaining ridges. From the rows of houses, people from Graywood Snake's clan watched with somber eyes, many singing and calling final wishes to their departed Elder.

"So, where are the souls?" Salamander asked.

"Hovering close to the bones, you know that." The Serpent paused in his Singing. "Why do you ask?"

"Because of the people," Salamander replied quietly, keeping his head down as was respectful toward the dead. "They call out to Graywood Snake, but what is left of her in the basket is soulless meat, correct?"

The Serpent grinned humorlessly. "That is the way of people, Salamander. The living see the Dead everywhere. It hurts nothing and makes the living feel better.

Perhaps the Dead hear all of the calls. I don't know, and worse, I can't find out until I, myself, am dead."

They passed the last of the ridges with their mourners, and walked out onto the beaten grass beyond. To their right, the Bird's Head rose high and resolute into the yellow-hot air. The ramada at the top looked fuzzy and wavered in the humidity. Bright fabrics that had been tied to the sun poles hung limp and heavy.

As they walked toward the distant forest, insects chirred and whizzed around them, transparent wings glittering in the white light. Looking to the south, across undulating dimples of old pits, Salamander could see Dying Sun Mound, flat-topped and green at the end of the causeway. On this day a group of children and dogs chased across the low-walled expanse of the mound, flinging a leather-wrapped ball back and forth with sticks. Their shouts and barks barely carried in the heat.

Sweat broke free to stream down Salamander's body and mix with the juices that streaked his buttocks and legs. He batted at the growing number of big black flies that buzzed around, drawn by the odor of fresh wet flesh.

Their route took them past the southern end of the huge borrow pit. As they rounded the rim of the deep pit, Salamander could look down into the dark waters. Insects broke the surface, and a flight of ducks exploded from the green weeds that lined the shore, their wings whistling as they battered the air.

Salamander was wishing for a drink by the time they made the forest margin. Entering the shadows provided the slightest relief from the searing sun, but the hot wet air seemed to press in close.

The Serpent led the way along a narrow trail

beaten into the leaf mat by the passing of tens of tens of tens of bare feet over the ages. They walked under the arching span of hickory and beech trees before stepping into a small clearing thick with old brush.

"Clay Fat needs to send someone to burn this brush next winter," the Serpent muttered.

Each of the clans had a spot like this, removed from the Sun Town by a short walk. Here, in a small clearing, the cuttings were disposed of.

Salamander glanced around, seeing the thick brush. Old branches, worn gray by weather, poked out of the clusters of palmetto, privet, and honeysuckle. Raspberries were forming, the fruits green and lush. They would produce a harvest that no one would come to collect. A thousand spiderwebs laced patches of white in the branches.

"They catch the flies and beetles," the Serpent said, noting his interest. "For some creatures, there is good hunting around the leftovers of the Dead."

A crow cawed above. Since the night of his initiation, he had grown more than a little leery of crows. Salamander looked up, seeing the black bird alight on the waving tip of a branch to watch with one beady eye. Only then did the white droppings that marred the leaves and branches catch his attention. No wonder the place looked so lush. Death fed life here, be it the carrion eaters or the plants. He swung the basket down, reaching in to help the Serpent remove slimy strips of muscle, skin, and viscera. These they draped around on the brush, easy at hand to the scavengers. More crows called in the treetops, eager for the coming feast.

Salamander batted at the flies as he laid the last of Graywood Snake's body onto the sagging branch of a privet bush. He realized the crunchy stuff under his feet was maggot casings.

"Evil spirits!" the Serpent cried to the open sky. "Stay here, and away from the souls of our departed friend. This is your place! Take what you will of what we leave here, and be content. Come no closer to Sun Town, or I shall have to do battle and destroy you."

Salamander swallowed hard. He never felt safe when they made these deposits. His Dreams, always uncertain to start with, were labored after he and the Serpent processed a body. That he involved himself in such doings irritated his wives to no end—perhaps explaining his willingness to help the Serpent with his grisly chores.

"Come, my friend." The Serpent turned and led the way back into the forest. "We have finished this portion of our duty. All that remains is to help Clay Fat fire the house tonight. I shall have Bobcat do most of the Singing. I think he is ready for that."

They walked in silence as they retraced their tracks. Breaking into the open again, the sight of the Bird's Head to the north and the children playing on Dying Sun Mound to the south reassured Salamander.

"Mud Stalker came to see me last night," the Serpent said offhandedly. "Knowing that Bobcat had been called to Ground Cherry Camp to attend a broken leg, he asked me to find another to help with the Elder's body."

Salamander shot him a glance. "He did?"

"It appears that some do not approve of your interest in acquiring the arts necessary to handle the dead."

"That is not their concern." Salamander swung the

basket back and forth, slinging the loose gore from its stained bottom.

"You are not happy in your marriage," the Serpent stated.

"You have divined this on your own, have you?"

"Do not mock me. You have been married now for almost three moons. And a Speaker for your clan for nearly as long. I can feel Power and trouble gathering around you."

"Mud Stalker is disappointed with me. I haven't always voted the way he would like. And Mother, I don't understand. She mostly just stands there, eyes lost on the distance. I have caught her talking to Cloud Heron's ghost when no one's around."

The Serpent sighed. "What about your Dreams?"

Salamander ground his teeth, then admitted, "They come sometimes. Many Colored Crow has come to me since the night of my initiation. Sometimes I fly with Masked Owl. He tells me things."

"Such as?"

"He tells me to watch out for certain people. He gives me glimpses of faraway lands. Sometimes he warns me of things."

"What things?"

Salamander shook his head. "I'm sorry, Elder. They are between Masked Owl and me."

Carefully, the Serpent said, "You are aware that Mud Stalker and your wives are plotting?"

"Oh, yes. Though why they insisted that I marry is beyond me. And why, for the sake of Snakes, did they appoint me to the Council? I just sit there. I'm an embarrassment. Look at me! But for the political necessity, I wouldn't be made a man yet. Who ever heard of a boy like me sitting in the Council?"

The Serpent slowed as he reached the deep borrow pit. With care he stepped over the edge. The slope was steep, but a narrow trail had been worn through the thick green grass and into the brown earth. A misstep meant a nasty tumble through the weeds and grass and into the stagnant water below. Salamander started as a snake slithered rapidly away. He could see the plants moving as the reptile wound along the slope. Wood snake? Or water moccasin?

At the bottom, the Serpent crouched on a thin strip of beach and splashed his hands into the water. Cleansing had to be done on the western side of Sun Town, every bit of blood, liquid, and tissue washed away. The borrow pit pond was the perfect place for these ablutions. With great care, the Serpent washed his hands, taking time to pick the dried blood from under his fingernails. "Bide your time, Salamander. You are meant to be a joke. It is the revenge Mud Stalker has planned for your mother and clan."

"It humiliates me," Salamander agreed as he stepped to one side and perched on the steep slope. He bent forward and dunked the basket into the water, seeing minnows, tadpoles, and insects swimming away. He sloshed it back and forth before hauling it out, ripping a handful of grass free and scrubbing the insides to remove the stains.

"And what does a salamander do when a raccoon is snorting and sniffing around a fallen log? Does he run out immediately in search of insects?"

"Of course not."

"There is a lesson in that." The Serpent rubbed at a

blood spot on his forearm and looked up pointedly. "Do you know what it is?"

"I didn't want to be a member of the Council." Salamander tipped the basket to dump the red-stained water out. "I didn't ask for any of this."

"Sometimes the best people are those who didn't ask for the responsibility."

"Sometimes they aren't."

"Power chose you, Salamander. At each important event, it has settled around you like a blanket. Just as it did atop the Bird's Head and at your initiation." He paused, looking down at his hands again, inspecting them to make sure they were clean. "I won't be around to help you much longer."

"What are you talking about?" Salamander bent down and began washing his hands.

"I'm talking about the future. What is to come. You are so young, my friend. That is your strength and your weakness."

"That doesn't make sense."

"Listen to me!" the old man demanded. "Something is coming, something I cannot see over the horizon of time. I am an old man, and I will probably not live to see this thing happen. My friends are dying. Graywood Snake was younger than me. Elder Back Scratch is ailing and will die soon—leaving that witless Sweet Root as Clan Elder. Cane Frog will be lucky to survive another winter. Who can tell how many moons I have left? This, however, I know: Learn from your Spirit Helpers. Learn from the world. Do not seek fame, or revenge, or any other petty gratification. Do you hear me, Salamander? *Be who you are!* That is why Power chose you."

"Be who I am?" He glanced at the old man in puzzlement.

"Exactly. And be it smartly. You are caught between Masked Owl and Many Colored Crow because they saw something in your souls. Dreams are crossing here. Different paths to the future. Like those crossed lines I carved into your chest, you are the place between the North and the South, the East and the West. You lie between Masked Owl and Many Colored Crow. A battle is being waged, and you are the key."

"What battle? What are they fighting over?"

The Serpent shook his head slowly. "It is an old thing between them. They are brothers, you see. Masked Owl and Many Colored Crow. They take other forms at times, sometimes wolves, ravens, eagles, lions, bears, but one is always light, the other dark. Forever separate, forever bound, but never in agreement. They pull the world back and forth between them."

"And I am supposed to bring an end to this?"

"No. You are just supposed to help one side win for the time being."

"But how can I be part of this? I don't even have a Spirit Helper to advise me. Not even Salamander."

The Serpent made a face. "Are you *that* dull-witted?"

"How do you mean?"

"Many Colored Crow sits atop the Men's House during your initiation. Masked Owl takes you flying in your Dreams. Boy, just *what* do you think a Spirit Helper does, anyway?"

Salamander blinked, a cold shiver running down his back despite the dripping heat. *No wonder he laughed*

W. Michael Gear & Kathleen O'Neal Gear

*when I asked if Salamander would consider being my Spirit Helper.*

"That's right," the Serpent told him fondly. "Just be yourself, Salamander. That will save you. So long as you do not lose yourself, do not become like the others. If you forget who you are, become like them, you are going to be crushed like a caterpillar in a lizard's jaws."

# Chapter Eight

Evening had settled on Sun Town the way it did in the days after the solstice—with great rapidity. Water Petal sat to one side of the ramada, her back propped against one of the support poles. Her infant, a son, suckled noisily at her left breast. As it worked the brown nipple, the baby's little fingers kept grasping and flexing, as if he didn't have enough to occupy him in the busy pursuit of filling his belly.

A low fire smoldered under the ramada's northern edge, that location receiving slightly more protection from the intermittent summer rains. Wing Heart tended it by adding another branch from the pile Salamander had brought in from the forest.

Lost in thought, Salamander studied the circular wicker framework of the new house that rose immediately to the west. Still unroofed, the walls looked like a huge round basket sticking out of the ground. Poles had been dug into the earth and saplings woven between them to harden as they dried. This in turn would eventually be smeared and plastered with clay and allowed to cure before brush was piled against the walls and set on fire to harden it. Only then would the pole rafters be put in place for the roof. Saplings, again, would be woven across them to provide a lattice to which shocks of grass thatch could be attached.

Salamander turned, studying the preoccupied look on his mother's face. *What is wrong with her?* Was this the woman he had known, and so often feared? Where once a cutting sharpness lay behind those dark eyes, now only emptiness remained.

Wing Heart had decided to rebuild on the location of Uncle Cloud Heron's house rather than her old one. Though she'd never said, Salamander suspected that she couldn't bear to build where she had burned her son's bones. It didn't make sense, but then, where Wing Heart was concerned a great many things didn't make sense anymore.

"Moccasin Leaf is continuing to spread her poison," Water Petal announced. "She is spreading the story among the lineages that Salamander, with the advantage of two wives, is unable to plant a child in either one."

"White Bird has only been married for three moons," Wing Heart answered absently.

Both Salamander and Water Petal flinched at the use of her dead son's name. Oblivious, she continued, "I'd been married for six before Black Lightning planted White Bird in my belly. And, if memory serves, Pine Drop's mother, Sweet Root, took nearly a year to catch." Wing Heart turned and settled herself at her loom. A half-finished kirtle hung there, the center decoration consisting of a bird woven out of the whitest hemp thread she could find. Her fingers rose like thin brown spiders to the warp and began plucking the threads.

Water Petal turned her attention to Salamander. "You are lying with them, aren't you?"

"Of course." Great joy that it was. He looked out at the night with a bitter feeling in his breast. In addition to the worry over his mother's frequent lapses and odd snatches of conversation with dead people, his nights with his wives bore down on him like rough sandstone on soft wood. The memory of Spring Cypress pulled at his souls like a tightening cord. He could feel his heart hammering, the blood running hot in his veins. Snakes, he had wanted her with a desire that had burned him. Why wasn't it that way with Pine Drop and Night Rain? Both women had bodies every bit as well shaped as Spring Cypress's.

"Salamander?" Water Petal's voice dropped. "How often do you mount your wives?"

He shifted uncomfortably. "When they tell me to." The admission felt like drawing a rose stem through an open wound.

"Snakes!" Water Petal cried, startling the baby, who spat out her nipple and gave a lusty bawl. She maneuvered his mouth back into place and resettled his fabric-wrapped body into a more comfortable position. "I suppose each time they *let* you exercise your rights as a husband, it is a week just before or just after they've been in the Women's House?"

He nodded, wishing they could talk about something else.

"Salamander," Water Petal's voice dropped, her eyes taking Wing Heart's measure as she asked, "is it fun? Do you enjoy coupling with them? Or have they turned it into work, a thing that must be endured?"

"Endured." He ground his teeth, taking his own suspicious glance at his mother. "It wasn't as if our marriage was something any of us looked forward to."

"Salamander, there is talk that you may not have heard. Moccasin Leaf overheard it in the Women's House. It seems that..." She winced as if her teeth hurt.

"That Pine Drop is bedding that Frog Clan man, Three Stomachs." He finished for her. "How did he get that name, anyway?"

"From the way he eats. What would fill three men barely lasts him until his next meal. But that's not the point. Is it true?"

He nodded. "I have seen them. One of the advantages to being invisible is that it's easy to pass unnoticed. They plan meetings any chance they get." He paused. "At least she enjoys coupling with him."

"Rot her crotch away," Water Petal hissed. "You know what she's doing by putting you off, don't you?"

"Yes, Cousin. She is avoiding having my child. Though why she would mate with Three Stomachs is beyond me. None of his children have lived. His wife, that Rattlesnake Clan woman, has borne him five stillborns."

"Of course," Water Petal noted, putting the pieces together. "If she does have a child by him, and it's stillborn, it reflects on you." She shook her head. "Do they hate us that much?"

"More, I'd say." Salamander reached out, fingering the polished wood in the ramada's support pole. "But do not concern yourself."

"Indeed?" Acid, like cactus juice, laced Water

Petal's voice. "Do not concern myself about the woman who seeks to insult my cousin, not to mention the Speaker of my clan?"

"It is not time yet," Salamander told her. "She isn't conceiving any child by Three Stomachs."

"Snakes and Lightning, Salamander! It's his seed he's planting inside her slippery tube!"

"Please lower your voice." Salamander shot her a hard look. "Not everyone in Sun Town need be part of this discussion."

"And *how* do you *know* that his seed is not already growing in your wife's womb?"

"I have my ways." He watched his mother as he spoke, but Wing Heart seemed oblivious, a slight smile on her lips as she worked the loom. This world might have been but a shadow of the world she saw. "You must trust me, Cousin. She will not conceive, and she suffers as a result of her roaming."

For the first time, Water Petal's expression softened. "That makes me feel just a little better, Cousin. It gladdens my souls to hear that you are carving at least a little revenge off her slim body. Would you mind telling me how you're accomplishing this feat?"

"It is not revenge, Cousin. And, no, I will not tell you how I deal with her infidelity." He noticed a young man hurrying along the embankment toward their ridge. A slim fellow, Salamander couldn't place him in the gloom. Then he recognized that loose run: Little Needle. "Cousin, you must trust me about this."

"Thank the Sky Beings, I hope this is something that you're learning from the Serpent? People talk about that, too, you know. Many wonder what to think of you. It's not like you will step into his shoes when he dies. He has made it clear that Bobcat will. As to why you help him with the death rituals, well, it seems depressing to me."

"He needs me."

"So do other people, Salamander! Your mother, the Clan Elder, could use a little help on the house she's building. But for Yellow Spider, it's a wonder we've even raised the walls!"

He stood, stepping out from the ramada as Little Needle came jogging up, his breath rising and falling.

"Salamander?" the boy called.

"Greetings, Little Needle. What brings you at a run? Not more gossip about my wives, I hope." He glanced back, unable to read Water Petal's expression.

"No." Little Needle managed between puffing breaths. "But I'm glad you have heard these things about them. Especially Pine Drop. Did you know that she's been—"

"Yes, yes, go on." He clamped a hand on the boy's greased arm and dragged him into the shadows of the ramada. "What brings you here?"

"Jaguar Hide!" the boy cried. "You wouldn't believe it! I talked to my cousin, Bluefin, who was fishing in the south. He has a set of gill nets placed where the channels are draining out of the swamp. He went to check them, and who should be waiting but Jaguar Hide! Bluefin thought he was dead! But then Jaguar Hide asked him his clan. And when he told him Owl Clan, Jaguar Hide asked him to carry a message to Elder Wing Heart."

"What message?" Water Petal stood and stepped forward. Salamander didn't need to see her quick glance at Wing Heart.

"Cousin," Wing Heart interrupted, surprising them all, "Speaker Cloud Heron and I will hear what Jaguar Hide says." She turned her head in the darkness, though how she could still work the loom baffled Salamander. "Tell me, Little Needle."

"Jaguar Hide wants to come here!" Little Needle had stopped bouncing from foot to foot, puzzled at the mention of the dead Speaker. "He wants to meet with you, declare a truce between our peoples. He wishes to know if you will speak in the Council and grant him safe passage to come and see you?"

Wing Heart had stopped weaving, her form a dark shadow in the gathering night. For a long moment she remained frozen, then said in her old familiar voice, "Yes, Little Needle. I will speak for him. Send word: Owl Clan guarantees his safety. Let him come and tell the Speaker and me what is on his mind."

"Don't do this, Elder." Water Petal turned to stare at Wing Heart's dark shape. "Whatever he is after, it is no good. And we have never been weaker."

"We are *Owl Clan!*" Wing Heart snapped. "No one challenges our authority. Let him come!"

Water Petal's sagging posture betrayed her defeat. No matter what, Wing Heart remained the Elder. Her word was final.

Salamander turned back to his friend. "Go. Tell Bluefin that the Elder will see Jaguar Hide. I take it that he has a way of getting the message to the Swamp Panthers without ending up skewered on a pole in their village?"

"He does. Jaguar Hide gave him instructions on how it was to be done."

"Then you had best get a good night's sleep," Salamander told him. "It will be a long trip through the channels tomorrow."

"Yes, Speaker." Little Needle turned, trotting away into the darkness to find his mother's house on the third ridge.

"What does Jaguar Hide want?" Water Petal repeated to herself.

"He will bring trouble," Wing Heart said from her loom. "I have no doubt of that. Don't worry, Cousin, it is nothing that the Cloud Heron and I can't handle."

Salamander could feel Water Petal's unease as she studied the Elder. White Bird, Cloud Heron, they cropped up in Wing Heart's conversation as if they had never died. Maybe this was just what his mother needed to bring back her old confident self. Was she still canny enough to deal with the terrible Swamp Panther warrior?

*Masked Owl, why haven't you warned me about this in my Dreams?*

Pine Drop followed the deep forest trail through the gathering dusk. A heavy fabric sack hung over her shoulder and weighted her down with freshly picked bladderwort. The plant was her excuse to walk a half day's journey to the south and had taken her but a finger of time to collect. The rest of it she had spent satiating herself on Three Stomach's male member. In the beginning she had hesitated taking him as a lover. The man simply had no brain to go along with that magnificent body of his. The reason for his prodigious appetite was directly related to the fact that he had a lot of body to feed. Three Stomachs was big, muscular, hardy, and endowed with an incredible vitality. His male part was built like the rest of him: huge. The sight of his hardened organ had frightened her the first time, but to her delight, he was skilled enough to prepare her womanhood to accept it without discomfort.

She winced, placing a hand to her abdomen. While she would have liked to blame the cramps on Three Stomachs and the oversized root he slipped into her, the painful irritation had started earlier that week. And Night Rain, too, complained about it. The malady didn't affect her seriously, but was annoying, peaking about midway through her moon.

*You should see the Serpent about it.* Yes, she should, but the idea of discussing such a problem with someone who was close to her husband rankled. What if the old shaman went straight to Salamander to say, "Your wife is having female trouble the week before and after she is bedding her lover."

That assuredly wouldn't do. And, rot take it, why hadn't Three Stomach's seed planted in her womb? It was common knowledge, spoken of in the Women's House, that a woman took about midway in her cycle. Snakes knew, the man had pumped her full enough times in the passing moons. His own wife had conceived in the last moon. She and Three Stomachs were hoping that this sixth child would be the one who lived.

She followed the trail out from the canopy of trees south of her clan grounds and trudged toward the distant curve of Sun Town's ridges. In the gloom, she could see the lines of houses, some haloed by cooking fires.

"Greetings, Niece." Mud Stalker's voice startled her. He was sitting in the grass, his head and shoulders barely visible. "Sorry to frighten you."

"Uncle!" She took a breath to resettle her heartbeat. "I didn't expect to find you out here."

"Nor did anyone else." He grunted and climbed to his feet, then gestured toward home. "I had hoped that you would take this trail back. I need to talk to you. Several things have happened. First, I don't think you should see Three Stomachs again. At least, not as a lover. We are starting to hear talk."

"Let them talk." She matched her stride to his, the bag of bladderwort swinging from her shoulder. "I could care less if people know I'm dissatisfied with Salamander now, or later."

"Ah, yes, but I do care." He studied her in the darkness. "You are not pregnant, I take it?"

"I won't know for another half-moon, Uncle. Let's see if I have to retreat to the Women's House, shall we?" She winced, slowing, a cramp tightening just below her navel.

"Are you all right?"

"Yes, Uncle." She made a face and forced herself to straighten. "It comes and goes. I'll be over it in a week or so."

"Here, let me take the bag." He reached for the sack. "What's in it?"

"Bladderwort. I'll look like a perfectly dutiful wife when I prepare it for our household." She glanced at him, walking with one hand pressed firmly against her abdomen. "So, tell me, Uncle, have you found a lover for Night Rain yet?"

"She must be handled a bit more judiciously." He

had his head cocked, his strong left hand knotted around the sack of bladderwort. "Has she mentioned any young man besides Saw Back? Anyone that might have caught her eye?"

"No. And I have even suggested several. She's very young, Uncle. She thinks only as far as Saw Back."

"She's a woman, no younger than you were when you married Blue Feather."

"I loved him." She shook her head, relieved that the cramp was fading. "Give her time, Uncle. She is younger than I was at her age. She has always been unsure, and for the moment, she is confused and unhappy. Marriage hasn't been what she expected, and I think it will take a while for her resentment to pass. When it does, we can find a man to pair her with. Until then, forcing her to do so might cause us more harm than it will do good."

"We agree." He paused. "You can stop seeing Three Stomachs without regret? This thing between you, it hasn't gone to the heart yet, has it?"

She laughed at that. "No, Uncle. It hasn't gone to the heart. I don't mind locking hips with him, but I would hate to be married to him. I think he only has a single thought in a day, and not a very interesting one at that."

"Good. He shouldn't be much of a problem. He has had affairs before and never made a pest of himself afterward. If you gently tell him that you can't see him anymore, he should just shrug and walk away."

"Indeed, Uncle? You know a lot about him, then?"

Mud Stalker chuckled. "Let's just say that he has proven useful when it came to placing women in compromising positions. Depending upon the woman, and depending upon the nature of her indiscretion, a great deal of leverage can be acquired by the party who happens to *stumble* over them in the act. Politics is partly flexibility, partly being smart, and partly leverage."

"I will remember that."

"Good." He made a smacking with his lips. "A runner went to Wing Heart tonight from Jaguar Hide asking for the Owl Clan's support in safe passage to Sun Town. What one of our kinsmen overheard at the canoe landing was that Jaguar Hide wants to make peace between our peoples. He evidently still thinks that Owl Clan is preeminent."

She already guessed where this was headed. "You want me to find out what this is really all about?"

"I do. And I want to know if it is to our advantage to let Owl Clan make this peace, or whether we can use this as an opportunity to cut yet another support out from under them."

"Such as?"

"Such as allowing Elder Wing Heart to promise safe passage, then ambushing Jaguar Hide on his way home." He made a gesture. "Not that we would have to do it, mind you. Deep Hunter would have more than a passing interest in bringing that Swamp Panther cutthroat to justice."

She nodded. "I see." A hesitation. "My husband and I don't talk, you know."

"That is another reason for interrupting your affair with Three Stomachs. At least until the whispers dry up. We don't want him to find out. If he does, he could become completely alienated, and as much as I would love to humiliate him and Owl Clan, it is a bit soon for such a revelation."

She glanced at him. The notion of taking Three Stomachs to her bed had been bothersome in the beginning. What if she did conceive? And what if the child were stillborn? Given the man's incredible potency, she had convinced herself that it had been a combination of bad luck and his wife's infertility that had led to the five dead infants his wife had delivered, but what if it wasn't? That she hadn't caught in three moons was starting to worry her—as were the cramps during the weeks of her heightened fertility.

That thought having lodged between her souls, she cocked her jaw. Just how deep did Mud Stalker's hatred run? Deep enough to place his own kin at risk? She shook her head, unwilling even to consider that the uncle she had known and looked up to all of her life could even contemplate such a thing. No, he was acting in the clan's best interest—and in hers and her sister's.

*Leadership depends on these kinds of things.* The words lingered in her thoughts. *A leader cannot be like the rest of the people. More is demanded of him. To be a leader means giving up part of yourself for the rest of your clan.*

She had taken those adages into her souls as her infant body had taken her mother's milk. With the exception of a few times as an adolescent girl lost in daydreams, she had never questioned it. Now she found herself a confidante of the Speaker, her mother in line to be named Clan Elder, and married to the Speaker of Owl Clan, dolt though her husband might be.

*I am in the center of my clan's leadership.*

"You have grown silent," her uncle noted.

"Thinking about what it means to be a leader, Uncle. About the things we have to do. Until now I have never really understood the words I have heard all of my life. About a leader's responsibility to her people."

"And now that you understand?"

"It is a terrible burden, Uncle."

"Yes?"

"One I will carry." She felt a tingle in her loins and tensed against a cramp that didn't intensify. "I will see what I can learn from Salamander about Jaguar Hide's purposes in coming here."

"Good. I am so proud of you, Niece. So very proud." He made a gesture. "You should know, your grandmother is dying. She may not last the night."

"I should go to her."

"Yes," he replied. "And think of what her death will mean for your future."

# The Serpent

We humans spend so much time working to shrink the miraculous to the size of our own pettiness that it's a wonder we manage to get anything else done.

Our lives are filled with miracles that we do not see. Every time a hawk shrieks or a bear roars, it is the visible breath of the Creator entering our world.

But we look and look away.

Each time a raindrop lands, our world is clothed in the glory of its greatest possibilities.

But we go inside our houses where we can't see it.

We are too preoccupied with who might be saying bad things about us to care that the wildflowers have bowed their heads in profound gratitude and the vines have spread their arms in prayer.

That is the challenge we face. It is only when we allow ourselves to experience the divine presence each moment that we live our lives to the fullest.

And that is the dilemma. It is a summons to wonder

*that most of us will turn our backs upon in favor of belittling someone else.*

*Are we really so terrified to look into the Creator's eyes?*

*What do we fear we will see?*

*The primary purpose of a miracle, after all, is not revelation. It is redemption.*

# Chapter Nine

The night after Back Scratch's funeral, Salamander blinked his eyes open and listened to the sounds. Birdsong had sent its first melodies through the darkness. Dawn couldn't be more than a hand's time from breaking over the eastern horizon. He reached out and lifted the deerhide, aware of Night Rain's sleeping form where she lay beside him. His second wife was snuggled against the wall, her back to him. She shifted, some sleep-ridden sound deep in her throat as he slipped from the covers into the cool air and resettled the deerhide over her shoulders.

The events of the previous night came tumbling out of his sleep-heavy souls. After Wing Heart had excused herself and gone to bed, he and Water Petal had sat up late, discussing the implications of Jaguar Hide coming to Owl Clan. Did it mean that he had heard of their weakness, or did he still come to them believing that he dealt with the most prestigious of Sun Town's clans? Assuming the former, did he have designs on Wing Heart, seeking to further damage her standing among the clans? Or would this be the challenge that would snap her out of her endless mourning for her brother and son?

Salamander stretched in the dark shadows and glanced at the door, a bare gray portal to the predawn outside. Moving in silence, he tied a cord around his waist and pulled his breechcloth into place.

Under his bed he found the wooden box that contained his herbs. The sweetgum wood had been decorated with an interlocking owl motif, the wings of one blending into the wings of another to encircle the box. Opening it, his fingers encountered a soft leather bag in one corner. This he lifted and loosened the drawstring. He took a pinch, sniffing to ensure he had the right mixture. A quick glance ensured that both women were hard asleep. He dropped a dash of the powder into the stewpot. Sniffing his fingers again, he confirmed the ingredients: wild ginger, licorice root, dog bane, milkweed, and rue. Both Pine Drop and Night Rain were destined for another day of female discomfort.

He wearily returned the herbs to his box before closing it and restoring it to its place under the bed. From the clay pot beside the box he scooped out a liberal handful of rendered bear grease laced with pine resin. This he smeared liberally over his arms, legs, face, and belly—protection against the hordes of stinging and biting insects.

Finished, he reached for his atlatl and darts. To his dismay, one of the long cane shafts caught on the deerhide hanging from Pine Drop's bedding.

"Huh?" she mumbled. "What's wrong?"

He could see her shifting, sitting up under the soft

hide. "Nothing. I'm sorry. It's still early. Go back to sleep."

"Salamander?" she groaned. "Snakes, the sun's not even out yet."

"Shush, go back to sleep." He started for the door.

"Wait. Where are you going?"

"Out to greet the sun. And then hunting."

"Have a good hunt." She started to roll over, then stopped short as if suddenly thinking of something. "Wait. I'm coming with you."

He froze. "Why?"

"I'm your wife. Can't I come with you if I want to? You might be able to use some help."

He could feel his souls sinking. "I might be gone for most of the day."

"It's all right. Night Rain can do the chores. I brought us bladderwort from one of the bogs down south. She can boil it and drain it."

Fortunately, she couldn't see his face while he waited for her to stand, tie her kirtle around her waist, and grease herself.

"Drink some of that stew," he told her insistently. "If you don't, you'll be chewing sticks in two hands' time."

She crouched, lifting the ceramic pot and drinking deeply of the mixture. That, at least, brought him a little satisfaction.

"Wretched Snakes," she said as she replaced the bowl and wiped her lips. "The fire is stone dead, and that tastes like swamp muck."

"It's food," he reminded. "You'll need the strength." He wondered what he was going to eat. It wouldn't do to go begging breakfast from Water Petal as he'd been doing for the last couple of months while he laced his wives' food with the Serpent's potions. It might turn into a very long day for his stomach.

He led the way out into the morning. Moisture rode on the southern breeze, speckling his skin and filling his nostrils. In the darkness, he could see tufts of mist curling along the ridge. The line of domed houses seemed to solidify as if from fragments of dreams as he and Pine Drop walked along the earthen berm to the first gap. From there he crossed to the Southern Moiety commons and cut across for the ramp leading up the eastern side of the Bird's Head.

"Do you do this every morning?" she asked.

"Yes." It had become a ritual with him. The last place on Earth he wanted to be was in Pine Drop's house when his wives awakened. Having begun with such low expectations, their relationship had been deteriorating ever since. It had been safe to assume that they wanted as much to do with him as he did with them.

He passed the Council House and started up the long ramp. It never ceased to amaze him that his ancestors had built such a triumph. He often tried to wrap his comprehension around the number of baskets of earth that had been dug, carried, and piled to create the Bird's Head. The sheer size of it filled his souls with awe.

He had taken to sprinting up the long climb and chafed now that Pine Drop was clambering along behind him. Still, he hurried as much as he could, hearing her breath begin to strain when not even half-way up.

"Is there some pressing hurry?" she called from behind.

"Normally, I run up this."

"Well, go." She waved him on in the foggy grayness. "I'll see you at the top."

Thus freed, he ran, enjoying the pull in his muscles as he dashed to the top. He came to a halt just past the ramada and filled his hot lungs with the cool air. As he turned back to the east, he could see the faint graying of the horizon. The south wind pushed at him, a last faint filtering of stars visible through the heavy air as they began to fade in the east.

She emerged out of the mist below, thin and well formed, her movements female and sinuous as she climbed. Her hair, loose and long, swayed with each step. Were it anyone but Pine Drop, the moment would have been enchanting. As she neared, her image grew into Spring Cypress's. A fantasy that passed as she raised her face to his.

"Now what?" she asked, a tone of resentment barely hidden.

Salamander seated himself and dug into the moist soil with his fingers. "Now we wait."

"Just wait?" She turned, staring out at the graying world around them. Her breathing slowed as she paced back and forth.

He found the little stone owl he had been carving and the flake that he had buried beside it the morning before. Wiping the black clay from it, he resumed his carving.

"*That's* what you do up here? Just sit and carve?" She pointed at the stone image in his hands.

"Why don't you go back and sleep? This can't be pleasant for you."

He could make out her features now. She was a striking woman, her round face balanced with a thin nose and perfect cheeks. She comported herself with a proud bearing and quiet dignity. He could see her teetering on the verge of stomping off. At the last instant, apparently by force of will, she relented and plopped herself down beside him to stare out toward the eastern horizon. The light there had begun to yellow.

He asked, "Why are you doing this?"

She mulled over the words before she said, "I thought that, perhaps, we might try spending some time together." She was winding her gleaming black hair into tight ropes, only to flip them free and repeat the process. "If we are to live together, we must build some trust between us."

"All right." He shot her a wary look.

"Do you hate me?"

The question caught him by surprise. "No. I don't hate you. I just don't like you."

She stared out at the distance, arms crossed as she leaned forward. He could see her expression tensing, as if she were fighting a pain in her stomach. Returning his concentration to the little red owl, he carefully began the notch that would separate the figure's feet.

After several heartbeats, she said, "Just because we are married doesn't mean that we can't be friends."

"That wasn't the impression I had when I first moved into your house."

"I'm sorry."

*Ask her if she is just friends with Three Stomachs.* He resisted the impulse, thinking instead of how Salamander was when Raccoon was sniffing around his log.

"Sacred Snakes," she whispered, and he looked up. A band of red had burned across the far northeastern horizon. Before them, Sun Town was wreathed in silvered mist, only the black tips of the rooftops protruding in curving rings.

"It's beautiful," she continued. "I had no idea."

"That's why I come here. For this one moment of the day, everything in the world is at peace, locked in beauty. In this instant, my souls Dance in joy and breathe the miracle of life."

The distant fire of morning had illuminated her eyes with an unearthly shine and cast her smooth face in orange. Her lips were parted, and she moved her hands from her belly to the spot between her breasts, as if to feel the beating of her heart.

"...My souls can Dance in joy," she murmured absently, "...breathe the miracle of life."

"Watch this." He raised a hand, anticipating the moment as the sun cracked the horizon and shot a seething sea of red across the mist. It rolled toward them, flicking color from the fingers of mist that deepened as the filaments of dawn threaded in to illuminate Sun Town itself in a warm orange glow.

"Beautiful," she whispered, her face alight with joy.

Her expression stopped him. He had never seen her look this way. Monsters of the deep, she hadn't actually allowed the morning beauty to touch her souls, had she?

"On clear mornings"—he watched the glowing world of color—"you can watch the sun as it moves through the Sky. The turning of seasons is marked as Mother Sun makes her way north and then back south. If you pay close attention, you can see her pass each of the ridges."

"This is a thing the Serpent taught you?"

"Among others."

"And there is Power in this?"

"There is Power in many things. Humans just don't always understand them. Most of the time, we refuse to hear the voices the world uses to speak to us. Listening for them isn't something that comes naturally to people."

She studied him, her face profiled in the red light. He had the sudden urge to reach up and trace the line of her forehead and straight nose. To follow the hollow onto her full lips and around her chin.

"Do you really hear those voices?" she asked in an oddly shy voice.

"Some of them." With reluctance, he had to remind himself that this was the same woman who had been in Three Stomach's arms yesterday. That, coupled with her sudden interest in sharing his day, brought wary reality back to roost between his souls.

"Well, come," he said, carefully replacing his owl in its hole and covering it up. "We ought to get on with our hunting. I was thinking of taking a canoe and loading it with fish traps. The water level has dropped enough that the channels are forming."

She looked uncharacteristically sad as she sighed and stood up. "Yes, I suppose so."

*Wouldn't it be wonderful if we really could live like this, share not only moments of beauty but the heart, too?* A bitter laugh formed in the back of his throat. Such things were not meant for him. He might as well consider walking across the surface of the water.

# Chapter Ten

**W**ho *is this man?* Pine Drop turned her head, cheek resting on the flattened wood of the canoe bow. From that angle she could surreptitiously watch Salamander's face while at the same time keeping the blue heron in her sight.

A midday sun beat down, the air muggy and filled with insects who rose, fell, and circled on gleaming wings. Birdsong filled the backswamp forest, and the rich odor of wet earth, water, and plant life penetrated her nostrils.

Their canoe rested in a marshy shallow, partially lodged in a stand of swamp grass that obscured their outline. Herons were keen-eyed birds, among the most difficult to sneak up on. Nevertheless, by patience and stealth, Salamander had eased their canoe within a stone's easy pitch of the tall bird. Through the stems, she could see it as it hunted the lily pad-filled shallows. The graceful heron took one sure step, then, several heartbeats later, another. Between each step, the heron stopped, serene, its head slightly cocked, an alert eye on the dark water.

"He is so precise," Salamander whispered. "No movement wasted."

*This is a day of revelations.* She considered both the heron and her husband anew. She had known herons ever since she was a child. Her people hunted them: their meat was prized, the bones were used for awls and flutes, and the feathers served as personal adornment at ceremonials and special occasions. Through all those years, she had never observed a living bird up close—let alone for any length of time. She had never peeked into another creature's life, never even considered that it might have a personality and unique characteristics.

The same way her husband, Salamander, did. Who *was* he? *What* was he? That morning in her presence, Salamander had transformed himself from a fool to a mystery. Clearly uncomfortable with her presence, he had been aloof, hesitant, and protective. After the miracle of the morning sunrise, they had walked down, loaded his canoe with fish traps, and paddled out into the channels to bait and set the traps. In the process, Salamander had stopped them under a low-hanging cypress to watch as one of the large yellow-and-black spiders spun a beautiful web between the branches.

At first, she had chafed at the inactivity, baffled by the rapt expression on his face. It had finally occurred to her that, for the first time, his guard was down. She was seeing him as he really was. The wonder she saw reflected in his face was the image of his true souls shining through. Then, in an effort to understand his fascination, she had really paid attention to what the spider was doing.

Strand by strand, the spider enlarged the spiral of its web. Each action was like a carefully practiced Dance. The gossamer threads were spun and carefully set in place by a graceful manipulation of the legs.

"I've never realized how perfect their webs are," she had remarked. "Isn't that curious? In all of my life, I've never watched one being built."

"People are too busy," Salamander had remarked offhandedly. "We are in such a hurry to feed our bellies that we forget our souls."

"So tell me, what does a soul need for food?" she had asked somewhat sharply.

She had never seen his eyes like that. They looked ancient, knowing, like tunnels to the infinite. He said, "Beauty, peace, and tranquility."

For a moment, she mulled his words. "What about authority, prestige, and security?"

"Tell me something, Pine Drop. Are you happy with your life? Don't just answer for the sake of answering. Think about it. When you close your eyes at night, do you take a deep sigh and say to yourself, 'Feel the joy in my souls. Thank the Sky Beings that I have had such a good day.' Then, do you look back over the wondrous things you saw and experienced that day?" He smiled shyly. "Tell me the truth."

She had searched his eyes, then lied. "Yes, I do."

A knowing smile had been his only answer before he turned back to watching the spider.

His question had unsettled her, as had his serene presence as they finished laying out fish traps. He had seen the heron, and drifted them silently into the marshy flats where they now watched the bird through a screen of grass. Pine Drop actually took the time to study him with the same scrutiny she applied to the wondrous heron.

"How do you answer that question, Salamander?" she whispered softly. "Do you go to sleep happy every night?"

He shrugged slightly where he lay beside her in the canoe. "Depends on the day. On a day like this, I will. If I have to spend the day involved in clan dealings, I won't."

"You're a Speaker. You have to deal with those things."

"Responsibility can kill the souls," he whispered.

"It can also fulfill them. It is what you make of it."

"The difference is where you find responsibility. Is it responsibility to yourself, to your lineage, your clan, or your people? That's the soul killer. Responsibility to self, however, fulfills."

"So, what are you doing today?"

"I am feeding my souls."

"And when people are looking up to you as Speaker?"

"My souls are dying." A pause and a gesture. "Watch."

The heron took a half step and froze. Balanced on one foot, it shot its head forward, the long yellow beak flashing into the water. It lifted its head in a sinuous motion, flipping the silver fish in the air and swallowing it. Only then did it gracefully insert its raised foot into the water.

"Isn't that remarkable?" Salamander's voice was reverent. "A person couldn't do that, not with that kind of balance. Did you see how the heron just seemed to flow? At the Creation, Heron must have done something wonderful."

"Why do you say that?"

"Because the Creator gifted Heron with so much grace and beauty."

"People generally don't think of herons that way."

"People usually don't receive the kind of gifts that you and I have just received."

"You think this is a gift, being able to spy on a heron this way?"

"Of course."

"Why?"

"Because my souls have been fed. How about yours? What will you tell yourself tonight when you lie down to go to sleep? Will you look back on today and smile as you remember the sunrise? What about the way the spider's legs moved so precisely to place each strand of web? Or the way the heron moved?"

She evaded giving an answer. "Does it bother you that people think you're a fool?"

"No one wants to be thought of as a fool. They just don't understand, that's all."

"Why don't you do something about it?"

"What? Change myself? Try to be White Bird? I can't be like him. He was who he was. I have to be who I am. Not only that, it's not worth it. I won't give up Power just so that people will like me."

"What do you mean, give up Power?"

She could see the reservation return, and he said nothing, eyes on the heron, who had stepped farther away.

"Is that why you spend so much time with the Serpent? He's teaching you the ways of Power?"

Salamander shrugged. She could sense that she was losing him again, so, after a pause, she said, "You are right. About souls, I mean, and what they need for food. When I go to sleep at night, I don't feel very good about myself." She felt nervous as she added, "I am usually too exhausted to think about anything but who did what to whom. I repeat conversations from earlier in the day and worry about what I should have said. Sometimes I repeat them over and over, as if I'm practicing conversations that are forever gone. That or I worry about all of the things I didn't get done or have to do the next day." She made a face. "So, no, by your standards I guess I don't go to bed happy."

"I'm sorry to hear that."

"Why should you be concerned about what I feel?"

"Because, like me, you are trapped. You didn't want this any more than I did."

"Would you change it?"

He turned then, a warmth in his eyes that made her heart skip. "Oh, indeed I would."

"But you are Speaker for your clan. You are Owl Clan's leader! People look up to you. You are one of the most important men in the world. There are only six Speakers, and you are one of them. Do you expect me to believe that you would give that up?"

"In a heartbeat."

"To do what?"

As he considered, she watched his gentle eyes, seeing the complexity, the turmoil behind them. Something about him sent a shiver through her, as if for the first time she could see the depth and breadth of his souls. No man had ever looked at her with such infinite patience and understanding. Snakes, he was three summers younger than she was, but that look sent a tingle through her souls. Did Power really possess him?

"I would ease other people's souls," he finally answered. "I want to learn all the hidden things. I want to know how a firefly glows without getting hot. How snakes move without feet. Why ants can carry things that are bigger than they are."

"And why bears don't have tails?"

"Yes!"

She laughed for the first time. "And how mushrooms can grow without roots?"

Frightened by their rising voices, the heron leaped into the air, flapping away on liquid wings.

"Mushrooms don't have roots? That's one I have never thought of," Salamander remarked thoughtfully.

"Hanging moss doesn't have roots either," she told him, smiling. "Why not? It's a plant, too."

"See! There are so many things. Everywhere you look there is a mystery hidden, and it's so wonderful. Why is it that some people never seem to grasp the wonder?" His expression saddened.

"What?"

"Mother never understood."

After an awkward pause, she said, "I think you have had a lot of nights when you didn't go to bed happy either, Salamander."

That shy smile slipped past his lips. "Perhaps not. But I have learned to live with it. I cherish the memories. Like today, just now, watching the heron. Talking with you like this. After a day of dealing with Mother, I take them out, share them."

"Share them? With whom?"

He just smiled wistfully.

"Do you hate her?"

"Who, Mother? No. I know who she is, who she had to be for the clan and the People. I understand what it meant to her. I don't think she can stand the pain anymore."

"Is she all right?"

"No. I'm worried about her."

"People are talking."

He nodded, obviously unwilling to discuss it.

Did she dare? Was this the right moment?

"What does Jaguar Hide want from Owl Clan?"

She saw the change in his eyes, felt the coolness as he straightened and picked up the paddle. "We'd better be getting back."

"Are you going to meet with him?"

"The Clan Elder will give him safe passage."

"For what? Why would he—"

"I have to be getting back. I'm sure that you have clan business to attend to."

At his abrupt tone, she nodded, sat up, and reached for her paddle. As they pushed the canoe out of the shallows, it was as though something delicate and precious had suddenly turned cold.

Mud Stalker sat in the ramada as the evening fire crackled and popped, thankful that one of the youngsters in his lineage had thought to bring a supply of wood. The day had been busy, his authority called upon to mend a rift between two brothers over a woman and to make a judgment in a case of fish stealing. In the first instance, he had forbade either brother to see the woman, a member of Rattlesnake Clan. Perhaps they would learn a valuable lesson in this: Kinsmen did not compete with each other. Acting in such a manner had been disrespectful of the clan.

In the second case, he had found against the thief, requiring him to forfeit his canoe and to deliver one basket of fish to the aggrieved family per moon for an entire cycle. That the thief had been from Snapping Turtle Clan, and the victim from Owl Clan, had made his day more than a little sour, but with two neutral witnesses from Alligator Clan observing the theft, he couldn't have found any other way.

The fire popped, and he slapped at the mosquitoes that came with the fall of night. Despite his greased skin, they seemed unusually bloodthirsty. They kept flying into his ears, somehow aware that the insides were vulnerable. The soft whining of their wings was about to drive him mad.

He had a length of cane before him—the shaft for a new atlatl dart. To compensate for his bad arm, he had the shaft pinched in the crook of his right leg and clamped in his worn teeth. Staring from the corner of his eye, he reached out with his left hand and carefully placed a stone point into the grooved end of the cane. This next was the delicate part. Careful not to jiggle the point loose, he retrieved a length of damp sinew from the bowl before him and carefully maneuvered a pretied loop around the point. When it was in the right place he pulled it snug. In the process, he barely noticed someone coming to take a seat opposite him. Whatever they wanted could wait.

Having immobilized the point, he wound the sinew round and round the shaft, pulling it tight enough to keep the point in place. As he came to the end of the sinew, he formed a complicated knot, bending and rolling the fine thread between his fingers. Switching his grip, he took the shaft in his left hand and used his teeth to yank the knot tight.

Satisfied, he studied his work in the light of the fire. The point lay straight, perfectly aligned. The thick wrap of sinew would dry and shrink, tightening into a hard, immovable hafting.

"It always amazes me to watch you do that," Pine Drop said by way of greeting. He lifted his new dart and balanced it in his good hand. She had seated herself across the fire from him. He tried to read her expression but couldn't decipher the complex frown that marred her young forehead.

"Where have you been all day? Night Rain was here, and there, and the other place looking for you. She wasn't entirely sure what you wanted done with that bladderwort. In the end, I think she boiled the whole sackful. It took every pot in the house." He cocked his head. "Is she feeling all right? Her stomach seemed to be bothering her."

"It's nothing," Pine Drop answered. She had her legs bent before her and was rubbing her hands along her smooth muscular shins. "I was out with Salamander all day."

"Ah. And?"

The preoccupied look deepened. "Nothing." Her expression betrayed puzzlement. "Such an odd man. We watched the dawn from the Bird's Head. Why have I never done that before?"

"I have no idea."

"After that we went fishing."

"That's good." He suddenly understood her thinking. Smart girl. Men liked to talk when they were fishing. For some reason, it directed their thoughts to important matters, unlike hunting, which might deepen a man's thoughts but had to be conducted in quiet and discipline.

"Is it?" she wondered. "We spent more than two hands' time watching a blue heron stalking the shallows. Another two hands' time was spent studying how a yellow spider spins its web."

"I assume that you talked during these things?"

She nodded absently. "About everything but his clan. We talked about patience and organization, and what humans refused to hear or learn. Thinking back, none of it made sense." Her lips bent with irritation. "Do you know that I've never watched a spider build a web from nothingness before? Or seen that a heron flips a minnow in the air to swallow it?"

"Fascinating, I'm sure. I don't suppose that Jaguar Hide came up in any of these conversations?"

"No." She gave him a flat look. "When I grew desperate, I even asked him straight out." She paused. "I think he was expecting that question. I'd swear that he gave me a faint smile after that, a sadness in his eyes. The only thing he would tell me was that Wing Heart was going to promise Jaguar Hide safe passage, and that beyond that it was clan business."

"That was it?"

She nodded, her fingers still moving up and down her thighs.

"You didn't press him?"

"Of course I did, Uncle. But his entire manner had changed. I might just as well have slapped him."

He ran his fingers along his new dart. "I don't suppose you took the opportunity to lie with your husband? That usually loosens a man's tongue."

Her eyes fixed on his, dark, penetrating, and the effect left him unsettled. "It wouldn't have been right, Uncle."

"What's not *right* about it? You're his wife! Wives couple with husbands. It's what they do."

"After having been with Three Stomachs the day before?"

"You know why we're doing that."

The corners of her mouth tightened. "It wasn't that kind of day," she muttered. "Excuse me, Uncle. I was up with the dawn. I'm tired."

"Don't forget, with Back Scratch's death your mother is confirmed in the Council in three days. We need to prepare a feast for her, and we want you and your sister there for her confirmation. Dress in your finest." He paused, failing to understand her irritation. "And don't stop working on your husband. I'm sure you're smart enough to pry this information out of him."

"I doubt I'll see him anytime soon, Uncle. Not after today."

"What? Why not? He sleeps in your house, doesn't he?"

"That's about all he does." She rose gracefully, her parting glance upsetting his protest before she strode off toward her house on the third ridge.

He frowned as he fingered his new dart. Firelight danced in yellow waves along the cane shaft. *What just happened here? What did I miss?*

# Chapter Eleven

T he Council House was filled. The six clans occupied their respective sections along the edge of the ring. While a great fire was built in the center at night, on daytime occasions such as this, a smoldering log in the middle of the fire pit sufficed. The afternoon sun was slanting at an angle from the northwest. The shaft of light illuminated Mud Stalker and his sister Sweet Root, the newly appointed Clan Elder.

Wing Heart studied her new opponent and tried to concentrate. Sweet Root. This was Sweet Root. Elder Back Scratch was dead. Dead. Just like Graywood Snake. Just like White Bird. Cloud Heron...dead.

When? She blinked, confused.

The terrible ache in her souls continued to muddle her thoughts. As the meeting continued, she kept hearing Cloud Heron, his deep voice booming as he stepped out and addressed the Council. She could see him there in the slanting sunlight. Watched as he raised his hand and spoke so eloquently to the crowd. His voice, so clear and resonant, echoing in her souls.

*Look at him! Isn't he magnificent? Has there ever been a Speaker as grand as Cloud Heron?*

She tried desperately to focus her attention on Sweet Root, but tears tugged at the corners of her vision.

Sweet Root was speaking, her voice sounding far away. She remained a handsome woman, her hair still midnight black despite her age. She might have delivered eight children, two of whom had lived, but her body remained slim, only a thickening of her waist evidence of the seasons she had spent carrying children in her womb. She had been tattooed around her flattened breasts, down the midline of her belly, along the arch of her shoulders, and across her chin. Another pattern of concentric circles had been tattooed on her abdomen between the navel and pubis in an effort to increase her fertility, and that pattern was now obscured by the dust gray kirtle she wore.

Wing Heart glanced about, looking for Cloud Heron. She had just seen him, addressing the Council. Not a moment before. He had to be here somewhere. *Where is he?*

Snapping Turtle Clan was well represented on this day, as was their right. Not only did Speaker Mud Stalker sit proudly as his sister was confirmed as Elder, but so did both of the woman's daughters, Pine Drop and Night Rain. The girls had dressed resplendently: Brightly colored headdresses made from painted bunting feathers perched atop their gleaming black hair, and yellow shawls of tanned young alligator hide hung from their shoulders. Each of their kirtles was tied immaculately at the waist.

*Such beautiful girls. Very worthy of White Bird.* She

looked around, losing her thoughts. *Where is White Bird? He should be here for this.*

"*Dead*" a voice echoed in her head.

"No, not dead," she snapped in irritation as she glanced around, seeking to identify the speaker. It was impossible. Absolutely impossible. He lived, yes, that's right. Something held him up. Something important.

"As my first act as Clan Elder," Sweet Root's raspy voice called, "I must ask this Council to consider the matter of Owl Clan's invitation to the Swamp Panther leader, Jaguar Hide."

Attention turned in Wing Heart's direction. In the eye of her soul, Cloud Heron was sitting behind her, his age-lined face somber as he steepled his fingers. She waited for him to speak.

Another memory drifted into focus, and she watched her son, White Bird, as he stood, alive, strong, straight, raising his hands to accept the cries of approbation that had risen from the gathered Elders, Speakers, and the crowd outside the confines of the Council.

*Look at him, Cloud Heron! How proud he stands, his back straight, the sunlight beaming down on his head. Look at the smile, the ease with which he accepts leadership!*

"Elder?" Water Petal said from behind.

"What?" Wing Heart blinked, her son vanished. She turned, but Cloud Heron was nowhere to be seen. Her souls staggered, only to remember her brother sinking into fever, his body wasting over the long moons. A nightmare image—a yellow tongue of fire—leaped from a torch to ignite the roof of the house that held his cleaned bones.

*You are alone!* Her souls shriveled at the knowledge.

"I was..." She blinked as she tried to find herself, to recall what was happening. Glancing around, she realized that everyone was waiting, waiting for her. "Cloud Heron, tell them," she muttered.

At the stunned expressions on Water Petal's and Moccasin Leaf's faces, she whirled around, searching. Where was Cloud Heron? She had just seen him, his hand up, voice ringing as he addressed the Council.

"Where did he go?" she wondered.

"Who, Elder?" Moccasin Leaf had a horrified look on her face.

"Tell them." Wing Heart looked into Water Petal's eyes, and waved at the Council. "Just...tell them." She tilted her head as she tried to understand what was happening. If Cloud Heron hadn't brought this up, who had? Surely this was something that Water Petal had mentioned. She must know. "Speak for me."

Water Petal swallowed hard and stepped forward. Moccasin Leaf's eyes might have been deer-bone stilettos, piercing her souls with hate and embarrassment. Seated on a palmetto mat, young Mud Puppy watched her with wide, frightened eyes. Mud Puppy? What was he doing here?

"Does this Council not deserve the Elder's respect?" Sweet Root demanded. "Does Wing Heart not speak for her clan when it comes to allowing an avowed enemy to step into our midst? I may be new here, but even as a freshly made Elder, it would appear that I have more respect for these proceedings than the revered Elder from Owl Clan."

"If the Council will hear my words," Water Petal stepped forward, a curious tremor in her voice.

"I, for one," Sweet Root immediately answered, "wish to hear from the Clan Elder."

"She's not well!" It was Mud Puppy's voice. He was on his feet, stepping out in front of Water Petal, his fists clenched at his sides. He wore a beautiful white mantle, one that shone in the afternoon sunlight.

Wing Heart turned, blinking hard. *Why is he here?* This was a place for Speakers recognized by the Council, not uninitiated boys. "Where is my brother? Where is Cloud Heron? Why isn't he here?" Fear bloomed within her like a lotus.

It was Water Petal who swung around on one heel, deftly catching Wing Heart's elbow. "Come, Elder. Let's get you home. The Speaker can handle this." But fear lay in Water Petal's eyes.

"Yes," Wing Heart agreed, quick with relief. "The Speaker can handle this. Cloud Heron always knows what to do."

She was being led away as she heard Mud Puppy say, "The Elder meant no disrespect. If the Council will just be patient..." A roar of voices erupted in answer.

Cold shivers ran down Salamander's body as he shot a quick look over his shoulder. Water Petal was leading his mother away, one hand on her elbow. Even from this distance, he could see his mother's face—a stricken look etching her once-indomitable features.

He swallowed hard, turning his attention back to the jeering calls of the Council. His heart hammered at his ribs, fear bright in his veins. Behind him, Moccasin Leaf was hissing something in poisonous tones.

*I can't speak to the Council! I'm not a Speaker!* He nerved himself to step out into the open where a Speaker should stand. His skin had the hot nervous prickle of embarrassment. For a moment, he couldn't find words.

He glanced at Clay Fat, only to read disappointment in the appalled expression on his face. Turtle Mist, beside him, looked horrified. People shifted on their feet, clearly uncomfortable. Deep Hunter sat with his jaw cradled in his right hand, head tilted forward as he glared out with hard eyes. Stone Talon was shaking her head, tsking sounds coming from her toothless mouth. Three Moss, her hand on her mother's shoulder, gaped incredulously.

Cane Frog demanded, "What is happening? What do you see? Tell me, Daughter! Who is doing what?"

Salamander turned his pleading eyes to Mud Stalker, only to encounter a burning intensity, a hard smile on the man's thin lips. He stood behind Sweet Root, cradling his ruined right arm. Long white heron feathers had been inserted into bands on his upper arms so that they stuck out like snowy wings. Where she stood, a pace in front of him, Sweet Root might have been tasting something delicious, her eyes half-lidded and blissful.

"The Elder is sick!" Salamander cried. "Just leave her alone. Let her rest. She'll get better. She will."

He hated himself, embarrassment growing hotter with each beat of his heart. They could see the sweat breaking out on his face now. See his losing battle as his muscles began to tremble.

Sweet Root asked loudly, "Do I speak for the

Council when I say that no *sick* Clan Elder should be dealing with Jaguar Hide within the limits of Sun Town? What has Wing Heart done? Asked the leader of the dreaded Swamp Panthers to come here? A foreigner, allowed to walk unpurified into our midst? And bringing what with him? A black cloud of curses? Witchcraft? Will he unleash disease and misery among us?"

A roar of agreement went up, members of the Council nodding and bobbing their heads.'

"Then we will meet him on the Turtle's Back!" Salamander shouted, hoping at least to mollify some of the sentiment against his mother. Snakes and lightning, what had happened to her?

"Why meet him at all?" Deep Hunter asked from where he sat.

"To find out what he wants," Salamander answered, his stomach curling and twisting inside him. He had fastened his eyes on Pine Drop and Night Rain. Their expressions jolted him: a mixture of pity, embarrassment, and loathing.

"Why did he send a runner to Wing Heart?" Mud Stalker demanded as he stepped forward to stand beside his sister. "What is his business with Owl Clan? Why didn't he ask to speak with the Council?"

"I don't know." Salamander tried to swallow the knot in his throat. Their eyes were boring through him, seeing his quaking souls. Why had Mud Stalker insisted he take his brother's place? Surely anyone could have known he wasn't supposed to be a Speaker.

"Perhaps," Mud Stalker said evenly, "there should be some representation from the Council at this meeting? What do you say?" He took another step forward, where he could meet the eyes of the others. "An old enemy comes, and we should allow him to meet only with Owl Clan? To broker what sort of deal? Something that leaves the rest of us out? Or something which, for our own safety, we should know about?"

"Alligator Clan agrees," Deep Hunter remarked. "We will send our delegates to this meeting to see for ourselves."

"As will Frog Clan," Elder Cane Frog called, her sightless eyes alone blind to Owl Clan's humiliation.

"Eagle Clan will be there, too," Stone Talon called. "Speaker Thunder Tail will represent our interests."

"So will Rattlesnake Clan," Clay Fat agreed, his voice less strident than the others.

"Owl Clan votes no," Salamander said in a futile and small voice. Atop everything else came the sting of defeat. He had just spoken for his clan for the first time, and been party to its worst defeat. "It is our business."

"Not anymore," Mud Stalker replied coolly.

When Salamander turned and walked back to his seat, Moccasin Leaf's face was livid, her jaw grinding as white rage mottled her features. Had she a club at hand, he didn't doubt that she would have crushed his skull on the spot.

The canoe slipped silently along the channel, its wake spreading in a long V over the brown water. A muggy heat hung in the still air, heavy and deadening on the lungs. Overhead branches of sweetgum, bald cypress, tupelo, and water oak wove into an impenetrable mat of green draped with vines, flowers, and hanging moss. On either side, ferns, brambles, and tangled vegetation carpeted the banks.

Turtles plopped off logs and dived for the depths as the canoe passed. Birdsong accompanied them, as did the whining of the insects. The smell of vegetation, mud, and stagnant water cloyed in the nostrils.

Anhinga dipped her paddle resolutely as she propelled them forward. She could feel her uncle's piercing stare as it ate into her back. The knowledge that he doubted her sent a flame of anger through her.

Anticipating her, he said, "Remember, this must be done slowly, thoughtfully, and with great skill."

"I *know*, Uncle."

"The gravest danger is time. It will lull you, soften your resolve. You will look around you and begin to see these people as not so different from us."

"You have told me this time and time again."

"I will tell you yet again," Jaguar Hide insisted. "Think, Anhinga! You are going to marry a man. You will live with him, day in and day out. You will look into his eyes, watch his smile. You will welcome his body into yours. His child will begin to grow within you. Do you understand what I'm saying?"

"Yes, Uncle. That by pretending to fall in love with him, I really will." She shook her hair, flipping her raven locks in a dark swirl. "Looking at my back, what do you see?"

"Outside of a healthy and attractive woman?" He hesitated. "The scars are healed."

"Yes, but you can still see them." She drove her

paddle vigorously into the water. "And so can I. I can run my fingers over them, feel the ridges, and remember the pain. Those are the things I do when I am awake. I remember what each wound felt like when they inflicted it. Over and over, I see the bodies of my companions. See what they did to them. It is better when I am awake, Uncle. I can shut most of the memories out of my head. When I am asleep, the terror comes. The Dreams wrap around my souls, and I relive every moment, watching them be cut apart, their hearts, livers, and intestines ripped from inside their bodies. I see those animals squatting over ruined faces, defecating into bloody eye sockets. Unlike being awake, I cannot stop the Dreams, Uncle."

He paddled silently behind her for a moment. "The past cannot be killed, Anhinga, but it can be built anew. It is that which you must guard against. You will be tempted."

"I will be *strong!*" she insisted. "I have no life left. At the Panther's Bones, I had to look into eyes of Mist Finger's relatives, see Cooter's sister, wince as Right Talon's mother's eyes asked me, *Why?* I had no answer for them, Uncle, only the ache in my heart that I was alive, and their sons and brothers were not."

"No one holds it against you."

"I do," she snapped. "And I'm the only one who matters."

After a long silence, he asked again, "Are you sure that you want to do this thing? It is fraught with danger."

"It isn't a matter of wanting, Uncle," she told him hollowly. "I must."

With a leaden heart, she continued to paddle

doggedly toward her destiny. In her souls she was already delighting in the surprise as she drove a deer-bone stiletto into White Bird's heart. But before that, yes, she could be patient. She could wait for years if she had to. It would make the act all the more terrible for the witnesses.

# Chapter Twelve

"I felt like such a fool!" Salamander cried as he reached out from the bobbing canoe and grabbed at the duck-shaped wooden float. He caught it, pulling it toward him. Straightening in the canoe, he reeled in the cord that hauled the wicker fish trap to the surface.

He sat in the stern, Water Petal in the bow. The center of the narrow hull was cluttered with pointed wicker fish traps. Each was the length of a man's leg, two hands wide, cylindrical, with a funnel-shaped opening that allowed a fish to swim in, but not out.

Water Petal remained silent as Salamander grasped the wet staves and pulled the trap from the opaque brown water. A single buffalo fish flopped inside. He placed the trap across his lap and untied the door that allowed him to reach in. He caught the fish behind its gills and pulled it from the trap. Using a round rock, he bashed it in the head and dropped it, quivering, into a basket.

"I've never felt so worthless in my whole life." His

thick fingers retied the cord after he closed the hinged trap door. "I couldn't think of anything to say. I was so embarrassed and shamed."

Water Petal picked up her paddle, propelling the canoe forward, steering with the blade. She glanced over her shoulder, checking to see that her son slept soundly in the moss-padded cradle. "Salamander, don't blame yourself. No one expected the Elder to react that way. She was like a ball of soil in a rainstorm. She just melted away."

"My brother wouldn't have made a fool of himself."

"Perhaps not, but he's dead, and you are the Speaker." She shook her head. "I'm not sure how this happened, but it has. Like it or not, you are the Speaker. Sick or not, your mother is the Elder. At least she is until Moccasin Leaf can marshal enough support from the clan to dismiss her."

"She has started on that," Salamander noted. "It will take her a while to get concurrence from the outlying camps. It's the middle of summer. People are off every where, hunting, collecting, making a living."

"I don't have much hope," Water Petal told him heavily. "As bad as it was on you, I watched any chance of succeeding Wing Heart vanish. Without her, our lineage is too weak."

Salamander's heart fell. She didn't hold it against him, did she? "Water Petal, I didn't do it on purpose."

She glanced back at him over the pile of fish traps and read his expression. "No, not you, Salamander. I don't blame you. By the Earth Monsters, I don't know how this happened so fast. It's as if Power just blew through like the south wind and left us broken and beaten."

"I am still Speaker." He considered that. "Moccasin Leaf might be able to have Mother removed, but as Speaker..."

She turned, expression thoughtful. "Finish that. What were you about to say?"

"Mud Stalker wanted me as Speaker. He saw more clearly than anyone. I would love to know how. He has wanted our clan to be disgraced for years. He brokered the marriage with White Bird and placed me right in line to succeed my brother if anything happened. It's as if he knew White Bird was going to die."

"Salamander, no one can foretell a lightning strike."

"No, but having seen the things I have, it makes me wonder."

"What? That Mud Stalker would have killed White Bird? Do you know what an awful chance he would have been taking? Murdering another clan's Speaker would destroy Sun Town, split the clans right down the middle! It would mean war...between us! At best he would be hunted down and murdered! His family and lineage cast into exile, or maybe even killed!"

Salamander stopped short, images reeling in his souls. "Blessed Owl," he whispered.

"Yes? What?"

"It's me!"

"What's you, Salamander?" She was focused on him now, the canoe drifting listlessly toward a lush green bank. As the spring flood had receded, it had left behind a braided web of channels like this one that crisscrossed the wide Father Water's floodplain.

"It's me that he's been counting on. He's been ahead of me all along. He is counting on me to be a failure."

Water Petal said nothing, her expression pinched.

Reading it, Salamander smiled sadly. "I know, Cousin. We're relatives: you, Yellow Spider, and me. Outside of Mother, we are the last of our lineage."

"It's not your fault, Salamander." Water Petal turned away, her hands slipping up and down the paddle as if agitated.

"It isn't time yet," Salamander said gently.

She turned, caught off guard. "Time for what?"

"To take back what is ours."

"I don't understand you."

"I'm not sure I do, either. Cousin, I am going to need an ally."

"Salamander, what are you talking about?"

"I'm not sure yet. But when I know, I'll tell you, all right?"

"You're starting to sound as crazy as your mother."

"Let's hope the rest of the clans think so." He smiled for the first time, pitching the fish trap atop the pile. "The next float is just up there. That's the last one that Pine Drop and I set. I say we cut up this crappie for bait and make another set in the next channel."

For the first time since he had caught his cricket the night White Bird returned from the north, he actually felt tendrils of hope.

Accompanied by six of the enemy's canoes, Jaguar Hide and Anhinga paddled ever closer to Sun Town. It had been a trial for Anhinga, meeting those canoes full of Sun People and traveling side by side with them. In the narrow channels, the enemy were so close that she could reach out with her paddle and tap them. They were propelled by muscular young men, their bodies greased and wearing their best. Colorful feathers were tucked into armbands, hair was done up in high buns and pinned with bone skewers. They wore layers of necklaces across their swelling chests that proclaimed Sun Town's immense wealth. Curiosity and danger reflected in their hard gazes as they paralleled her course.

To keep her nerve, she ignored their called questions, allowed Uncle to do the talking, and kept her back straight, eyes on the channel before her.

She considered it her first challenge, one that she had met, smiling, but remaining aloof enough to keep them at bay. She was, after all, Swamp Panther, the niece of the most noted warrior in the history of her people.

Two other canoes had shot ahead to carry word to Wing Heart that Jaguar Hide was nearing. In spite of her vow of self-control, Anhinga felt a quickening, a thrill and fear mixing within her. She was entering the camp of the enemy to take up a new and secret life.

"Easy," her uncle whispered behind her as they followed a winding channel past a stand of bald cypress, the boles knotted and thick where they rose from the still water. There lay Sun Town, dominating the high bluff across a sun-silvered lake. Dark soil was exposed on either side of the canoe landing, and up high she could see the Father Mound topped by the dreaded Men's House.

Once before, she had been brought here to be carried up that slope, degraded and bound—and there, during that foul day, she had suffered while her life was destroyed.

"Are you all right?" Jaguar Hide asked gently. "You haven't taken a stroke in half a dozen heartbeats."

"I was just seeing the past, Uncle." She speared her paddle into the water, driving them forward. She watched as an incredible number of people began to spill down the bank, a host of them launching canoes. The slim craft pointed in their direction, sunlight flashing on paddles as they pushed their craft forward.

"Sobering, isn't it?" Jaguar Hide asked from behind. "That is a lesson, Anhinga. Look at their numbers. And you and your fellows thought to bloody their nose?"

"Does this have a point, Uncle?"

"It does. When you are setting out to harm a great beast, the only way you can deal it a mortal blow is to strike at its heart. Swiftly, without remorse or pity. You must drive your blade true and straight, lest the beast kill you before you can escape."

"I have already figured that out, Uncle."

One of the lead canoes had closed and was turning sideways, a tall man in the bow, his right arm oddly cradled. "Greetings, Jaguar Hide," the fellow called. "I am Mud Stalker, Speaker of the Snapping Turtle Clan. I am to direct you to the Turtle's Back." He pointed with a muscular left arm. "It is that hump of land there with the gum trees. We shall have our council there."

"Snapping Turtle Clan?" Jaguar Hide muttered. "What do they have to do with anything?"

"Beware, Uncle. A great many things may be happening that we are unaware of. Just get me to Owl Clan, and all will be made right in time."

In a loud voice, Jaguar Hide called, "Accompany us

to that place. We have come in peace to see the great Elder, Wing Heart. It is time to bring an end to this senseless killing and raiding."

"Especially as it has cost you so dearly," Mud Stalker agreed in a jocular tone.

"I will drive a dart into his body myself," Anhinga swore under her breath.

"Careful, Niece." Jaguar Hide's smooth voice warned. "Patience is the straightest dart in a hunter's quiver."

When they landed at the small island, it was to encounter a mob. "Not quite what we had expected, is it?" Anhinga asked.

"No, indeed," he replied as he shipped his paddle and stepped out into the warm water. In one hand he retrieved a sack of smoked fish as an offering. In the other he carried his stone-headed axe. A tool equally useful in felling a tree or a man.

Anhinga nerved herself and reached for the sack that contained her personal possessions. The crowd parted, the way leading up to the shadowed base of the sweetgum tree. There a contingent stood, all dressed in finery, skin greased, colorful feathers adorning their bodies.

"Courage," Jaguar Hide whispered as he passed.

"You, too," she shot back as she fell into step at his side. That short walk, surrounded on both sides by ranks of the enemy, every eye on her, was one of the most terrifying moments of her life. If this were a trap, they would be prisoners before either could react. Death was not nearly as frightening as the prospect of having her tendons cut and having to live the rest of her miserable life here as a slave.

By the time they reached the standing Elders, Anhinga was more than ready to run. Snakes and rot, could they see how scared she was? Even her tongue had stuck in her mouth. But for the grease on her skin, sweat would have beaded and gleamed as it ran.

"Greetings, Elders," Jaguar Hide cried smoothly as he came to a stop. In that instant, he was the noblest man Anhinga had ever seen. Not a sliver of fear was visible in his demeanor or expression. The sunlight played in his silver hair and danced on his broad shoulders. "I am Jaguar Hide. You know me."

"Indeed we do," the tall man, Mud Stalker, replied as he stepped through the crowd to stand beside a middle-aged woman. "We have come to hear what you want from us."

"Peace!" Jaguar Hide cried. "Nothing more, nothing less."

"Peace?" a chubby man asked. He had a moony face, his belly like a giant smooth brown squash. What would have normally been pleasant eyes looked skeptical.

"Peace," Jaguar Hide answered. "In the last several cycles, we have had too many of our young people murdered."

"That is a strong word." A grizzled old woman stepped forward. "I am Elder Stone Talon, of the Eagle Clan. My son and several of my cousins were butchered by you and your sneaky warriors, and over what? A couple of flats of sandstone?"

Anhinga discovered that she couldn't swallow. Fear had gripped the bottom of her throat until breathing was hard.

*Find yourself, curse you! If you can't face this, how are you going to stay here among them?*

"Butchered is precisely the word." Jaguar Hide lifted his arms, the axe held high. "Murdered, killed, slain, what does it matter what we call it? The effect is the same, be it in Sun Town or in the Panther's Bones! We wail and grieve for the lives and souls of our dead loved ones. How many generations have we done this? More than I can relate. Can any of you tell me when this started, how far back?"

A voice called, "It began just after the Creation when the Hero Twins began to battle each other. We have been fighting ever since." The speaker, what looked to be a mere boy, stepped to the fore. Thin, he might have been half-starved. His face was taut, as if he were frightened by speaking out in the presence of his Elders. He pinned Anhinga with large dark eyes that seemed to fill his bony face. "It goes back forever."

That voice! It touched Anhinga's souls. She noticed that the Elders had turned disapproving eyes on the skinny boy, distaste in the set of their lips.

"The boy is correct," Jaguar Hide agreed. "And I, for one, am ready to try something new."

"Why?" A muscular brown man, his face deeply lined by countless days in the sun, asked. "I am Deep Hunter, Speaker of the Alligator Clan, and I would know why Jaguar Hide, who fought so many battles and killed my brother, would come here asking for peace."

Anhinga watched her uncle's face, seeing the slight tic in the corner of his eye. Yes, he knew this Deep Hunter.

"Greetings, Speaker. It has been a long time since you and I faced each other."

"We could take that up where we left it." Deep Hunter's voice had dropped to a growl.

"We could, but it would make more sense if we didn't." Jaguar Hide fingered his axe and stared out from lowered brows. "I have grieved enough in one lifetime, and caused enough others to grieve, that I would find another way."

"Why?" the middle-aged woman beside Mud Stalker asked. "I have been told all of my life that you hate us. What has changed your mind?"

Jaguar Hide smiled, his voice firm. "Oh, I do hate you. Do not believe for a moment that anything we do here today will stop that."

Anhinga tightened as a ripple ran through the crowd.

Jaguar Hide let it hang for a moment before adding, "But I can still hate you without killing your young people. I can hate without hacking their dead bodies apart in a futile attempt to frighten their souls. I can hate you without having to bury one of my young men or women every other moon."

Uncle thrust a hard finger toward Deep Hunter. *"And so can you!* You can hate us without killing us!" A pause in the tense silence. "Who knows, perhaps as we are taken by other means of death, our young people might not hate as we have. Perhaps they will do things differently than we did."

"I still do not understand this," Mud Stalker said warily. "What do you have to gain by peace?"

"The lives of my young people." Jaguar Hide cocked his head. "And you, and your clans, have sandstone to gain, as well as your young people's lives."

"We can take your sandstone anyway," Deep Hunter growled.

"Yes, you can," Jaguar Hide agreed. "But at what price, old enemy? Your nephew? Your grandson?" He shook his head. "I am not here to trick you. I am here to offer you sandstone in return for leaving us alone. I am not fool enough to think that we will remake our world, or forget our hatred and live like brothers. I want to try this for a couple of summers, that is all. Who knows, it may be that we really *enjoy* hunting and killing each other and burning our children's bones in grief." His sad smile seemed to touch them more than the logic of his argument.

"How will this work?" the skinny boy asked before the others could.

That voice! Yes, she knew that voice. But from the darkness, hands fumbling at knots. The sweet words, *"I'm cutting you free,"* echoed in her memory. This forward youth, *he* had been the mysterious shadow in the night?

Uncle said, "From this moment, you will not raid our territory. In return we will allow one canoe per moon to come and take sandstone. If you wish to send two canoes for sandstone, the second must bring gifts for my people. That is all." Jaguar Hide crossed his arms.

"And how do we know you will keep your word?" Deep Hunter's jaw was cocked.

"I bring my niece, Anhinga. I will marry her to the son of Wing Heart, Elder of the Owl Clan. Wing Heart's reputation has traveled far and wide as the greatest among you. We believe that she, of all of you, will see the advantages to this agreement between our peoples."

The words caught the Sun People by complete surprise, but before the Elders could speak, the skinny boy cried, "Owl Clan accepts your offer, great Jaguar Hide."

The boy stepped boldly forward, and for an instant, Anhinga expected his mother to leap from wherever she had been hidden in the crowd to drag him back.

"No, you don't," Mud Stalker growled, narrowing an eye as he studied the boy.

"*Owl Clan* accepts!" the boy fired back, effectively silencing Mud Stalker. The tension between them couldn't be mistaken.

"Who *are* you, boy?" Jaguar Hide asked, obviously surprised.

"I am Salamander, son of Clan Elder Wing Heart and Speaker for the Owl Clan."

Laughter broke out, and Anhinga could only stare as a cold shiver, like a whisper of Power, coursed in her veins. Mud Stalker was glaring daggers at the boy.

"Where is Wing Heart?" Jaguar Hide demanded.

"The Elder is ill," the boy replied, his dark eyes fixed intently on Jaguar Hide. "I have offered to accept your conditions. Yes, or no, revered Elder? Will you marry your daughter to Wing Heart's son, or were your brave words something else?"

Anhinga turned, seeing her uncle's eyes glitter as he said, "I meant what I said! I came here seeking peace!" He looked as if he had just pulled his arm from a hole and found a water moccasin wrapped around it.

The boy took another step forward, offering his

hand to Anhinga. "Then, as of this moment, I accept this woman for my wife."

"Salamander!" a young woman cried from the crowd. "What are you doing?"

He ignored her, his gaze burning through Anhinga's shock as he said, "Do you agree to take me as your husband?"

"Yes." Her reply came involuntarily.

Salamander glanced at Jaguar Hide. "I presume that you have brought the traditional gifts of food. If you will distribute it to the assembled guests here, it will formalize the arrangement between us."

Anhinga stared at Salamander's extended hand, frozen in the moment.

The young woman from the crowd—a baby at her breast—elbowed her way forward, panic on her face. "Salamander, what did you just do?"

"Water Petal, I just cast myself adrift in the Dream," he replied with a weary smile. "I just wish I knew where it will carry me."

Anhinga placed a hand to her throat. She couldn't breathe. Chaos seemed to erupt as the stunned crowd realized what had just occurred. Everyone began talking at once, crowding around her and the skinny youth who took his place so naturally at her side.

*Blessed Panther, what have I done to myself?*

# Chapter Thirteen

S houts of disbelief drowned the questions being called by others. Aware that he had trapped himself, but unsure how, Jaguar Hide reached into the sack of smoked fish and began handing it out. The boy, first in line, stared into his eyes, taking an oily chunk and thrusting it into his mouth as if in defiance.

Those eyes! Jaguar Hide shook his head. He had seen eyes like that, but never before in a child's face. A child's? The boy—the young man—was Speaker for Owl Clan? Had that been a joke? It was only later, in the milling swelter of people, that he had learned about White Bird's death and the dissolution of Elder Wing Heart's souls.

*White Bird died over three moons ago! Elder Wing Heart discredited and soul sick? Why haven't we heard?* The question shifted back and forth between his souls.

At times the remoteness of their swamp, safe as it was, left them far removed from the activities of other peoples. Nor, obviously, would the young Owl Clan man he had contacted have admitted to these scandalous happenings within his clan.

Jaguar Hide returned his attention to the present, listening as he handed out gifts of smoked fish. He kept an eye on his niece, watching her as she stood, half in shock, at the youth's side.

"How can Salamander just up and marry her?" a woman was asking her companion. "He didn't even ask his clan!"

"He's the Speaker, that's how."

"But his mother, she should have been consulted," another declared hotly.

"Who? Wing Heart? She's lost her souls: all she does is sit at her loom and Dream of the past."

"You think Wing Heart retains enough of her wits to tell him no?" another asked.

"I'll tell you what," a man insisted, "when Mud Stalker insisted that Salamander follow his brother, he dealt a deathblow to Owl Clan."

So it went, people passing him, collecting pieces of the rapidly vanishing fish, and through it all, he had no time to discuss this unsettling turn of affairs with Anhinga. She looked as if her own souls were floating, white-faced, back stiff, while the skinny man-boy who stood beside her accepted the well-wishing of individuals.

"So, you have your peace," the gruff voice interrupted Jaguar Hide's reeling thoughts.

He centered himself on the threat hidden in that deep voice. Turning, he met Deep Hunter's narrow stare with his own. "We have *our* peace. You and me, old enemy."

Deep Hunter shot a look over his broad shoulder to

where Anhinga and Salamander stood in the center of a knot of people. "It didn't quite turn out the way you expected, did it?"

*How could he know?* Old reflexes from countless Council sessions and clan meetings came to his rescue. "You tell me. Is that boy really the Owl Clan Speaker?"

Deep Hunter nodded, amusement in his eyes. "He is indeed, confirmed by the Council after his brother was stuck dead by the Sky Beings."

"Then, being only somewhat familiar with your laws, his action carries a great weight with your Council."

Deep Hunter sensed the trap. "It does, but his decision to marry your niece does not bind the Council. We will discuss this peace of yours. We can still dismiss it out of hand."

Jaguar Hide handed the last piece of fish to Deep Hunter before folding up the bag. "I understand that. But Owl Clan is bound, isn't it? If the other clans should decide not to accept my offer of peace, it would appear that Owl Clan will have a singular and unlimited source of sandstone. And—excuse me if I'm unsure of your ways—that would grant them a great deal of status, wouldn't it?"

"Status, prestige, authority, it comes and goes like the wind, old enemy. Look at how Owl Clan has fallen, from the top to the bottom, and just within a few moons."

"They could rise again, just as quickly, I would assume. And yet another clan could fall like a dropped stone. A lesson I would well remember, Speaker." Jaguar Hide grinned wickedly. "If this could happen to the great Wing Heart, I'd say none of you is truly safe. Wouldn't you?"

"You didn't come here seeking peace." Deep Hunter's eyes were probing.

"Ah, old enemy, but I did." He gestured at his niece, looking like a surprised deer suddenly surrounded by a ring of hunters with nocked darts. "Let's you and I see what the future brings, hmm?" Somewhere deep down between his souls, a voice cackled in raucous laughter. No matter the way of it, his weapon was planted. From here on, he must hope that Anhinga was as tough and single-minded as he believed her to be.

"Welcome to the future, Deep Hunter."

Night Rain ran as she had never run, breath pulling at her throat as she sprinted full tilt across the plaza to her clan grounds, passed the first two ridges, and rounded the borrow pit. She charged along the row of houses, her kirtle napping, her young breasts bouncing. She leaped a barking dog that rushed out to intercept her. The cur continued growling and snapping at her ankles. Ripping a stick from a firewood pile outside her cousin's house, she paused long enough to smack the dog along the side of its head before charging headlong past the last house and into her yard.

"Sister! *He's married!*"

"What?" Pine Drop asked, poking her head through the door. Ground smilax root covered her hands in a paste.

"Salamander! He's married!" She was gasping, one hand to her burning throat.

"Well of course he is, you silly toad. To us!" Pine Drop had an irritated look on her face.

"Yes, to us! And to this Swamp Panther woman!" She pointed to somewhere behind her. "It just happened! Out there...on the Turtle's Back. I told you you should have come!"

"What on earth are you talking about?"

"Jaguar Hide! The Swamp Panther! The meeting he wanted with Owl Clan? It was to make peace. This Anhinga is part of it."

"Who is Anhinga?"

"His new wife! Salamander married Jaguar Hide's niece to seal the agreement! It just happened!"

Pine Drop looked confused. "He wouldn't have married this quickly. He'd need time to discuss it with his clan. This must be some sort of joke."

"No, I swear, Sister, Salamander just took this woman for his wife. It happened so quickly no one could do anything about it. It even caught Mother and Uncle by surprise."

"So, what are we going to do about it?"

That question caught Night Rain flat-footed. "I don't have any idea."

"What did Uncle say?"

"He told Salamander no. And then Salamander defied him in front of everyone. Uncle is fuming."

"What did he say to you?"

"He said to come and tell you. Right away!"

Pine Drop's brow lined, puzzlement mixed with disbelief. "Well, he's certainly *not* bringing her here!"

Night Rain's gasping had slowed to deep breathing. "Sister, this isn't good, is it?"

"I don't know," Pine Drop said softly, her gaze

growing absent. "Maybe I just need time to think, that's all."

The sun had dipped below the high embankment of Sun Town to cast a blue-green shadow across Morning Lake. Puffs of cloud gleamed as they continued their endless march north from the gulf.

People slowly trickled away, taking to their canoes to paddle back to the landing. Salamander paused for a moment to gather his thoughts. The afternoon had passed like one of the whirlwinds that ripped out of late-summer thunderheads.

Several clumps of young men stood in furtive groups by the shore, talking over the day's events as they studied their canoes and shot curious glances back at Jaguar Hide. Salamander couldn't help notice the stacked atlatls and darts lying inside those narrow hulls. Something about the way they waited, the way they stood, quickened his souls.

Jaguar Hide stood to one side, his head bowed as he studied the charcoal-stained dirt at his feet. His face was a deeply lined mask, the thoughts hidden, almost brooding. If Salamander could read the set of his shoulders, a terrible nagging worry lay within the man.

Salamander glanced at his new wife. Jaguar Hide had every reason to be worried, most likely about his current situation. His life was under the protection of a broken and impotent clan. Anhinga, however, looked absolutely miserable and terrified, as if she were once again some sort of captive.

"Do not be frightened," he said as he turned to her. "I think this was meant to be."

Her eyes were partially hidden by the fall of her long black hair. She stood with her arms crossed under her breasts, the nipples like darts pointed at his souls. "Who are you?" Her voice was laced with frustration.

"I am Salamander, Speaker for the Owl Clan, as you have heard over and over this day."

"*Who* are you?" she repeated more vehemently. "Why did you step out today? You're no Speaker. The Sun People only choose old men for Speakers."

"This time they chose me. It happens, but very rarely."

"Why you?"

"Because my brother was killed. He was struck by lightning. I was made Speaker in his place."

"That makes no sense." Her beautiful face trembled as if she were fighting sudden tears.

"It wasn't supposed to." He narrowed an eye. "They made me Speaker in order to discredit my clan."

"It worked."

He smiled. "Yes. For the moment. Come, we must talk with your uncle." But she didn't move as Salamander walked over to where Jaguar Hide stood lost in his musings. "Elder? Are you staying the night on the island?"

"I think not." He lifted his head to scan the sky. "It will be dark in a couple of fingers' time. That will be good enough." His smile turned predatory. "Were I to stay here, boy, I'm not sure my souls would find my body alive in the morning. There are men here who wouldn't trouble themselves over a silly little agreement made between you and me. And, as I have discovered, the great Wing Heart's authority is a thing of the past, so I doubt she could protect me." He shook his head, eyes taking in the waiting youths. "No, better that I take my leave as dark is falling. By the time a pursuer catches up, I will have vanished into the channels like the fog."

"As you wish, Elder."

The old warrior studied him as if he were a piece of meat. "Are you a fool, or a joke, boy?"

"I am Speaker for the Owl Clan." He couldn't help meeting that gaze. "I am supposed to be a joke. The spirits will decide who laughs longest."

"I see." He turned his attention to Anhinga. "I will be going. Take care of my niece. If you don't, I will hear about it, and when I do, it will take you a long, long time to die."

The way he said it made Salamander's blood chill. This man had been raiding from the swamps when Salamander's mother was but a suckling. It took no stretch of imagination to believe the stories about the number of men Jaguar Hide had killed.

The Swamp Panther Elder turned and walked toward the shore. He bent over the canoe, laying out what Salamander determined were sandstone slabs. Then, without a word, he pushed the canoe out, jumping lithely into it. The craft didn't even rock as the old warrior settled in the stern, picked up his paddle, and pulled the canoe around.

"Wait!" The cry strangled in Anhinga's throat as she rushed up, staring in disbelief, a slim hand to her throat. In a louder voice, she called, "Uncle?"

He raised a hand to her, but didn't look back as he stroked vigorously for the channels. The young men, clustered as they were, were caught by surprise. Salamander could see them, talking in hushed tones before they raced for their canoes.

"Let him go," Salamander called. "No matter what your orders, it is only right! He came according to his word: Owl Clan has guaranteed him safe conduct."

"He killed my father!" Saw Back, of the Alligator Clan, cried passionately.

"Animal," Anhinga hissed under her breath.

"And your clan has killed more than one of his kin in return," Salamander replied as he blocked their way to the canoes. "I said let him go."

"Who are you to give someone in Alligator Clan an order?"

"I am Owl Clan's Speaker. I stand in the Council and know its wishes! If you push this thing, it will be between your clan and mine. Do you want to come and explain that to the Council?" Salamander crossed his arms.

Saw Back picked up a pointed paddle engraved with alligators and stepped up to Salamander. "You're the smallest whelp in the litter, Mud Puppy. I don't care that you were made some Speaker! You're barely off the nipple yourself, and you want to give *me* orders?" He smiled as he gripped the paddle. "Move out of my way!"

"Go ahead. Strike me, Saw Back. Do it right and break a couple of bones. Better yet, kill me." Salamander took a step forward, aware that the youths were watching, waiting, a keen anticipation in their eyes. "Deep Hunter will be so pleased when he has to defend his clansman in the Council. You see, it's not just me, but the very notion of a warrior striking a Speaker. It sets a precedent that the Council can't allow, no matter what they think of me."

Saw Back stared at Anhinga, taking in her perfect body. "I think after I smack some manners into you, I'll break your wife in for you."

Salamander took another step forward, crowding him. "No, you won't."

"Why?"

"Because your mother will be crying as she burns your bones."

That brought laughter from the youths. They were crowding around now, that hunter's gleam in their eyes. They were primed to fight, to kill.

Saw Back had to take a step back to tap his chest. "You'd kill me? Here are my souls, Mud Puppy, come and take them."

"I am Salamander," he replied calmly. "As long as you do not defy the Council, I won't take your souls. But if you push this thing, I will. Not tonight, but some-time when—"

"He's getting away!" Needs Two, another of the Alligator Clan hunters called as he looked over his shoulder.

Jaguar Hide's rapidly moving canoe was halfway to the channel.

Anhinga backed away. From the edge of his vision, Salamander watched her pick up one of the pointed paddles. The way she held it assured him she hadn't considered using it in the water.

A handful of young warriors eased off to one side and bent to shove one of the canoes out.

"I said, *leave him alone!*" Salamander pointed a

finger at them. "As a member of the Council, I *order* you."

Saw Back made a face. "You couldn't—"

*"Fool!"* Salamander shouted into his face. "The Council could care less what *I* order, but as a Speaker, it would make an exception. Would Deep Hunter want it whispered around that a Speaker can be disobeyed? This isn't about *me,* Saw Back!"

"He's almost to the channels!" Needs Two cried as he hopped from foot to foot, unwilling to take action on his own.

"Well?" Salamander cried, walking between them, his hands waving. "What is it? Are you going to attack me? Are you going to throw a burning ember into the tinder of clan relations? Why don't you run and ask Deep Hunter if he wants a fight with Owl Clan? That wasn't in the orders, was it? No, just go kill Jaguar Hide! But Owl Clan has made a bargain since that order was given." He thrust a finger at Anhinga. "You would kill my wife's uncle! I would have to seek retribution!"

They looked confused, half of them fingering their darts as they glanced out to where Jaguar Hide's canoe slipped into the channel, vanishing behind the bald cypresses.

Salamander gave a frustrated sigh, hoping that fear sweat hadn't broken out on his hot face. "All right, get off the island. I have things to attend to with the Serpent. This woman must be cleansed." He made shooing signs with his hands. "Stop pestering me, and think about your actions before you go against the Council."

"I'll leave in my own good time," Saw Back insisted.

"Hey," Sour Mouth, another of the Alligator Clan

youths called. "Come on! He's made it into the channels!"

Salamander smiled as they turned, trotting for their canoes.

"Why didn't you fight them?" Anhinga asked. The paddle was clutched in her hands, ready to be swung at the nearest foe. Her eyes were on the two canoes lancing out into the lake, hot in pursuit of her uncle.

"We couldn't have won." Salamander shrugged. "All we needed to do was give Jaguar Hide time to get off the lake. He's in the channels now. In a finger's time, it will be dark. Long before Saw Back and his warriors could possibly catch up." He paused. "Sometimes the best way to win is by not starting a fight in the first place."

She gave him the same disbelieving look she'd been giving him all day. "How did this happen to me?"

"I cut you free one night and started it all," he reminded.

"But why did you offer to marry me? It wasn't your place."

"Because, I think *he* wanted me to."

"Who? Who wanted you to?"

He turned again, looking at her. She stood half a head taller than he did, her body a slim silhouette against the darkening sky. Her long legs, the curve of her hips under the kirtle, and her round pointed breasts were softly bathed by the twilight.

"Has anyone ever told you that you are the most beautiful woman in the world?"

She just stared at him in wonder.

# Chapter Fourteen

Does it make any sense that your people could drag me right up to the front of your Men's House the last time I was here, but this time I have to be cleansed?" Anhinga demanded, her hands clenched in her lap as she stared at Salamander's lean form across the fire.

"I have never thought of it that way," he answered, a puzzled frown on his forehead.

The fire burned before a low hut made of woven palmetto leaves. It stood beneath the sweetgum, having sheltered countless travelers and Traders. This, Anhinga had learned, was to be her bridal home during the cleansing of her souls.

Around them a halo of insects insisted on swirling, most of them to be eventually sucked into the flames. In the night sky, a thin sliver of Father Moon shone between the clouds and cast patterns of silver across the blackness.

"I could have brought all kinds of evil into Sun Town. Believe me, for all the terrible things I wished on your people, they should have died of a terrible wasting disease, their muscles turning to pus, their skin becoming a mass of boils." She glared her hatred at him.

His large dark eyes seemed to swell, and her souls stumbled. What was it about him? His people considered him some sort of comic fool, but when she looked into those eyes, it was as if they drew her souls down into their brown depths. He made her skin shiver with a curious excitement that she couldn't understand. Was it because she was destined to kill him? Is that what made him such a novelty?

"If you hate us so, why are you here?" he asked softly. The fire popped, sparks rising between them.

"My uncle wants peace." She could see he didn't believe her so she countered, "Why, in Panther's name, did you cut me loose that night? I was your brother's property."

He took a deep breath. "For the same reason that you came back. We are tied by Power. You and I."

She bit off a bitter smile before it could touch her lips. *Yes, bound by Power! It has brought me here to destroy you, fool!* Aloud she said, "You took a great risk setting me free."

"Yes." He shrugged, looking curiously vulnerable as he eyed the fire. "The vision isn't clear yet, but you should know that you're not the only one trying to destroy me."

*By Panther, does he hear my thoughts?*

"I don't know where Masked Owl is taking us, or how it is supposed to end. All I have is my wits, but everyone else has theirs, too." His smile went crooked. "However, until they destroy me, I shall do my best to care for you. I don't understand the balance of it, but for all that White Bird would have done to hurt you and demean you, I shall do everything the opposite."

She frowned, unable to see the sense in that, but willing to accept its oddity given the alternatives. "I still don't understand why you spoke out. You could have let the others find a husband for me. Perhaps Deep Hunter, or that Mud Stalker."

"I told you." His eyes had become passive again. "We are tied. When I recognized you, I knew that was why he asked me to free you. So that you could come back. You came here to marry White Bird, the man who captured you and hurt you. You were meant for me. I realized that in a flash of understanding."

"But I still have to undergo this cleansing?"

He nodded. "It would be most unpleasant if you didn't."

"It was *most* unpleasant the *last* time I was here."

For a long time, he said nothing, just stared into the fire.

"I heard that you are already married."

His smile might have been a ghost. "Yes, to two women in Snapping Turtle Clan. Pine Drop and Night Rain."

"So, I am a *third* wife?"

He steepled his fingers, brow lining. "This will be difficult. Among my people, a man goes to live with his wife, in her territory."

"Among mine, too. So, what is my territory? This little heap of mud in the middle of a lake?"

"For the next six days it is." He seemed oblivious to her anger. "After that I will build you a house in Owl Clan territory. I know just the spot. You will appreciate it, my brother's bones were burned there."

Owl Clan territory? Good, things were beginning to look up. It would place her in the middle of the enemy, in a position where one day she could drive the terrible dagger of revenge into their hearts.

"I will work the rest out with my other wives." He mused, seeing it all in his souls. "Which will be interesting in its own right."

"They will not resent me? Try to make me miserable for taking you away from them for part of the time?"

Amusement, like faint and distant lightning, flickered in his face. "I could be wrong, but I doubt it. Like you, they were not particularly pleased to marry me—especially after my mother's souls began to loosen. I imagine that the nights I spend with you will relieve them. Perhaps, after you come to discover your situation, you may be just as grateful for them."

She took a deep breath against the tightening she felt in her chest. Tonight, she should be bedding her enemy, taking the first step on the long passage to final revenge on Owl Clan. Instead, she was here, removed from Sun Town by their silly fears of spiritual infection, talking to this unusual boy. The top of his head only came to her chin. Unlike Mist Finger or the others of her suitors, he was mostly thin bones. Hardly the ideal of the young warrior-hunter that had filled her fantasies.

*Wait until he's asleep, steal a canoe, and head south.*

"And do what?" she asked aloud, eyes fixed on the fire. He seemed not to hear as she imagined her uncle's face, saw the expression of disappointment in his eyes. It had been bad enough during the months that she healed in the Panther's Bones, living amid Mist

Finger's, Right Talon's, Cooter's, Spider Fire's, and Slit Nose's families. What made her think that after this second failure, it would be any easier?

Armed with the stony beating of her heart, she stood. He was watching her as she stepped around the fire and reached her hand out to him. When he took it, a curious tingle ran through her. His eyes seemed to grow as she pulled him to his feet. For a long moment, she looked down into his fascinating eyes, seeing the growing desire.

She held his hand as she walked to the small shelter, ducked inside, and loosened the knots that held her kittle. The fabric slipped smoothly over her hips to settle beside the moss-covered bed.

He had frozen, mouth parted, his eyes fixed on her body where the fire cast its feeble light. The vein in his neck was pulsing, his chest rising and falling. When she untied the knot that held his breechcloth, it fell away to reveal him, taut and ready.

Her own heartbeat had begun to pound, a warm sensation spinning itself inside her hips. She lay back on the bedding, watching him with a building anticipation. The faint firelight played across his thin body as he lowered himself, his skin sliding warmly across hers.

Instinctively, she wrapped her arms around him and felt the life burning brightly within him. Her breasts tightened as his chest met hers. She was leading him to her, thrilled as his penis slid inside her.

She was thinking about how she was going to kill him when the liquid waves of ecstasy burst through her pelvis. She gasped, taken completely by surprise. Nothing in the naive experimentation of youth had prepared her for the likes of this.

Moments later, he, too, shivered and tensed, a strained sound choking in his throat. Then his arms cupped her shoulders, and he buried his face in her hair.

Atop the thick thatch of the Women's House, the rain sounded like a continuous whisper rather than a drumming. The runoff beat a staccato as it spattered into pools of water that in turn dribbled off to the sides of the Mother Mound. The building was large, filled with baskets and pots that contained the ceremonial items provided by each clan for its women. Each moon, when a woman's cycle came full, she came here, to attend to herself through the menstrual period.

The time she spent in seclusion with her sisters provided a respite from the never-ending trials of life. She had time for reflection, attention to the spirits, and a break from the normal routine of running a household. Children, husbands, and relatives could not constantly pester or demand her attention. Here, surrounded by women, she could catch up on gossip, hear news of other clans, build friendships, and strengthen ties with friends and acquaintances. The walls of clan politics tended to soften. Negotiations took place, and problems could be solved in a more relaxed environment, woman to woman, without the pressures of others bearing down.

Night Rain had put off leaving for the Women's House until the last moment when she discovered herself spotting. Like her sister, she had suffered intermittent cramps for the last several moons. Even the

swelling and tenderness in her breasts wasn't an indica-
tor. She should have known, however, from the moods,
and the fact that her cycle had begun to coincide with
her sister's.

She removed her bark rain hat as she stepped into
the low doorway. The building, large and rectangular,
was oriented north–south atop the low mound. The
doorway opened to the west, while on the east, two
large windows were situated so that the first rays of the
morning sun shot light into the two rooms, one for the
Northern Moiety, the other, hers, for the Southern.

She nodded to the clusters of women who sat in
clan areas along the walls. They were working at tasks,
making beads, others twining cord. Some ground pieces
of hematite against slabs of Swamp Panther sandstone
in the endless process of crafting net sinkers. They
nodded, smiling and waving as Night Rain crossed the
room. She rounded the small central fire and located
Pine Drop where she sat on a furry buffalo hide, the
hair flattened from long use. She lowered herself onto
the space her sister opened for her and placed her sack
of provisions and her rain hat to one side.

"I thought you'd be following close behind me."
Pine Drop smiled. "I take it you left a stew for
Salamander?"

Night Rain snorted. "Why? He's still over-building
a house for that wild Swamp Panther woman. I swear, I
hope she chokes on the Serpent's cleansing. I don't trust
her. She's evil. And why, Sister, do you care if he eats or
not? He and that barbarian are the talk of Sun Town!
*We* are mentioned by everyone! You should hear the
things they're saying. That somehow it was *our* fault.
That we couldn't conceive, that you were off with

Three Stomachs, that we hurt his feelings so much he had to go to a barbarian for companionship! People are laughing at us and not just him!"

Pine Drop stopped short, a pale look washing across her face. She had been grinding ocher on a sandstone tablet. Beside her sat a small pot of grease with which to mix the bright red color. "I should never have listened to Uncle."

Night Rain cocked her head. "What's wrong with you? For nearly half a moon, you've been different. Something's changed."

"Nothing has changed."

"Yes, it has. You haven't spoken a single word to Three Stomachs. What did he do to you?"

Pine Drop widened her eyes expressively. "As you can see, Sister, he did nothing to me. I should be happily at home, delighted with the notion that my moon was late, assured that I was pregnant. Yet, here I am, taking my share of absorbent from the pot, trying to figure out why I'm barren."

"You're not barren. It just hasn't taken is all." Night Rain resettled herself, reaching into the sack she had brought. From it, she took root cakes, dried fish, and smoked deer meat to put into the stone bowl her lineage left for storage. She slipped out of her shawl and massaged her breasts, wincing at the ache. "Snakes, why has my moon come to be so miserable?"

Pine Drop stared at the smoking fire pit in the center of the room. A flame flickered in halfhearted effort as it slowly chewed at the bottom of a blackened log. "I don't know. I just wonder, is all."

Night Rain perked up at that. "Yes?"

Her sister shook her head. "I never had these problems, the unending cramps, I mean, until I started coupling with Three Stomachs. It's as if..."

"What? Snakes! Don't drag this out. Tell me."

Pine Drop tilted her head, asking in a whisper, "Do you think we're being punished?"

"By whom?" Night Rain leaned forward, searching her sister's face. *What does she know? What does she suspect?*

*She is more intimate with Mother and Uncle's plans. Have they told her something?*

"Power," Pine Drop answered, a hand covering her mouth. "Spirits. Something."

"Why would you think that?"

She shook her head as though baffled. "It's just a feeling."

"A feeling?" Night Rain shifted, glancing covertly around the room. "What happened the day that you and Salamander were gone? Remember? The day you left me the bladderwort?"

Pine Drop smiled slightly, then her perplexed look returned. "It was..."—she seemed to be searching for the right word—"...fun."

"Fun? A day with Salamander?"

Pine Drop raised her hands and dropped them. "You can't understand."

"That's drilling the bead in the center. You're right, I *don't* understand. I think he's about as much fun as a lump of mud. He hasn't so much as broken a smile since we've been married. He's a dupe, Pine Drop. People laugh at us behind their hands. I can't wait until Uncle says the time is right to divorce him. I just thank the Sky Beings he hasn't crawled into my bed for nearly a moon."

Pine Drop's lips pinched. After a long pause, she said, "How does it make you feel now that he's spending his time with that Swamp Panther and not us? I mean, doesn't it bother you that he prefers the companionship of some wild barbarian to ours?"

"Eats Wood says it's the same woman White Bird captured during the raid at Ground Cherry Camp. The one who escaped so mysteriously in the night. Remember? She took Red Finger's canoe? He says it's a Swamp Panther plot, that she came here to do something terrible to us in revenge for what we did to her and her friends."

"Eats Wood is an idiot."

"Well, so is our husband."

"Is he?" Pine Drop wondered. "I've heard Uncle and Mother talking about it. About this marriage. They want to believe like Eats Wood, that it is some terrible plot hatched by Owl Clan with the Swamp Panthers to hurt the clans, but they are both worried they might be wrong."

"How so?"

She shook her head. "Think about it. Wing Heart has lost her souls. Any action Water Petal would take is instantly challenged by Moccasin Leaf. The fight between the lineages has paralyzed Owl Clan. Salamander is the Speaker, but everyone thinks he's a fool."

"He is."

Pine Drop ignored her. "Nevertheless, this *fool* now has an alliance with the Swamp Panthers, and Owl Clan receives a canoe load of sandstone every moon." She gestured around, pointing.

At every location at least one, and generally several pieces, of sandstone were lying on the packed clay floor amid pieces of wood, leather, and stone. The material was essential to Sun Town. The finishing of most stone tools and all woodwork depended on the abrasive quality of the sandstone. Anything that needed to be smoothed or fitted had to be ground, and Swamp Panther sandstone was the perfect abrasive. She opened her other hand, showing Night Rain the piece of sandstone she had been grinding the ocher on.

"Sandstone will not return them to authority," Night Rain declared. "Snapping Turtle Clan now occupies that position."

"We're not on top yet. Thunder Tail has been given leadership of the Council. But for us the vote would have been unanimous."

"Give Uncle several more moons, and we'll be on top. Just wait and see."

Pine Drop asked, "Did you know that Deep Hunter detailed men to kill Jaguar Hide? Our husband managed to delay them. Somehow he kept Saw Back's party on the Turtle's Back just long enough so that Jaguar Hide escaped into the channels. Salamander baited them, confused them, and the Swamp Panther got away. Deep Hunter was furious. He stalked back and forth in a rage for a whole day. He still can't understand how he was thwarted, but he exiled Saw Back to Yellow Mud Camp for four moons."

"Delayed how?" Night Rain was curious for the first time. "Saw Back is a really a handsome man. He's Alligator Clan, and well, you know, I've been thinking that after we're through with Salamander, he'd make a fine husband."

Pine Drop gave her a sober look. "You'd better hope he can placate his Speaker. That, or, assuming we are ever *through* with Salamander, you had better plan on enjoying your life in Yellow Mud Camp."

"Having a man like him to share my bed, I could stand the climate over there. I'm surprised that he didn't just ignore Salamander. Everyone else does."

"Perhaps, but Salamander talked Saw Back out of fulfilling his Speaker's orders. And Deep Hunter blames Saw Back, not Salamander." She seemed to retreat again, lost in her thoughts.

"You've been preoccupied ever since he married that barbarian." Night Rain shook her head. "It's not a disaster! It frees us! Think, Sister. Why does he need us? He's got her, a barbarian, for a wife. That makes him more of a freak than he already is. I think we should ask Mother and Uncle to get us a divorce."

Pine Drop was nodding absently. "Perhaps." A pause. "What could he see in her?"

Night Rain stood and walked to the large ceramic pot that held the mixture of cattail down and hanging moss. At just the mention of sharing a bed with Saw Back, her flow increased.

When she returned, Pine Drop was still looking confused.

"Sister, who cares what he sees in her?"

Pine Drop airily replied, "I just wonder, that's all."

# Chapter Fifteen

A nhinga stepped out of the canoe and planted her feet firmly on Sun Town's muddy landing. Above her on the high bluff she could see the hated Men's House. The old Serpent stepped out of the canoe behind her, helped by Salamander. He was studying her, eyes prying at her souls, perhaps sensing the danger she brought to his people.

Anhinga walked warily behind her husband. Husband? The word still startled her. Of course she had known she was coming here to marry the man she was going to kill. Knowing and anticipating, seeing how it would be in the soul's eye, was one thing. In that vision she was smiling as she stepped into White Bird's arms, every essence of her being fixed on his painful death. He had been a tough and cunning warrior. A hero worthy of Anhinga's wrath.

Now, six days after she had first laid eyes on him, she walked behind a skinny boy possessed of pain-haunted eyes. His hair was mussed, and she could see most every bone in his body. He walked with an ungainly amble, his souls off somewhere distant, lost in Dreams.

*Where, Anhinga, is the glory in murdering this simple boy? He has neither craft nor cunning, and shows all the wariness of a rotten stump.*

Patience. She would wait. Besides, the ordeal of having undergone that flat-faced Serpent's "cleansing" made the souls cry out for someone to kill. Miserable though she had been, she was Anhinga, niece of Jaguar Hide. The last thing she would allow these foolish Sun People to see was any hint of weakness.

The old Serpent watched her, his brown eyes like keen shining stones behind those folds of sagging skin. He might have been a fish eagle perched on a low branch, trying to peer below the surface of her skin for a glimpse of her souls. She had given him nothing, bearing the sweats, purges, chants, and smokings as if they were but a pleasant relaxation. By Panther Above, she *would* kill someone for that!

She fought a grim smile as she remembered the last time she had staggered down this very slope, the darkness had been complete, her body and souls filled with pain and horror. This boy had been with her then, too. Where she had left this place broken, shattered with grief, an escaped slave in the night, she came back in triumph as the wife of a Clan Speaker, walking head upright toward the small knot of people who had come to watch.

Salamander called greetings to some, nodding to others as they passed. One by one, Anhinga met their eyes, seeing one or two faces she thought familiar. And, yes, there was that one! The pus-sucking chigger who had twisted her nipple. She willed her face into a bark-solid mask, avoiding his narrowing eyes. Did he recognize her? Cleaned as she was, dressed in a finery of feathers and finely woven cloth?

Then they were atop the bluff and turning northward. She had seen this place through pain-blurred eyes, but now, from a different perspective, it took her breath. How huge! The immensity of Sun Town hadn't registered when, as a captive, she lay blinking against a headache, bound and trussed, watching her friends being butchered. Now she saw the incredible height of the huge Bird's Head to the west, the span of the house-topped ridges that arched around her like the jaws of an immense monster. The entire place was open, mantled in green.

And the sky! She looked up in awe. She came from a forest people. She had never seen so much of the sky! Mother Sun beamed down on her, hot and bright. The sensation stunned her, left her feeling exposed, alone, and vulnerable. Never before had she been less than a stone's throw from trees. Even at the Panther's Bones, when she stood on the high Sun Mound, it was but an island among the trees.

Unnerved for the first time, she swallowed hard.

"It is something, yes?" the old Serpent asked from where he followed her.

"I hadn't realized. The size of it!"

"The world crosses here," Salamander said, turning his thoughtful eyes to hers and smiling shyly. One by one he pointed out the clan grounds. "And this building"—he stabbed a finger at the rectangular building that topped a mound overlooking Morning Lake—"is the Women's House. Where you will have to go when your moon comes full." Uncomfortable, he asked, "Uh, is that anytime soon?"

"Perhaps," she replied offhandedly, her attention on the place. That would be unbearable, sitting in there for four days surrounded by hostile strangers, avoiding their prying questions, enduring their presence. "I might just go to the forest, if you don't mind."

Salamander gave her a short nod. "If you would be more comfortable. Up ahead are the Owl Clan grounds. There, that first ridge, is where my lineage lives. I am building your house there, next to Mother's. It is a good location. From the front door you can see straight out across the lake to the east. Every morning the sun shines right through the doorway."

"There was no house there?"

"There was. My brother was burned in it after lightning killed him. It happened right there." He indicated a place on the edge of the borrow pit. Several wispy goosefoot plants stood on the spot, the trilobed leaves insect-chewed. "He was planting that goosefoot when he died. We don't touch it." He gave her a serious look. "It is not for us, do you understand? It belongs to the Sky Beings."

*After dark, I shall be sure to urinate upon the spot.* "Who am I to question the Sky Beings?" she asked.

He led her around the borrow pit to the toe of the ridge. It was a stunning location. The view was the finest she had ever seen. At her feet the bluff dropped away to the shores of the lake, a moderate-sized body of water. Two canoes were trolling a net behind them, or so she assumed given that the occupants were paddling mightily, their bows pointed outward, and each trailed a rope into the water. Beyond them an endless vista of sweetgum, tupelo, bald cypress, and water oak stretched in a vast forest that merged into the distant horizon.

Looking northward, she counted out the five ridges to a low bank of trees. "What is there, beyond the sixth ridge?"

"A deep gully," Salamander told her. "Beyond that a wide trail runs to the north, to the Star Mound. There, at the summer solstice, we thank Mother Sun for returning to us again and bringing the world to life. For the rest of the year it is a guardian against the Dark Powers."

She nodded, thinking how similar their beliefs were to her own. At the Panther's Bones, her people retreated to the high rise at the north end of the village to conduct their summer solstice ceremonies.

"Our house will be there." He pointed, a hesitation in his voice.

She looked behind her, seeing a collection of building material beside a burned circle. Charred posts still protruded from the ground. Grass had grown around the black outline where the heat from the burning house hadn't killed the roots.

"My brother's bones were burned there." Salamander looked even more frail.

*Good! May his souls watch as I couple with his brother. May he scream his warnings from the Spirit World onto deaf ears. May he wail as I avenge my people upon his family.*

She could feel the Serpent's piercing gaze boring into her back. She realized that a grim smile had come to her lips. Salamander was watching her, brown eyes large. "It was the way of Power," he said simply. "Everything is."

To cover herself, she said, "It will make a wonderful house, husband. The sooner we finish, the better. Who is that?" She pointed to the elderly woman who sat under a ramada not ten paces beyond, her body bent over a loom.

"That is Elder Wing Heart, my mother."

She heard the worry in his voice. "You say her souls are loose?" Before he could answer, she added, "I would meet your mother. Your family is now mine, husband. Introduce me."

Reluctantly, he led her forward. A wooden pestle and mortar stood halfway between the house locations. Charcoal and old cooking clays were scattered about, as were bits of stone: flakes and crumbled sandstone, the latter looted from her own lands, no doubt. She cataloged the belongings under the ramada: cordage and fibers, several soapstone bowls, bark plates, a ceramic pot half-full of cloudy water, and an array of bone needles and combs.

The woman held her attention. She looked used up, wrung out, and discarded by life. Despite the drawn lines in her face, she still carried a regal air. She would have been attractive once, could be again if her eyes weren't lost and roving. She still sat erect, her strong fingers caressing the fibers with a lover's touch.

"Mother?" Salamander asked softly as he bent down beside her. She seemed oblivious to his presence, her head tilting back and forth, smiles rising and falling on her lips. Her expression kept changing, as if she were having silent conversations inside her head. "I have come to introduce you to Anhinga. The niece of Jaguar Hide. Elder, we have a new daughter for you."

Wing Heart continued her weaving. Her son's

words might have been the droning of insects for all the attention she paid.

"Mother?" Salamander touched her shoulder, looked unhappily back at Anhinga. "I want you to meet my wife."

"Yes, yes, White Bird. Go tell your uncle. And don't let that idiot little brother of yours miss supper tonight. He's probably off looking under logs or something. Now, go on, and don't bother me. The Speaker and I have things to do. Plans to make before the next Council."

Snakes! This was Elder Wing Heart? By the evil mist, how could she have come to this?

"It's all right," Anhinga said softly. "There will be times in the future when her souls are closer." She smiled at him, allaying his discomfort and reaching out to take his hand. "Our life together is just beginning. I am sure there are tens of tens of things to do." She glanced cautiously at the old man. What did he suspect? "We have a house to build, and it must be a grand one, worthy of a Clan Speaker. Let us start there." She led the way back past the pestle and mortar and surveyed the charred circle. "This must be cleared."

Patience. Her uncle was right. The Serpent kept watching her as though she were a copperhead loose in a children's play area.

She ignored the old man and his seeing souls. Her first concern was to lull Salamander. She smiled at him. "We shall build a grand house here, and when it is finished, we shall make a great feast for just the two of us. When we are full, we will lie on a thick buffalo blanket and you shall fill me in the light of a happy fire."

W. Michael Gear & Kathleen O'Neal Gear

He smiled at that, as if seeing a fantasy in his souls. "I would like that."

A memory flashed...a human liver, rising high into that wide-open sky above Sun Town. It flipped and jiggled as it rose, sunlight flashing on the wet, gleaming surface. For a brief instant it stopped, hanging magically before beginning its rush to the Earth. She remembered the sound so clearly: a hard splat! In a crystal image she saw the tongues, pink and fast between white teeth as the camp dogs licked up the pieces.

# Chapter Sixteen

A large turtle, a slider, lay on its back in the center of the coals. Its head and legs had been lashed tightly with green vines so they didn't protrude and burn. The flesh steamed, hissing and sending aroma around the activity area between the houses. Salamander's nostrils kept catching hints of it on the wind. He glanced back from his precarious position atop the thatching of his new roof. The house they had built on the location of his old one was almost completed.

Elder Wing Heart sat under the ramada, preoccupied with her incessant weaving. Her nimble fingers plucked at the warp and weft stretched between the peeled poles. This fabric, nearly complete, was a series of white birds on a brown background. One of the most beautiful pieces Salamander had ever seen. Even Anhinga had stopped short, gasping at its beauty.

The sky was overcast, gray with a thick bank of clouds that threatened even more rain. It cut the muggy heat that made a man's bones want to wilt. The teasing wind, rising and falling, carried the warm moist scent of the forest, grass, and trees while it promised moisture.

Salamander had never built a house before, and but for Water Petal's advice and guidance, he'd have made a bad affair of it. Together, the three of them—he, Anhinga, and Water Petal—had excavated the foundation holes, planted the uprights, woven the lattice, and plastered the walls.

They had retrieved longer poles and wrist-thick lengths of cane from the floodplain forest, their quest taking them a day's paddle down the winding channels while they searched for just the right sizes of bald cypress. Power laced the wood, making it more resistant to rot than other kinds. Sweating under the sun, they had stepped the largest of them for roof supports. The rest they muscled up, setting them on the wall and interior supports as rafters. Slim cane stringers had been laid crosswise and tied in place with peels of freshly stripped bark. Vines had been interwoven to form a lattice both to support the thatch and to allow it to be fastened tightly.

Thatch, as Salamander found out, wasn't as easy as it seemed. After the backbreaking labor of cutting the grass and bundling it, care had to be taken to pack the sheaves and tie them. Placing the bundles was as much art as it was hard labor.

Salamander used a length of cord—material provided by Water Petal's husband, Darter—to pull the last bundle tight. "Watch your hand. Here it comes," he called as he slipped the bone needle through the thatch.

"Got it," Water Petal called as she grabbed the needle tip inside and pulled it through.

Salamander watched the cord pull tight,

compressing the sheaf, and could imagine her knotting it and cutting it with a stone flake. He turned, perched like a big bird at the peak of the roof. "How does it look?"

Anhinga had her hands placed on her hips, her head cocked as she studied the final product. "It is a house, husband. At last, it is a house."

He grinned, enjoying the harsh accent that came with her speech. Their languages were mutually intelligible, most of the words the same, but sometimes the usage led to incomprehension, and sometimes mirth. He'd been shocked when she referred to his penis as "your slug." She had been stopped short in confusion when she found out his people called a vulva "a canoe."

Water Petal ducked out of the interior and looked up, satisfaction on her face. "We are finished."

"Tonight we shall conduct the proper ceremonies to bless it." Salamander turned himself on the wooden ladder they had manufactured—two poles lashed together with thick rope—and balanced carefully, his toes seeking a purchase as he backed down. Water Petal and Anhinga reached up to steady him as he clambered down the last steps.

He helped them lower the ladder and looked up at the dull green thatch. Freshly cut grass couldn't be used; it would rot and disintegrate. The cuttings had to be seasoned, dried to just the right consistency before being bundled.

"I feel better seeing a house there," Water Petal told them with a sigh. "It reminds me of better days." She turned to look at her baby where it lay in wrap of moss-lined fabric.

"How is he?" Anhinga asked, pointing at the child.

"Still asleep, thank the Sky Beings," she answered. "He cried all night. I dabbed a bit of nightshade paste on my finger and touched it to his tongue before coming over here."

Anhinga narrowed one of her eyes. "That must be done with care." She was inspecting the little baby.

"He has to sleep," Water Petal answered, turning back. "Perhaps it will keep his bowels quiet. For the last couple of days milk goes in and moments later, water comes out. I've wiped his bottom until it's raw."

To Salamander's eyes, his little cousin didn't look healthy. The delicate skin around the infant's face had shrunk and taken on a dark cast. The baby fat had disappeared from sticklike arms.

"My best thoughts are for him," Anhinga said.

Salamander watched the interplay between the two women. Anhinga and Water Petal had reached some sort of uneasy coexistence. Not friends, not enemies, but during the hard days since the completion of Anhinga's cleansing, a careful toleration had developed as they had labored together to build Anhinga's house.

Looking toward the ramada, Salamander could see his mother, oblivious, her hands working the shuttle as she talked to herself. He dared not step closer, or he would hear her carrying on a conversation with her dead brother. He wondered if she could hear his Dream Soul talking in reply. If so, what was his dead uncle saying? Why didn't he send her souls back to her?

Instead, he inspected the turtle. It's once-yellow belly had mottled. The black spots that marked the scoots were now blotched with ash. "He's about cooked. Every new house must have turtle for the first meal."

"Why?" Anhinga asked.

Salamander was admiring the way her long black hair hung over her round breast, to be teased aside by the wind. "Among our people it is said that Turtle's Power is imparted to the new house. Wherever Turtle goes, his house protects him, keeps him from harm."

She frowned. "My people eat snails as a feast when a new house is occupied. For the same reasons. Snail always has a house, no matter where he travels." She pointed. "Your turtle there, his house didn't keep him safe from your fire."

Water Petal's lips twitched with irritation. Salamander, however, smiled, replying, "And I'll bet your snails' shells don't save them from your boiling pot, either."

"I have sassafras and cedar root," Water Petal told him as she hid her expression by inspecting the cuts on her hands. "I'll bring them tonight for the first fire."

"Why?" Anhinga asked.

"Cedar smoke cleanses," Salamander told her. "And my people believe that sassafras-root smoke brings good luck. For the same reason, we must not reenter the house until we have made necklaces of flowers, so that all the thoughts and words that people share inside will be sweet."

Anhinga studied him through sultry brown eyes, the look barely masking the turbulence within her. His souls thrilled. Not only was she the most beautiful woman he had ever seen, but the danger communicated by her large dark eyes drew him like a spell.

"What is it with you two?" Water Petal asked, sensing the tension between them. "I swear, when you look at each other it's like rubbing fox fur on a winter day. The very air crackles and sparks."

"It is the Power between us, Cousin." Salamander turned toward Water Petal. "Anhinga and I are tied by a curious bond." The secrets of their relationship would be beyond her, and he dared not try to explain about what happened under their blankets. His aunt might be young and adventurous herself, but somehow, Salamander doubted that anyone could comprehend the intensity of his matings with Anhinga.

"It must be something." Water Petal sighed, reaching down to scoop up her sleeping baby. "You've turned the clan on its ear with this marriage. I swear, Moccasin Leaf begins to foam at the mouth if I pass within a stone's throw of her."

"She is what she is, Cousin."

Water Petal turned, eyes flashing. "So you say, but I believe that she has found the votes to remove Wing Heart as Elder."

Salamander's smile tightened. "All things in their time. You must trust me. That's all."

"And wait until they remove you, too?" Water Petal's voice tightened. "We're the last of our lineage, Salamander."

"What we are is never as important as who we are. We must wait and be smart."

But for the baby in her arms, she would have thrown her hands up in despair. "You exasperate me, Salamander." Then a slow smile crossed her lips. "But what else can I do? You're family." She turned. "I'll see you this evening."

"Thank you for your help, Cousin."

A final wave was all he got as she disappeared between the houses on her way home.

Anhinga had watched the exchange silently, her

arms crossed under her high breasts. "Is it not enough that you are Speaker?"

"She had thought to follow my mother."

Anhinga glanced sidelong at Wing Heart. "I have heard the stories. Your mother was once a great leader. Even Uncle respected her."

He frowned. "Perhaps she will be yet again. It is up to her souls to decide whether they will return or not. Not even the Serpent has been able to help her."

She turned those probing eyes on him again, her expression still guarded. The breeze was toying with her long black hair, dancing it around her slim shoulders with their faded scars. "What about Masked Owl?"

He stopped short, startled. "What do you know about Masked Owl?"

"You talk to him in your sleep."

"I do?"

"Not everyone talks to a Sky Being when they sleep." A suspicious look crossed her face. "Does he say anything about me?"

"Sometimes." He bent and began to work on the knots that held his two-pole ladder together. The rope would be reused, the poles cut into firewood when they dried.

"What?" she asked, stepping to the other end of the ladder and using an awl to loosen the knots.

Did he dare tell her? She was giving him that look, the slightly arrogant and dangerous one. "He said that you came here to kill me."

She stopped short, fingers frozen, eyes widening. Then, smoothly, coolly, she smiled, flashing her teeth at him. "I will not kill you anytime soon." A pause.

"Unless your heart stops tonight when we share that new bed in there." She jerked her head toward the house, shining black hair flowing with the motion.

It was, he thought, a most challenging affirmation of his suspicions.

Night's soft dark cloak still covered the skies as Pine Drop climbed the last several steps to the rounded summit of the Bird's Head. Her lungs were pulling, her muscles warn from the climb. She turned back to stare out at the charcoa east. Silence, as deep as the night itself, met her ears. She had left early, desperate to be at this place first. Would he come? She seated herself and clutched her jay-feather cloak about her shoulders.

Darkness smothered her.

Then the stillness stirred. She could feel Power gathering. Her skin reacted as it would to the faintest touch of flower petals. The air grew heavy, pressing down from above. She would have sworn she felt giant wings passing silently above. Her heart tripped, hammering at her chest. Every nerve in her body demanded that she rise and charge headlong down the steep incline that led to the open plaza, below.

She closed her eyes and forced herself to sit. With all of her will, she remained motionless, taking deep breaths of the night. It might indeed be late summer, but she drew the jay-feather cloak more tightly about her shoulders. The breeze that skipped out of the southwest chilled her to the very bones. It ruffled the bright blue feathers, teased a lock that had come loose from her head, and prickled the hair on her arms. Born of the chill or the spirits that hovered around her, a shiver tightened her spine.

*Snakes! Where is he?* Or had this been a fool's errand? *One fool for another,* her souls answered. Only an idiot would come here to this place on the edge of darkness and death. She swallowed hard. An idiot, or a man of Power.

He had sat on this very spot that morning. Curious, she tested the soil, finding a loose spot. Her questing fingers parted the dirt, feeling around until, yes, right there. She picked up the irregular stone. No bigger than a large pebble it lay cool on her palm. Rubbing the clinging dirt away her fingertips traced the recognizable shape of a little potbellied owl. The same one he had been working on that day, or another? How many of these had he crafted?

Pine Drop pursed her lips. There were so many things she didn't know about her husband. With the exception of one magical day, they had never talked. Never spoken as a woman did with her husband.

*You never made the effort.*

Was it her fault that he had married the barbarian? The morning after she had left the Woman's House, she had passed that way, seen the new house he had built Anhinga on the location of his mother's old one. Just the sight of that building had stung something in her souls.

Spiders and scorpions, why? What did it matter? Why did she care what Salamander did, or who he did it with, so long as it did not reflect on her, or her clan? It was an arranged marriage only, the interminable result of an attempt to align her clan with his. Or, it had been until Wing Heart's souls had fled. Now it was a political relic. Owl Clan was effectively emasculated. She, herself, had done her part in their undoing. She had helped to lower her husband's prestige by her dalliance with Three Stomachs.

It had been her duty to her clan, ordered by her mother and her uncle, not some wild impulse generated from her loins. She had done as her elders wished, and done it well. She had enjoyed coupling with Three Stomachs, and he had conjured sensations she had never experienced with a man.

*Then why don't you feel happy about it?*

Memories of Salamander's face haunted her. She remembered the expression he had worn every night when he entered their house. He might have strapped on a mask so that no one could read the thoughts behind it. With it, he had seemed impervious to her viper's tongue, and oblivious to her disgust when he climbed into her bed to perform his husband's function for her clan.

*It takes two to lie together with pleasure.* She had at least had a husband to teach her the ways. Embarrassed, she remembered her first fumbling attempts at coupling and how Blue Feather had patiently shown her the body's secrets. From the awkward manner Salamander had come to her, it had been his first time with a woman. He had been rudely jerked from boyhood and placed in his dead brother's bed, to sire children on his wives. Wives who took every opportunity to mock and belittle him. One day he had been playing with toys, the next he was Speaker. Then he had been thrust forward in the Council to explain his mother's very public spiritual disintegration to a hostile audience that wanted nothing more than his and his clan's destruction.

That was the same young man who had brought her

here to see a marvel. In a face that should have reflected revulsion at her mere presence, he had instead displayed delight as a heron hunted the shallows and a spider built a web. She recalled the happiness on his face as they paddled the canoe load of fish traps out into the channel, baiting and dropping them into the still waters.

*When did I ever see magic?* It wasn't a prerequisite for being Mud Stalker's niece.

For a few hands of time, she had been free. That notion surprised and saddened her. In an entire lifetime she had never enjoyed happiness like she had out paddling around with Salamander. At the height of it, she had ruined everything with a carefully crafted question when she tried to trick him into betraying his clan.

She reached down, patting her stomach below the navel. The cramps were gone. After this last period, she felt better than she had in moons. Had it been guilt over spearing herself on Three Stomach's giant member?

*By the Sky Beings, I'm tired of all this.* Perhaps this morning she could begin to put things right. A future might not exist for her and Salamander. She was, after all, Snapping Turtle Clan, and no matter that she might now disapprove of what her mother and uncle had asked her to do, she was nevertheless in line to one day become Clan Elder. If the clan leadership ended her marriage with Salamander, as they soon would, it did not mean that Salamander should have to hate her for the rest of his life.

If this were handled right, they might be able to make some agreement between them, a way to balance the competing needs of their clans with an understanding of each other. Surely a woman who might someday become Clan Elder could manage that.

Was it her imagination, or was the eastern horizon now gray? Yes, indeed it was. It would be soon, or not at all.

His form was a murky shadow among shadows as it passed the ramada. She could hear the soft whisper of his feet on the packed clay.

She took a deep breath, closing her eyes and rehearsing the things she wanted to say.

"Masked Owl?" he asked plaintively. "When you came to me last night, you told me to climb the Bird's Head at dawn."

Pine Drop started, staring around in the darkness. Was there someone else up here? Or was he talking to the Sky Being?

Salamander called, "Can we go flying again?"

She could see him now, his thin form barely outlined in the building gray. His skinny arms were raised, his head tilted up at the fading stars in the night sky. Her skin began to prickle as if bobcat fur were being rubbed across it. She swallowed hard, heart racing. Snakes and lightning, he *was* talking to the Sky Being!

"Is Water Petal's baby going to die?" he asked and cocked his head, listening. He must have heard an answer because he said, "I'm sorry, too. It will bruise her souls. Haven't my people suffered enough?"

He nodded, his eyes still fixed on the sky. "Yes, I understand. I just hurt for her, that's all."

Another pause. The light had grown enough that she could see his face: rapturous, and unless her eyes tricked her, glowing of an unearthly light. His eyes were pools of spinning darkness. She could feel her souls knotting and twining around themselves, frightened, frozen in place. Pus and blood, she wasn't supposed to be seeing this!

Her mouth had gone dry, her muscles tense, ready to leap to her feet. Frantic fingers wound into the blue feathers, crushing them, pulling some loose. Where she had cherished them for the beauty and warmth they provided, now she was thankful that their dark coloring helped to hide her shivering form.

"When they arrive I shall take very good care of them," Salamander said quietly. "Yes, I know." A pause. "In time, Masked Owl." He closed his eyes. "Just for the moment, can we Dance with the One. Just until the sun breaks the horizon? Take me on your wings, fly me up into the sky one more time."

In moments, the light would be bright enough that he couldn't help but see her when he opened his eyes. Pine Drop screwed a bit of courage from her terrified souls. Glancing up to be sure his eyes were still closed, she slipped over the rounded summit of the Bird's Head. Obscured by the brow of the great mound, she hurried away, placing each foot with care lest she slip on the dew-slick grass.

She sprinted down the final incline on the mound's southern shoulder and reached the level grass. Only then did she realize that the little stone owl was still clasped in her sweaty palm.

# Chapter Seventeen

The wind had changed, blowing down from the north and bringing uncharacteristically cold air with it. Bits of branches, flower petals, nearly ripe seedpods, and occasional leaves torn from distant trees went flying past.

Salamander walked with his back hunched against the blow as he tried to sort his churning emotions. The session in the Council that day had been particularly bitter. Moccasin Leaf had been given recognition and had asked if the Council would recognize a new Elder should Owl Clan present one. The vote had been unanimous: yes. When it came to Owl Clan's vote, he had stood and quietly added his yes to the vote.

Now his stomach ached at the memory. *Was it disrespectful? Did I betray Mother?* He had no answers, nothing that would help this feeling. The vacancy had to be filled, and it would not be with Water Petal. Not enough support existed for her among Owl Clan's lineages. Moccasin Leaf had done her job well. People were ready for a change.

Then, during other discussions, had come the periodic gibes and barbs concerning people who married barbarians. About their lack of respect, about their shiftlessness. He had watched Pine Drop's expression as the remarks were made. His wife had sat calmly in the rear of the Snapping Turtle delegation, her face reflecting nothing. She had refused to meet his eyes, even once.

So now he walked past the Southern Moiety's pole, its top decorated by streamers of colored cloth, feathers, and painted bones that dangled from leather thongs. He walked down the gap separating Alligator Clan from Snapping Turtle. Only a blind man would have been unaware of Elder Stone Talon as she sat at her ramada on the first ridge. She might have skewered him with a dart, so piercing was her glare.

He climbed onto the third ridge, walking eastward past the line of houses. When people spoke to him, he answered politely. He could almost taste their curiosity as they watched him pass, and he dared not look back as he approached his wives' house for fear that they were following in a parade to see what happened.

Salamander hadn't been here since Anhinga's arrival. For most of the time, both Pine Drop and Night Rain had been in the Women's House. Since then, well, he had been putting this off.

He rounded the last house. Night Rain was crouched under the ramada, grabbing up spilled cordage where the loom had been blown flat by the restless wind. She had laid a stone on a small ceramic jar full of red feathers, probably from a cardinal, that she had been weaving into the warp and weft.

"Can I help you with that?" Salamander asked, bending over beside her.

She shot him a scathing look. "No."

He nodded, backing away. This was going to be as bad as he had imagined. "Where is Pine Drop?"

"Inside. She took the stew in before it blew full of dirt. As if you'd care."

He took a deep breath and walked to the door as Pine Drop called, "Night Rain? Who is it?"

"Our *husband*, Sister. Evidently his barbarian camp bitch has given him time to come collect his things."

Salamander ground his teeth, a sinking in his chest.

"Come in, Husband." Pine Drop's face appeared in the doorway. "If you don't, you'll be blown away. Oh, would you mind helping Night Rain with the loom? Another gust like that last one, and she'll be blown clear down to the Panther's Bones." At that she smiled. "And, fortunately for us, you're probably the only man here with the ties to get her back without bloodshed."

The tone in her voice shocked him. Apparently it flattened Night Rain, for she made no other comment as he helped her maneuver the loom through the doorway while the wind tried to rip it away.

Inside he peered around in the gloom. To his surprise his belongings were just as he'd left them. Truth be told, he had expected to find them piled outside the door and reeking of dog piss.

Pine Drop resettled herself behind the fire. Newly kindled, the first flames were licking up around the sides of her carved soapstone bowl.

"It's still warm, but if you'll wait it will be hot soon." She looked up at him and smiled. "Please, be seated, Salamander. We have a lot to hear about."

He opened his mouth, but words stuck in the

bottom of his throat. Still mute, he seated himself, aware that Night Rain, too, was gaping.

"Sister?" Pine Drop asked. "Could you pour some of that raspberry juice from the gourd for our husband?"

"N-No!" Night Rain sputtered. "He can drink toad urine for all I care!"

To Salamander's complete surprise, Pine Drop reached out and slapped her sister hard across the cheek. "You will do as I say, Sister. Pour our husband some of that raspberry juice. *Now!*"

"No, it's all right," Salamander managed to blurt. "I didn't want to be any trouble."

Night Rain was speechless, her eyes wide, fingers to her cheek. She gaped in disbelief at first her sister, then Salamander.

"It is no trouble, Salamander," Pine Drop said. "It is only your due as our husband. And before I forget, thank you for the baskets of fish you had your kinsman, Bluefin, deliver to us. We really appreciated them."

"I would have brought them myself," he said through a tight throat. "I was busy. Every waking hour..." How did he finish that?

"It took me more than a half-moon to build this house," she replied reasonably. "You and your kin did it quickly."

Night Rain unsteadily reached for the gourd hanging on the peg by the door and handed it to Salamander. She was still stunned as she said, "You hit me!"

Pine Drop shot her a glance as she used a stone knife to slice sections of lotus root into the stew. "And I'll do it again if I ever hear you use that tone of voice with me."

"What has gotten into you?" Night Rain demanded hotly.

Pine Drop fixed her with a hard stare. "Responsibility, Sister. My lack of it, and yours."

"What?" Night Rain's face twisted.

"Very well, let's discuss this. Has our husband failed in any of his responsibilities to us?"

"He married that barbarian bitch!" Night Rain thrust a finger at Salamander.

"Our husband is Speaker for his clan." Pine Drop sat back on her haunches, hands on her brown thighs. "The Swamp Panthers came to Owl Clan, offering a daughter to them in return for an agreement to stop raiding. It was not our business what he did. Since that time, our husband has had to find lodging for his new wife." She lifted a wry eyebrow. "Or did you intend to welcome her here?"

Night Rain's mouth opened and closed as if she were a fish.

"That's what I thought," Pine Drop finished, then looked at Salamander. "You have behaved as an honorable man should." She lowered her eyes. "We, on the other hand, have not."

"I don't understand." To cover his discomfort, he sipped the thick raspberry juice. Sweet and delicious it helped to snap him out of his confusion.

Pine Drop met his eyes with an honesty he had never seen there before. "Salamander, we have behaved badly. You are our husband, and for as long as this marriage lasts, we are your wives. You have fulfilled your responsibilities to us without flaw. From this day forward, we will fulfill ours. Isn't that right, Night Rain?"

"What?"

Pine Drop might have been a stone. "I am the first wife, Sister. When it comes to this marriage, I have the right to expect obedience from you—something I have been lax in. You do not have to like Salamander, but you will treat him with respect. It is the way of our ancestors. You don't have to like it, you must only obey. If you have a problem with this, we will go out behind the house and settle it once and for all. Do you understand?"

Night Rain nodded in a daze.

"There, good. Let us start fresh, then." Pine Drop smiled when she looked back at Salamander. He had managed to keep his jaw from falling.

"Now," she began brightly, "what are your plans for tonight? Can you spend it with us, or must you go back to Anhinga?"

He tried to bring his racing thoughts together. "I told her I might not be back until morning."

"Good." Her eyes reflected concern when she said, "I want you to know, I have never seen the courage that I saw today when you voted with the Council on Moccasin Leaf's motion."

His voice turned hoarse. "Afterward I heard people whispering that I had shown disrespect for Mother."

"Did you?" Pine Drop asked.

"No. She cannot lead. She is ill. I, alone, am responsible for my clan. As much as I hated to do it, it was the right thing," he said woodenly, the wound in his souls opening.

She reached over and placed her hand on his. "Sometimes the right thing is hard to do, isn't it?"

He nodded, jarred by the sincerity he saw in her eyes. Snakes! Who was this new Pine Drop?

"I have to get air," Night Rain said, bursting for the door.

"Give her time," Pine Drop told him as he watched his young wife flee. "She still has a lot to learn."

"We all do," he murmured warily.

Anhinga watched the evening fall. The shadows cast by the rows of houses lengthened, the dome of the sky deepening in color. A trio of buzzards circled in a high spiral overhead, mocked by a single surly crow who dived and harassed them. Children's voices rose and fell as they engaged in a stickball game on the grassy Northern Moiety flat just across the borrow pit. Even the smoke from the evening fires seemed lazy as it rose into the quiet air.

Anhinga rubbed her arms, smearing the grease that kept mosquitoes from her skin. Casting an uneasy glance down the row of houses, she could see Water Petal's and sense the worry there. The little baby's fever had burned hotter, cooking life out of that thin and fragile flesh. She had seen it among her own people. It would be soon now.

*Here I am. Alone in the camp of the enemy.* She made a face and walked from her house, past the pestle and mortar, to the ramada where Wing Heart sat at her loom.

Anhinga cocked her head, watching the old woman's nimble fingers as they slipped thread back and forth through the warp.

"Hello, Elder," Anhinga called.

Wing Heart seemed oblivious.

Anhinga stepped over and seated herself on the cane matting. She snugged her knees inside her arms and studied the old woman's visage. Fleeting expressions seemed to shift like leaf shadows in a breeze. They rippled across the texture of the old woman's face, slipping among the wrinkles and hiding at the corners of her mouth. Her dark eyes, like midnight droplets, sparkled and danced, animated by some clinging remnant of her souls.

"My uncle always feared you," Anhinga ventured. "Do you remember him? Jaguar Hide? Does that name conjure any spark in your memory, old woman?"

The bony brown fingers never skipped, the vacant eyes never flickered.

Anhinga frowned and reached down. Salamander's adze lay forgotten on the cane matting. Anhinga picked it up, staring thoughtfully at the tool. The handle was the length of her forearm, and had been crafted out of the Y of a branch. The angle of the Y held a thin slate celt that had been set into the wood and bound by wraps of what looked like deer sinew. She tested the edge with her fingertip. Recently sharpened.

"Does it worry you to be here alone with me?" She studied Wing Heart from the corner of her eye.

Nothing.

"Your people killed my brother."

Wing Heart's eyes remained focused on a far horizon.

"Your son killed the man I would have married."

Wing Heart's lips twitched, and unexpectedly she said, "No, Cloud Heron. I don't think you should marry

Back Scratch." Her head dipped, as if hearing a reply. "Surely not."

Anhinga glanced around, seeing no one the old woman could be talking to. "What happened to you?"

"Thumper's a good man. Hard to believe he's kin to young Mud Stalker."

The adze balanced well in Anhinga's hand. She glanced around again, seeing that no one was close. In the shadows, it would be so easy. She could rise, drive the sharp stone head of the adze right through the Clan Elder's head. The body wouldn't be found until morning. She would be long gone, having struck the Sun People a terrible blow.

"I have hopes, Brother." Wing Heart smiled at that, her face lighting with joy.

Uncle's words came back. *"Wing Heart? She is the greatest of them. She and Cloud Heron remade Sun Town.*

*Oh, to be sure, they had started on the ridges and high mounds several lifetimes ago, but those two, they dominated the Council. What may have never been finished has been done in two tens of years under their leadership. Never forget: None is as crafty as Wing Heart."*

"You don't look so crafty now," Anhinga noted. Instinctively she reached out, brushing a mosquito from the old woman's shoulder where Water Petal had missed greasing her. "Panther's bones, you can't even take care of yourself."

The gray head bobbed in the twilight. "White Bird will return, Brother. I can feel it in my bones. With the spring. That's when we'll see him." When she smiled, a thin drop of saliva tricked from the corner of her mouth.

"He's dead, Elder." She pointed at the spot across the borrow pit. "He died there, remember?"

Was that a reaction? The old woman's smile dimmed, and pain glistened in her eyes.

Anhinga lowered her gaze, a heaviness on her souls. The smooth handle of the adze had warmed in her hand. She absently rubbed her thumb along the grain, then laid it to one side. What honor came from tormenting the tormented?

"Elder, you are drooling," she murmured as she reached for a bit of fabric and wiped at the corner of the old woman's mouth. "There, that's better."

She rose, stepping over to where the grease pot sat. "If you will allow me, you need a bit more grease or the mosquitoes are going to eat you alive."

"What is going on?" Mud Stalker demanded as he matched step with Pine Drop. She was carrying a grass-stem basket full of chinquapins. Midday sunlight peeked through low wads of clouds that scudded out of the southwest on a never-ceasing passage of the white-blue sky.

"Going on?" Her self-possessed look caught him off guard.

He tried to balance Night Rain's hysterical ravings against this calm young woman. "Night Rain came to me. She's upset. She says that you've either lost your souls like Wing Heart, or you've been witched. Which is it?"

"If it has anything to do with my souls, Uncle, it's that I found them." She gave him a smile too old for her age. She looked more mature than he remembered. The petty tightness at the corner of her mouth was gone. Her smooth brown cheeks seemed to have more color, and a serenity lay behind those dark brown eyes.

"I don't suppose you'd like to elaborate on that?" He cradled his ruined arm, fingers stroking the scars.

"Uncle, let me ask you a question."

"Go ahead."

"Do you expect me to be ready to step in as Clan Elder someday?"

"It is the natural order of things. The Sky Beings willing, I'll be long gone before your mother is, but yes, I fully expect our lineage to maintain its control. You are the logical one to follow your mother in the Council."

"I thought you'd say that."

"Oh, don't be ridiculous! You knew that full well. That's why I devote so much time to you." He realized he was scowling, too cagey a politician not to know that this was going somewhere he wasn't going to like.

"I have to learn to be an Elder," she told him. "I have to be worthy. To do that, I have to learn to think, to feel, and to lead. Do you agree?"

"Of course." Had he just stepped full under the deadfall?

"I was hoping you thought that way, because I want you to know that I will do my best for the clan. I need your advice in all things, as I need Mother's, but from here on, I am making my own decisions."

"You've always made your own decisions."

"No, Uncle. In the past I did as you said, as Elder Back Scratch said, and after her, as Mother said. But something has happened. I realized what I was becoming: Someone who only does the bidding of others, who can only follow orders, cannot give them."

"So, what does this have to do with Night Rain and Salamander? We are almost at the point where we can rid you of him. Once we replace Wing Heart with Moccasin Leaf, it will be time to castrate the little tadpole. A statement of divorce will do that as effectively as—"

"No, Uncle."

"What?"

"I don't want a divorce."

Mud Stalker grabbed her arm, pulling her to a stop. She stared at him over the basket rim. He searched her eyes, seeing a stubborn resolution there. "You will divorce him when *I* say so."

"The clan may not arrange a marriage without the consent of the parties. Nor can it break a marriage unless the husband and wife agree. I disagree."

"Night Rain doesn't. She thinks you've been chewing jimsonweed. I'm not sure that she's wrong. What is this crazy talk? Why are you defying me? I am your uncle, your clan's Speaker."

"Do you want my advice?"

"Given what you've said so far, probably not."

"Then hear it anyway. I think Night Rain should stay in the marriage."

Mud Stalker released her arm, shook himself, and asked, "Very well, Niece, since you've discovered all of these magical things, why?"

"Because she needs the discipline."

"I'm not terribly impressed with yours at the moment."

"Not discipline to the clan, Uncle. Discipline with

life, with responsibility. She's ready to run off to exile with Saw Back. You know, the Alligator Clan youth?"

"The one your husband got into trouble?" Mud Stalker nodded. "The one who was supposed to see to Jaguar Hide's death but let him get away?"

"He's not the sort we would want Night Rain to be married to. He's dumber than a cooking clay—and not nearly so durable."

"Obviously, considering it was Salamander who outsmarted him." Mud Stalker rubbed his jaw, seeing the logic of her words.

"And another thing, Uncle. We have been blinded by our own preconceptions."

He raised an eyebrow. "We have?"

"Why do you think Salamander is a stupid fool?"

"Because he is! Snakes, girl, four moons ago he was a weird little boy lost in games and silliness. Even his soul-scattered mother considered him to be an idiot and a failure. It took everything I had to maneuver her into marrying you to White Bird, and even more to ensure that addle-brained nit would follow his brother! By the Earth Monsters, who'd have thought that a bolt of lightning would deliver him to us like solstice supper?"

Her enigmatic smile cooled his enthusiasm as she said, "Watch him, Uncle. He is more than he seems."

"You would advise me? About that fool boy we put on the Council? He's a laughingstock!"

"For the sake of my clan, yes, I would advise you."

"But you won't divorce him?"

"No, Uncle. Not until he gives me a reason to."

He hated the resolve filling her large brown eyes. Rot it, there had to be some way of talking sense into the girl. "Well, so be it." An idea came to him. "After this last session in the Women's House, it is apparent that Three Stomachs hasn't been able to—"

"No, Uncle."

"You're right, Three Stomachs is out, but"—he narrowed his eyes—"have you thought about Speaker Deep Hunter? True he's a little old, but for the moment he absolutely *hates* Salamander for aiding Jaguar Hide's escape."

"No, Uncle."

"Deep Hunter is a Speaker, Niece. From a powerful clan. A man of real authority. Your coupling with him will balance some of the obligation we have to him. Not only that, but if this works out, if he can sire an heir, it might be a reasonable mating."

"No, Uncle."

"Well, it's probably early to talk about marriage. I can tell you, however, that he has had his eye on you. I watch these things. Red Finger is going hunting with him in the next couple of days. I'll have him delicately broach the subject. Trust me, Deep Hunter will oblige. And afterward, well, it will make him a little more amenable to our position in the Council."

"No, Uncle." She cocked her head, meeting his stare with defiance. "I am married. That's the tip of the snake's tail. The end. Find someone else." With that she walked away, her feet swishing through the tall green grass.

Mud Stalker frowned, trying to grasp where the problem was. Snakes, she wasn't really enamored of that skinny little idiot, was she?

# Chapter Eighteen

A
nhinga cursed and rested the heavy wooden pestle on her shoulder as she studied her thumb. The long dark sliver had run under the skin where it folded at the joint. She used her teeth to pull it, turned her head, and spat it out. The pestle had been made from a long pole, taller than she was. The bottom had been sanded round to match the hollow burned into the stump.

She glanced over her shoulder at the old woman seated at her loom. From the first glow of dawn to sunset's last light, she sat there, humming, talking to the dead, and weaving the most beautiful fabrics Anhinga had ever seen.

She had approached Wing Heart several times since that first night, cautiously seating herself and remarking about the weather, the taste of the stew, or the beauty of her weavings. Each time she might have been a leaf blown in by the wind for all the notice the old woman gave her. Sometimes she wiped up drool. Since the death of Water

Petal's baby, Anhinga had found Wing Heart's kirtle fouled. She couldn't stand the thought of the soulless Elder squatting in her own waste. Irritated by her compassion, Anhinga had sponged the woman clean before walking down to wash the fabrics in the borrow pit.

*I came here to kill her. Now I'm caring for her infirmities.* Anhinga slammed the pestle into the mortar, flattening more of the ground nuts into paste. As she worked, images kept swimming out of her memory. If she closed her eyes she could smell the fires of home. That blue smoke hung low in the trees surrounding the Panther's Bones. She could imagine the earthy scent of the swamp clinging in her nose with a blossom's intensity.

She could see Striped Dart, seated before a fire, his legs akimbo. He had that preoccupied look on his face, his smooth black hair pulled back into a tight curl and pinned to the side of his head. In the fantasy, her brother looked up at her and smiled.

Panther's blood! They'd had some times. She could see him again as he had been as a boy. How they'd played, she, Striped Dart, and Bowfin! Tag, hide-and-seek, ball games, and play war. She remembered splashing in the waters of Water Eagle Lake when they'd traveled east to the bluffs. The sun shone on their naked brown skin as they frolicked and dived in the murky depths.

Her mother's and father's faces formed as they had been then, young and in love, happy with their family. That had been so long ago, those golden summers, lost with the passage of time like water down the rivers of her homeland. Bowfin was dead. When she conjured her mother's face it was to see the lines of grief as she wailed over Bowfin's body.

Other memories rose to fill her. Firelight flickered as Mist Finger stood before her. She was on her stomach, propped on her elbows, her knees and toes digging into the soft black dirt. Her breasts had barely begun to bud, his shoulders only beginning to widen.

"I will be a great warrior!" he had said as he strutted back and forth before the fire, his walk an exaggerated mimicry of a great blue heron's.

"You'll be a lazy fisherman," Cooter had replied where he lay on his side, the firelight flashing yellow on his belly. "Me, I'm just going to make canoes."

"Canoes?" Anhinga had cried. "When you could be a great warrior and have pretty young maidens like me sing your praises?"

"I like making canoes," he had said simply. "It's an art to make a good one."

"I'll let the maidens sing *my* praises," Mist Finger had declared. "But, just for you, old friend, I'll use one of your canoes to carry them off into the swamp when I choose the right one."

They had all laughed at that. Now, over so much time, it echoed hollowly in her ears.

*I miss them.* She bent down, setting the pestle aside, and scraped the paste from the mortar bottom, placing it in a ceramic bowl. She studied the vessel for a moment. One thing was sure, Sun Town potters made better bowls than her people did.

That led her to remember Webfinger, the young potter at the Panther's Bones. She wasn't a known beauty, her face round but pleasant. Anhinga had spent hours sitting at her feet, watching those quick fingers as they worked. Through her magic a lump of mud was turned into a thin-walled hollow by means of pinching, scraping, and pressing with her palms and the wooden anvil.

*Home! What I'd give to be there now.*

"Excuse me?" A female voice caught her by surprise. Anhinga straightened, picking paste from her fingers.

The woman was young, comely, her breasts still firm, the lines of her belly unspoiled by the growth of a child. She wore a tan-and-black kirtle tied with a married woman's knot. Her gleaming black hair was tastefully parted down the middle and pinned on the sides of her head. A basket hung from the crook of her right arm. Her face caught Anhinga's attention, as it had a regal bearing. Something in those eyes made her alert. She didn't need to see the strings of beads, the tufts of exotic northern furs woven into her hair to know that this was a woman used to authority.

"Yes?" Anhinga instinctively rested her hands on the pestle. The solace of the stout wood reassured her. Not all of Sun Town's people could be counted on to be happy with her presence here.

"I have come to see you." The accented voice carried no hint of malice or anger.

"Assuming that your eyes work, you have succeeded. I am Anhinga. Daughter of Yellow Dye, who was daughter of Red Walnut, of the Sunrise Clan."

The young woman nodded, every manner correct and polite. "I am Pine Drop, daughter of Elder Sweet Root who is the daughter of Back Scratch, of the

Bluejay lineage of the Snapping Turtle Clan." She smiled soberly. "I am also first wife to Salamander, Speaker for the Owl Clan."

Anhinga started. Salamander had told her that his other wives could have cared less about her, as they had apparently cared so little about him. Yet here was this self-assured woman standing before her, bearing a basket.

"Is my husband available?" Pine Drop asked, her eyes straying first to the humming Wing Heart and then to the partially visible doorway of Anhinga's new house.

"He has gone," she replied carefully. By the Panther's blood, she hadn't come here to check up on Salamander, had she? "He is at his cousin's. Water Petal, do you know her? Her infant is dead."

The woman nodded, her eyes still taking Anhinga's measure. "Yes. I have just heard. I have come offering my clan's sympathy to my husband and his relatives." She indicated the basket. "Food for the family. Smoked raccoon, some boiled crawfish, and smilax-root bread."

"I wouldn't have thought you would care." The words just came out, surprising Anhinga of their volition. "Forgive me, that was not my right to say." Rot it, Pine Drop might be straight out of the pampered Sun Town elite, but that was no reason for rudeness. *And why do I care what she does or how she treats Salamander?*

Pine Drop lowered her eyes, smiling ironically. "If you know Water Petal, you have heard some terrible things about me."

Anhinga said nothing, guarding her suddenly impetuous tongue.

"I'm afraid most of them are true," the woman replied, raising her eyes again.

"You admit to lying with another man?" Anhinga asked, curious to see how far she could go. "Just like that?"

A slightly raised eyebrow was the only reaction she elicited. "Among other things." A pause. "I owe you no explanations."

"He said he wishes to spend the next few nights with you." Anhinga fingered the pestle, wondering why the woman's presence bothered her so. She had known from the beginning that he was married, not just to this woman, but her sister also. Multiple wives were nothing exceptional. Her uncle had *five*, but why did she feel so possessive about Salamander in the presence of this woman?

"My sister and I will be looking forward to his company." She hesitated. "I may be out of place, but if you need anything, come and see me. I was remiss not to have come to you sooner." Her smile seemed honest, warm. "You are alone among a strange people, your souls must be longing for home."

*Blood and spit! Is it that obvious?* "Thank you for your kind invitation. I shall discuss it with Salamander. If he approves, I may come and see you."

"And the Women's House?" Pine Drop asked. "Have you made arrangements?"

Anhinga jerked her head to the east. "I would prefer to seclude myself in the swamp. It would be better for all."

Pine Drop's expression tightened. "Out there? Alone?"

W. Michael Gear & Kathleen O'Neal Gear

Anhinga laughed. "What man is going to bother me in that condition? Do you think he would want to be close to a woman during her bleeding? And besides, I am Swamp Panther. To me it is more like home."

Pine Drop seemed to accept that. "As you wish, however, should you need, my clan would offer you space."

Anhinga's heart actually lightened. "Thank you, again. You are very kind."

"I am keeping you from your work." Pine Drop indicated the pestle and mortar. "I shall take this to Water Petal." She glanced uneasily at Wing Heart again, and added, "Do come to see me, even if it is just to visit."

"I will," Anhinga promised. And she would. Here was yet another opportunity opening before her. "It was nice of you to come here."

Pine Drop nodded and went on her way.

Anhinga watched the woman walk past Wing Heart's house and follow the ridge down to Water Petal's household with its grief and shattered dreams.

Anhinga placed more ground nuts into the mortar and began smacking the pestle home. The sound make a rhythmic *thump-tump thump-tump*.

The invitation to the Women's House had been unexpected, and something that, had the roles been opposite, she wouldn't have thought of had Pine Drop been at the Panther's Bones.

Anhinga frowned, removing the pestle. She placed a hand to her abdomen, trying to count the days. Her last menses had been just before leaving the Panther's Bones, had delayed it, in fact.

*You still have time. But soon. Very soon.* She

couldn't be pregnant, not only wasn't it time, but her stomach felt fine in the mornings. Whether she passed her moon or not, she had to get away. The four days to pass her bleeding would give her time for something she had just begun to plan.

# The Serpent

We are all frightened of the Stranger.
Probably because the Stranger is not nearly as far away as we think. She can come upon us suddenly, after an act of cruelty, the death of a loved one, or stumbling over an unknown dog in the forest. For no apparent reason, we cross some hidden border and the stranger is born. In a heartbeat, we do not even recognize ourselves.

*Our own fear with a face—that's who the Stranger is. And that is what makes her so very dangerous.*

# Chapter Nineteen

I n the two moons since Salamander's marriage to the Swamp Panther, Night Rain's irritation had grown. Late summer light slanted through the trees. From where she lay in the hunting blind, Night Rain could look up and see sunshine reflecting from the glossy green leaves of the magnolia. Great white flowers, the last of the summer, still whispered their scent into the sultry air. To either side, sassafras trees stood like resolute sentinels. The lobed leaves undulated on the late-afternoon breeze.

Deep Hunter stirred and shifted on the thin deer hide they lay upon. He propped himself on one arm, his appreciative dark eyes tracing the length of Night Rain's young body. She could see the pattern her body had made on his. The grease had been smeared on his chest, belly, and thighs. His penis lay limp, the scrotum that had been so taut moments ago had descended, lax in the heat.

She sighed, the warm tingling still fading from her loins. Snakes! So that was what it was all about? No wonder people made such a fuss about coupling. A glow of satisfaction still traced fingers of delight through her hips.

"You are so beautiful," he whispered.

She smiled as she studied the lines in his face. He might have been her grandfather's age, but his gnarly old body had surprised her. She hadn't understood that coupling could proceed slowly, gently, like a long leisurely soak in a warm pond. Her previous experience with Salamander had reminded her of the rapid way camp dogs joined, then faced away while locked, as if longing to be somewhere else.

"How do you feel?" he asked.

"Good." She stretched, dreamy, aware that his eyes were fixed on her supple body. "I didn't know it could be like that."

"You have only had boys." He yawned, smiling satisfaction. "And it pleases me that your Salamander is no better with his women than he is with his politics. Have you given any thought about what you will do when he's broken and dismissed from the Council?"

"This will be soon?"

"No, not for a while. Maybe next summer. A great many people want Owl Clan broken, not merely wounded."

She remembered her uncle's admonitions: *"Give him nothing but your body, Night Rain. This isn't some dazzle-headed youth, but a skilled Speaker, crafty in the ways of intrigue. Say nothing that will give him any advantage."*

She told him offhand, "I don't care. Just so long as he is out of my bed and gone for good. I have been told that if things are handled correctly, an alliance with

Alligator Clan might be considered." She lifted an eyebrow. "Currently, you only have one wife."

He chuckled. "Yes, and she is possessive. Trust me, you wouldn't want to move into her house with me. We have been together for a great many turnings of the seasons. She has her own ways of doing things, and I daresay, the pot would boil over within the first hand of time. I wouldn't want your tender flesh scalded by those waters."

Despite the warnings from her uncle, she said, "You have others from your lineage. Let's see, there's Saw Back."

"Yes, you'd think he was born of Owl Clan instead of mine." His expression soured. "You would be interested in a stone-headed boy like that? I still can't understand how anyone could fail in such an easy assignment. All he had to do was follow that murdering weasel into one of the channels and kill him! Jaguar Hide was alone, vulnerable. The added benefit was Owl Clan's abortive protection! It was a way of striking two birds with one cast of the bola."

Startled by his outburst, she placed a hand protectively on her breast. "But he was tricked!"

Deep Hunter's eyes narrowed, expression changing as he studied her. "Is this another one of his pathetic games? Did he put you up to this, little temptress? Are you playing with me? Hmm?"

The afternoon's warm delight had turned cold in her bones. Her uncle's warnings were spinning about in her head like bees. "No, I swear!"

She tried to recover her shaken confidence, smiling in what she hoped was a coquettish way. His continued silence and the chert-hard look in his eyes, indicated he was anything but fooled.

"You swear?" he finally said. "Really? That reassures me, little wren. So, did your uncle know that you were working for Saw Back when he mentioned this little tryst? Is he going to be happy when he discovers that you and Saw Back manipulated him like a leaf on the wind?"

"No!"

"And does your mother, the Clan Elder, know that you are using her position for your own scheming?"

"No!" Her desperation was growing.

"I think I shall have to extend Saw Back's banishment for trying to trick me like this."

She felt herself crumple inside, closing her eyes as she whispered, "No. It's no scheme, I swear it."

"Ah, swearing again? When I have caught you in the middle of a lie?"

"I'm not lying," she declared, on the point of tears.

"Indeed you are," he added smoothly, a glint in his eyes. "Either you are scheming with Saw Back, or you are scheming with me. If you weren't in some sort of scheme, you would be home, tending your household and your duty to your clan."

"This *is* my duty to my clan!"

"Then supposing we accept your desperate protestations and believe that you are not here for Saw Back's benefit. That would mean that Mud Stalker had an ulterior motive when he mentioned that I might meet you here. I wonder what that could be? Hmm? Care to share it with me?"

"I don't know," she pleaded, rising, frantic to escape as his hand clamped on her wrist.

"No, stay. I'm not finished yet." He nodded in triumph, a slow smile spreading on his lips. "You have made a mess of your seduction, my little wren. I have caught you in a botched attempt to wiggle your canoe around Alligator Clan's internal business." Satisfaction gleamed behind his veiled brown eyes. "What a story this will make in the Men's House. Every lip will be telling of how Night Rain will part her legs for those who can do her a favor. The young men are going to be snickering and offering favors every time you walk past."

"Dear Sky Beings," she cried, bolting up. "You wouldn't!"

He continued watching her, spiderlike in his intensity. "Wouldn't what? Make you a laughingstock? It would depend. You know, don't you, that you are already suspect in most people's eyes. You're married to that idiot Speaker. What would a little push do to you? Send you right over the gunwale, that's what. I suppose I should tell you, the water is deep and cold."

"Why?" she cried, hearing fear in her voice. "I am the daughter of Sweet Root, the Elder of—"

"I *know* who you are," he snapped. "That's what makes you even more vulnerable. Don't tell me you hadn't figured that out on your own." He raised one hand in a calming motion. "But it doesn't have to work that way, you know."

She swallowed hard, her thoughts scattered like a flock of frightened bobwhites. She could feel the tangling of his web around her.

"Let us say that what happened here today could stay between the two of us," he mused, releasing his hold on her wrist. "There is no reason to destroy you,

Night Rain. It would be unnecessarily cruel. All that talk, people laughing every time you passed. You've seen other women like that, living in constant shame, afraid to be seen in public. I can only imagine what the whisperings would be like in the Women's House."

Her breath shortened. It would be horrible. She was an Elder's daughter. Her uncle was the Clan Speaker. All of Sun Town would delight in tearing her down like an old ramada.

"What do you want?" she asked with a shallow voice.

"Oh, let's play this charade for a while." His smile broadened, rearranging the lines in his old face. "I rather enjoy teaching you the arts of your body." He ran his fingers down her side, along the curve of her hip and over the top of her thigh. "But don't think I would be ungrateful for your cooperation. Quite the contrary, actually." He studied her, seeing right through the front she put up, reading her souls. "What do you really want, Night Rain? Tell me the truth. I will know if you are lying."

She swallowed hard, thoroughly defeated. "I want to be somebody. Not a *second* wife to an idiot. Not a younger sister to Pine Drop. Everyone knows that Pine Drop is going to be Clan Elder someday. Snakes, she already acts like she is! You should see her. The way she orders me around. She treats me like a slave taken in war rather than a sister."

His knowing eyes had narrowed, watching her the way a hawk did a swamp cottontail. "Ah, honesty at last." He twisted a long lock of her hair around his finger. "Nothing is beyond attaining, Night Rain. Not if you ally yourself with the right accomplices. What you become, who you become, depends on you, on what you are willing to do to make your dreams come true."

She bit her lip, saying nothing.

He made a calming gesture. "You must understand, these things take time. They take compromise and dedication. Sometimes you must make difficult choices, decisions that place you in uncomfortable positions with your clan, and even your lineage." He shrugged. "You are here, coupling with me. That proves that those decisions are not difficult for you."

"You want me to work against my clan?"

He studied her, expression neutral. "Would you be Clan Elder one day? All you need tell me is a simple yes, or no."

Her heart sank in her chest. "Do I have any choice?"

"Oh, there is always a choice, little wren. I can tell that you enjoyed coupling with me. I can teach you more ways of kindling that fire within your hips. And, as an added benefit, I might be persuaded to send for Saw Back. If you are good, I might even allow the two of you to dally here in secret occasionally." His eyes narrowed. "I am told that Saw Back has come to absolutely hate your husband. He blames him for his misfortunes."

Night Rain's heart was pounding. Deep Hunter noticed, reaching out to place his fingers against the pulse in her neck. "Relax, little wren. In life, there is punishment and reward. If you help me, I will see that everything you want comes to you." He paused, searching her eyes. "Clan Elder?"

Mistrusting, Night Rain stared at him. "You could really do that?"

He nodded, so assured of himself that she couldn't help but believe him. "Of course. But only with the right accomplice." He leaned back, drawing her down beside him. "Tell me, Night Rain, are you that accomplice? Can you become my ally, knowing that with a little discretion, you can have everything?"

Her souls were trembling, but she hesitated. In that instant the memory of Pine Drop slapping her in front of Salamander flashed before her. She spoke almost without volition. "Yes, Speaker."

"Good," he whispered, bending close to brush his lips across hers. "Now, let me show you some new ways to throw tinder on a man's fire."

Water dripped in a line of rings as Green Crane, Trader of the Wash'ta People, lifted his paddle for another bite in the murky brown swamp. He had begun to question the wisdom of this journey southward to find the People of the Sun.

The canoe he and Always Fat paddled, slipped forward, powered by their muscular strokes as he glanced uneasily around him. Everywhere he looked, an endless pattern of green masked the trees. Through the few breaks in the foliage he could glimpse a dim world of black tree trunks wound with vines. The forest seemed to stretch on forever.

Ahead of them, the channel narrowed, ending in a verdant mat of reeds, duckweed, and flowering vines that swarmed over the fallen carcass of a bald cypress. The rotting trunk lay square across the passage, blocking any travel. The baleful eyes of a medium-sized alligator glared out at them from the scummy green surface. Turtles wearing forest-dark shells slipped from the protruding branches where they had been sunning themselves.

Green Crane shipped his paddle and looked back at his skinny companion. "We are lost."

"Good!" Always Fat made a face. His name was a jest. Always Fat looked like a walking skeleton. His ribs made a cage of his chest. Stringy arms held the paddle, and his knees looked like knobs in the middle of thick cane stalks. Mild resignation filled his long face. "I'm so glad you don't leave me baffled with hidden meanings. It pleases me that you can be so blunt when all I'd like to hear is something hopeful. Like, 'It must just be around the next bend.'"

Green Crane rubbed the back of his muscular neck as the canoe drifted forward. He and Always Fat were opposites, as well as inseparable companions. They had been planning this journey for a whole turning of the seasons, content to leave it hovering at the edge of imagination until Spring Cypress had arrived in their little village. Green Crane had been smitten at the sight of her. His attraction had only grown as he came to know her.

She was an enigma: A woman from Sun Town, that's all she would say. In the days it had taken to woo her, he had learned little more about her. He knew that she had come to his bed as a virgin, that she had left Sun Town of her own will over a broken love, and little else. One of the other Traders in his village thought he might have seen her before, and that she might have been Rattlesnake Clan, but he couldn't be sure of it, nor would Spring Cypress confirm the story.

She had just smiled sadly, and told him, "That life is dead."

Green Crane, however, wished to start a life of his own, one in which she figured not only as his lover, but as his wife. Among his Wash'ta people, a woman came to a man's clan with a dowry. Spring Cypress had arrived with nothing but a fabric bag slung over her back and her incredible beauty. Before his clan would allow him to marry, a payment had to be made. Her subsequent status within both clan and village would be dictated by the value of that payment.

The hide-covered load behind him consisted of an entire turning of the seasons' worth of Trading, dickering, hunting, and collecting. The bulk of the goods were from buffalo: finely tanned winter hides, smoked and dried meat, carved and polished horn implements. In addition, they carried lumps of silvery galena for ornamentation, different mineral pigments, raw hematite, and large quartz crystals, all of which brought a premium at Sun Town.

*"I shall ensure that you come to me as no woman has come to this clan in living memory,"* he had promised.

In that brief moment, her eyes had shone and she had thrown her arms around his neck, hugging her slim body to his. *"I cannot go with you, Green Crane. I cannot step into that place again. Not as I am now, a failure and a fugitive. My clan could reclaim me, hold me. I will not be their prisoner again."*

So he had come here, paddling down the White Mud River from his Wash'ta Mountain homelands. But somehow, along the way, he had become lost in the winding channels that led into narrow distributaries, dead ends, and ever-circling swamps of cypress and tupleo.

"How do people live in this mess?" Always Fat wondered.

"They must know the ways like we do the valleys of our home. I've heard of flatlanders getting lost, not being able to tell one valley from another."

"Mountains make sense," Always Fat reminded. "They have ups and downs. This place just has around and around."

Green Crane shook his head. He pointed a finger at the tiny patch of open sky over their heads. "Up!" He turned his finger toward the calm water. "Down!"

Always Fat pointed a finger over his shoulder. "Back."

They turned the canoe around and began paddling the way they had come.

After a hand of time they had retraced their way to the branch they had last taken. There, the canoe bobbing, Green Crane bent over, his hand cupping water as he slaked his thirst. "Tastes like tree roots and mud," he muttered.

"It could be worse." Always Fat pointed at the yellow lotus flowers in the shallows. "At least there's always something to eat here. Out in the western plains you can die of thirst and starve to death."

Green Crane glanced up at the sky, seeing the angle of the sun. By the Striking Eagle, had another day gone? "Well, from the sun, that way is west." He pointed.

"Hooraw! Saved." Always Fat lifted a mocking eyebrow. "Which way is Sun Town? For that matter, which way is anything?"

Green Crane considered the webwork of waterways around him. The hanging moss draping the low branches reminded him of green buffalo beards. Gaudy birds chattered and sang as they flew past. Two anhingas perched on a protruding log, unconcerned by a human presence as they sunned their wet wings in the afternoon.

"I don't think we could retrace our path even if we tried." Always Fat tapped his fingertips on his paddle. "So, we take the little channel, there."

"Why would that little channel take us through when the wide one we just tried wouldn't?"

"Because it's a way we haven't tried yet," Always Fat reminded. "If it turns bad, we'll come back and try something else."

Green Crane smiled as he shrugged, lifted his paddle, and drove them into the narrow channel. Many of his friends didn't appreciate Always Fat. But in the turnings of the seasons that they had passed together, Green Crane had come to value his companion's ever-present good humor. What a gift the gods had given him. No matter what the trial, Always Fat could only see the bright side.

The trees closed in, arching over their heads as they guided their slim canoe between the narrowing banks. Light dimmed, and the canopy overhead turned opaque. Green Crane ducked vines, batting away spiderwebs. "Are you sure about this?"

"No. But our canoe isn't stuck in the mud yet."

Tufts of leaves began brushing his elbows as he used the point of his paddle to push them along. The forest sounds tightened, bearing down on him. Gods, this was getting narrower.

He ducked a low branch, its bark scaly with moss

and algae. What he thought was a vine turned out to be a green snake that slithered away within inches of his eyes. He caught his breath, placing a hand to his heart.

"You all right?" Always Fat whispered.

"What if that had been a water moccasin?"

"We would have apologized when it bent its fangs on your tough hide."

At the sound of their voices, a dark shadow shifted in the Y of a tree. The panther cast a yellow-eyed glance their way, then leaped to the packed leaf mat, vanishing like a silent shadow into the gloom.

"Gods, that was a big cat!" Green Crane felt for his atlatl and darts. The fine white chert points had been chipped to an edge sharp enough to cut, but would he have time to prepare before some swamp monster plucked him from the canoe?

Always Fat swatted something off his head. "A centipede," he muttered. "I swear it dropped right on top of me."

"Precious Striking Eagle, just get me through this and I'll stay home, love my wife, and treasure my children."

"You haven't got a wife," Always Fat reminded. "Just the promise of a wife. Until you pay for her, you can't have children. You can't pay until you trade all this stuff with the Sun People for exotic goods we can't get at home."

"Must you be so cursedly pragmatic." He craned his neck, gaze following the winding vegetation up into the murky heights of the trees. Had there ever been a sky up there?

"I think it's a little brighter up ahead." Even as he spoke the watercourse widened. Within moments they were pushing the pointed bow of their canoe through a tangle of marsh ferns and out into the light.

"Pumpkin soup!" Always Fat cried. "Now where are we?"

Green Crane noted the shadows. "That way is west."

"Which way is Sun Town?"

"I have no idea."

"We could figure out where up and down are again."

"You think that would help?"

"Did it help last time? Wait. Who's this?" Green Crane turned his head seeing a low-slung dugout canoe heading his way. The center was heaped with long pointed baskets that he recognized as fish traps. A skinny youth sat in the rear, his hair parted in the middle. His greased skin caught the light as he paddled steadily toward them.

# Chapter Twenty

"Hello!" Green Crane called in Trade pidgin as he carefully stood in the bow and waved.

The youth raised an arm, apparently unconcerned as he paddled closer.

"Trusting sort," Always Fat noted. "Maybe strangers pop out of the hidden channel all the time."

"We are Wash'ta," Green Crane called. "Come to make Trade." He dare not say more until he found who the youth was, where he was, and if he were friendly. Green Crane could almost sense Always Fat's fingers as they surreptitiously rearranged his atlatl and a dart for quick utilization.

The youth dragged his paddle like a rudder to steer as his canoe glided toward them. He turned large brown eyes on Green Crane and nodded. Thin and reedy, he looked little more than a boy. A smudged white breechcloth was wadded around his waist, at his feet lay a pile of fish. An atlatl and darts rested close at hand. "I had hoped to find you."

That set Green Crane back. "You did? You knew we were lost?"

The youth cocked his head, those odd eyes seeming to enlarge. "Did you see an owl watching you?"

"We saw many things," Always Fat answered. "Alligators, snakes, and one very big panther." He jerked his thumb back at the bruised ferns they had just passed between. "Was that one of your spirits?"

"That might have been one of my wife's," the youth replied, an ironic smile on his lips.

"Where is your wife now?" Green Crane asked. What terrible thing had he led them into? He and Always Fat were lost in the swamp. Witches could capture them, devour their souls, and no one would ever find their remains in the maze of this terrible place.

"She has gone back to her people. I am to think she is in the middle of her moon. It is all right. She is lonely and homesick and needs time to plot with Jaguar Hide."

Green Crane shook his head, unable to quite grasp the meaning behind the words.

The youth stood then, balancing in the rear of the dugout. "I am Salamander, Speaker for the Owl Clan, son of Wing Heart."

"Of Sun Town!" Green Crane cried, his worry evaporating. "We made it!"

"We came to Trade," Always Fat repeated.

"I was told to seek out Owl Clan," Green Crane added, taking the skinny kid's measure. "Do you know a boy named Mud Puppy?"

The wry smile had a mocking quality. "I knew him very well."

"Knew? As in the past?" Green Crane felt a sinking

in his breast. "My Trade pidgin isn't very good. You mean he's...what? Dead?"

"He was *called* Mud Puppy," the youth said, "now is he known as Salamander."

"But you said you were Salamander." Always Fat shifted in the back of the canoe.

"I was Mud Puppy before I was made a man."

Green Crane slapped his sides. "We have come to find you! To show you this." He fished in his belt pouch to retrieve a little red stone owl.

At sight of it, Salamander's face brightened. "How is she?"

"Safe. Spring Cypress said to give this little owl to you when I saw you. To tell you it bore her safely to my people. Being safe, she would return the owl with great thanks. She thought you might need it to keep your own luck strong."

He made a pushing-away gesture with his hands. "It was a gift—not just for her journey, but for all of her life. She is my friend forever. Return it to her with my love and my fondest wishes for her health and happiness."

"You said you are Speaker?" Always Fat had his paddle balanced across his knees. "As in the Council?"

Salamander nodded sadly.

"But you are a...a..."

"A boy?" he supplied. "I'm afraid my body has not caught up with the age that this last turning of the seasons has branded into my souls."

"Can you show us the way to Sun Town?"

"It would please me to do so."

"How far?"

Salamander glanced at the slanting sun. "We shall

be there sometime after nightfall. You shall have to stay on the Turtle's Back until you are cleansed. Are you familiar with our ways?"

"We have heard of this." Green Crane reseated himself and collected his paddle. "We have only come to Trade. Not visit. Once we have done that, then we can return to our people. You need not bother with a cleansing."

They had not followed Salamander for even a hand's time when the youth looked across at them, asking, "Is Spring Cypress happy?"

"She is. Or rather she will be once we return with our Trade."

"She is to be his wife." Always Fat pointed at Green Crane. "He has fallen in love with her and makes this journey to acquire wealth to pay for her."

Salamander studied him thoughtfully across the short distance separating the canoes. "Are you worthy of her?"

Green Crane shifted. What was this youth to her? Who was he? An old interest of hers? "I would hope that I am."

"Do not hope," Salamander said soberly. "You must always *be* worthy. There is a difference, a matter of commitment that you would make when dedicating yourself to such a woman as Spring Cypress."

"Did you once hold hopes of marrying her?" Always Fat asked the question Green Crane couldn't.

Dreamy eyes covered Salamander's smile. "She was beyond my aspirations. She will have to tell you the story when she thinks it proper. Let us just say that she and I share a special bond between our souls. We had a single precious moment together that filled us both with

courage. She left rather than spend her life in misery."
He shot a measuring look at Green Crane again, as
though he were weighing his souls.

"I think," Green Crane mused in a voice only
Always Fat could hear, "that he is more than just a
green youth with a title."

"Indeed he may be."

In a louder voice, Green Crane asked, "Can you
help us conduct our Trade, Salamander? Say, for the
sake of Spring Cypress? Our success benefits her."

Salamander barely seemed to hear, as if lost in his
thoughts, but then said, "I am happy to advise you. By
that Owl you carry and the Spirit Helper who watches
over you, I will make you a most favorable Trade. Just
what did you bring, and what do you need?"

Green Cane knotted a fist in victory. He could
already imagine Spring Cypress's smile when he
returned with a canoe loaded to the gunwales with
finery.

The knoll protruded from the swamp like a floating
monster's back. Anhinga sat cross-legged on the dark
soil, her eyes on the lofty green depths of the cypress
forest. The canoe she had used to come here was pulled
up on the muddy bank. A fire smoked beside her, the
blue wreath rising pungently from the damp wood.
Mosquitoes hummed in a column, stymied by the
crushed gumweed she had mixed into grease and
slathered over her skin.

As she waited, she absently wound her finger
around and around a long black lock of hair. Her other

hand pressed against her abdomen. She was late, that was all. It happened to women who were worried, working hard, or under pressure in strange circumstances. Had anyone been more anxious than she married to a stranger in a strange land filled with enemies?

*You're all right. You haven't had the morning sickness. You don't feel different.* But how did a woman feel? She made a face. Surely Salamander couldn't have planted a child that quickly.

*What is it about him?* He wasn't what she had had in mind when it came to a husband. Her thoughts immediately went to Mist Finger, recalling his smile, the rolling muscles in his shoulders and arms. A man should look like that, have that brave glint in his eyes.

So why, she wondered, did skinny Salamander absorb so much of her? Her first surprise had come when they had consummated the marriage. That sudden and magical explosion in her loins had taken her by complete surprise, and better yet, he shot lightning through her each time they coupled. But his lure on her interest was more than that. His large brown eyes had a Power she didn't understand. He seemed to see past her skin, down into her souls. Most perplexing, he always smiled when she lied to him, as though reassuring her.

*He can't know that I am going to kill him.* It was impossible—unless his Spirit Helper had told him. She and Jaguar Hide were the only ones who knew the plan. Not even Striped Dart had been informed. They couldn't trust her brother to keep his silence. What, then, caused Salamander to give her that knowing look, the one that reminded her of a parent one step ahead of his errant child?

She lifted her lip, irritated at the very thought. Salamander? A step ahead of her? Everyone in Sun Town thought him a fool—with the possible exception of Pine Drop.

A fish jumped in the water beyond her camp. The thickened boles of bald cypress, tupelo, and overcup oak protruded from the still waters. Strands of hanging moss drooped, lacy and gray-green, and here and there thick patches of mistletoe had knotted and strangled their host's branches. The first fernlike needles were beginning to brown on the cypresses. A dry crispness hung in the air, a precursor of the winter to come.

Through the trilling of the songbirds and the hissing of the insects, she heard the hollow thunk of a paddle against wood. Movement caught her eye as Jaguar Hide paddled through the maze of waterlogged roots and protruding knees.

When he met her gaze across the distance, he smiled and raised a hand in greeting.

She rose gracefully to her feet and stepped down to the water's edge. He slid his canoe in beside hers as she offered him her hand, helping him to his feet. He groaned and made a face as his legs straightened. "Age," he growled. "Used to be I could live in a canoe."

"Hello, Uncle." She threw her arms around him, hugging his hard body against hers. "I see that you escaped the nasty Sun People. But I still haven't forgiven you for just paddling off like that."

He held her at arm's length, inspecting her from the parted crown of her head to her brown toes. "I came as soon as I got your message. What are you doing here?"

"They think I'm off to spend my moon in solitude."

Sudden fear leaped behind his eyes.

"Don't worry, Uncle, I passed that on the way here," she lied. "I wouldn't expose your souls to woman's blood."

"I would hope not." He grabbed a sack from the canoe and led her over to the fire. With a careful glance he studied her small camp. His gaze fixed on the tall, delicately leafed plants that grew on the far side of the small island. "What is that? Water hemlock?"

"It is indeed. People don't come here because the death plant grows here. Some think it taints the surrounding waters. We can meet here in private." She indicated a ceramic bowl resting in her canoe. "I bring water with me."

"Very well, you have exceeded all of my hopes. Tell me everything!" he cried, lowering himself beside the fire. "You are married, yes? To Salamander? You didn't kill him yet, did you? And what of Sun Town? What have you learned? What can we do to harm them? What is the truth about Wing Heart? Has she really lost her souls?"

"One thing at a time, Uncle!" She threw up her arms in mock surrender. She related her time in Sun Town, telling of building the house, Wing Heart's condition, and the collapse of Owl Clan.

"Tell me about this boy, Salamander. Is he really a Speaker?"

"He is. But most think him a young fool."

"From your tone, I take it that you don't?"

"I am not sure, Uncle. But fool or not, there are forces gathering to act against him. He has no allies except for his cousin, Water Petal, and she's ignored by everyone. There is a move afoot to replace him. They have already replaced Wing Heart. She is nothing more than a husk of a woman, like a pod stripped of its seeds."

"They have treated you well?"

She shrugged. "I am not one of their people. I am tolerated. Uncle, I can kill them anytime—with impunity—and escape in the night. I am unguarded. Not trusted, but not a prisoner, either. I think I should strike. I can be home before the next moon."

"I would prefer that you wait," he told her. "The time is not right. Not yet. Will it bother you to stay for several more moons?"

"Why?"

"Anhinga, think about this very carefully. You can learn about them, discover who their leaders are. Not just the ones now, but the ones who will lead in the future. You can come to know them as none of our people ever will, discover their strengths and their weaknesses. Do you see how such knowledge could be used to our advantage?"

She considered the passion in his eyes. Could she do that? Go back for a long period? She felt a tearing in her souls. "You ask: Would it bother me? A little. It is not pleasant, but not unbearable. The worst part is the loneliness. I miss friends. Family."

"You can come here. Meet me. At this place. Every time the moon is full. Sometimes I will bring your mother, or your brother. Any of your friends." He smiled. "Just as long as they don't learn what we are really about."

"In the end, I am still going to kill them."

He nodded. "Yes, but I think we need to reconsider given what you've told me. What good would it do to simply kill Wing Heart and Salamander? No one would notice that they were gone." He steepled his fingers, thinking. "Which clan is dominant?"

"No one is sure. Thunder Tail, of the Eagle Clan, has been voted leader of the Council. Snapping Turtle is gaining in prestige. Alligator Clan is fighting them." She smiled. "When Salamander delayed Saw Back's warriors and allowed you to escape, it infuriated Speaker Deep Hunter."

"He did that?"

"Most cleverly, Uncle. If for no other reason, we owe him for that."

"You are growing fond of him?"

"No, Uncle. I remember your warning. I constantly guard against forming any attachment to these strangers. I need only remember Bowfin, remember them butchering my friends, and my heart hardens."

"Good." He frowned, staring down at the soil. "In that case Salamander's action on my part has earned him a quick death, out of respect."

She took a deep breath. "I do not wish to, Uncle, but I will go back. I will wiggle my way into their confidence and learn what I can about them."

"Trust me, Niece,"—he smiled grimly—"it will make them that much easier to destroy."

# Chapter Twenty-One

From the heights atop the canoe landing, Salamander watched Green Crane's slim canoe as it paddled northward across the calm waters of Morning Lake. The wake, in the form of shallow Vs, trailed behind the long dugout, and the surface looked pocked where their paddles had swirled the water. He gave one final wave as the two Wash'ta Traders looked back. Each waved in turn.

"It is good," he told himself. "Masked Owl, see to their safe return."

*"If you ever need anything,"* Green Crane had said as he took Salamander's arm in a firm grip, *"send for the stone owl. I will come."*

"Make her a good husband," he had answered, before giving both Green Crane and Always Fat sturdy hugs.

Now he watched as they nosed their craft into the narrow channel that led north along the floodplain.

"So," Pine Drop's familiar voice said from behind him. "They are off."

Salamander nodded. "Indeed they are. I wish them safety and a speedy journey."

"I sincerely hope they don't get lost again." She stepped up beside him, tangles of her black hair curling around her shoulders as the breeze played with it. Her thoughtful brown eyes followed the Traders' canoe as it disappeared behind the willows.

"I think I explained the channels correctly."

She glanced at him, a question in her eyes. "Was it worth it? You almost stripped your clan for the meat and hides you received in return."

"Oh, yes, it was worth it." In his imagination he watched the canoe winding its way northward. "I have heard the talk. Others are saying that I make as poor a Trader as I do a Speaker."

"Do you, Salamander?"

"Would you believe me if I said there was more to this than the textiles, beads, carvings, medicine plants, and dyes?"

For a moment she hesitated, then said, "I think I would, Salamander." Her attention turned to his face as she said, "I think there is more to you than most people think." Her gaze went to the canoe landing. "Anhinga has still not returned?"

"No. It is but five days."

To his surprise, Pine Drop reached out and linked her arm in his. "Do you think she's coming back, Salamander?"

"Oh, yes. She doesn't want to, but she will. She can't stay away."

Pine Drop shook her head. "I don't like it. I mean the idea that she just goes out into the swamp for her moon. Anything could be happening out there."

He gave her a sidelong inspection. "Are you worried about her?"

"No, husband. I'm worried about you. Deep Hunter and some of the others might not be the only ones who are bitter about the past. I think you can wager that Jaguar Hide isn't acting in your best interests."

How much did he dare tell her? "No, he has his own plans."

"And Anhinga? There is talk. Eats Wood swears she is the same woman your brother captured in the Ground Cherry Camp raid."

"She is."

"What?" Pine Drop cried, using his arm to turn him so that she could stare into his eyes. Did all the women in his life have to be taller than he?

"We are bound, she and I. It is a thing I cannot explain. Something that no one but I can understand."

"You and Masked Owl."

He started, instantly regretting it as she read his expression.

Her voice dropped. "Is he real, Salamander? Does Masked Owl really come to you?"

He swallowed hard, knowing it made him look nervous, unable to help it. He bargained for time. "What do you think?"

She shook her head, a fragility in her eyes. "I don't know. I just don't know. Tell me, please. Tell me that it's just an act, a thing you do to keep your enemies off-balance."

That brought a wistful smile to his lips. "Pine Drop, why is it easier to believe that I'm making this up than it is to know that I converse with Masked Owl?"

She sank white teeth into her lower lip, searching his eyes, then said, "Spirit Power scares me, husband. I don't know what it wants from you, or from me. I just have a feeling, is all. And you, you're vulnerable, Salamander. You have a great number of enemies. Don't you understand, they are waiting to destroy you."

He reached out, running the backs of his fingers along her smooth cheek. "All but you and Water Petal. What has happened to you, Pine Drop? What do you see in me that the others don't?"

Her expression pinched. "I don't want you hurt. It is important that you understand that. I don't know what I can do to protect you. I have my duties to my clan, and I will attend to them, no matter what."

"I am forewarned, and I thank you for that. I wouldn't expect you to act against the wishes of your clan. Whatever you must do, I will understand. You must not worry about me. I will take care of myself."

She sighed wearily, shaking her head. "That doesn't make it any easier."

"It should." He turned his eyes back to the northern end of the lake, where the Traders had disappeared. "When the time comes, Wife, we must follow our hearts. Remember that I said that. Things are happening. Power is gathering."

She tightened her grip on his arm. "Come home with me, husband. The Snakes know where Night Rain is off to, but maybe she'll stay gone for the night. I would like to have you to myself for a time. Just you and me together for as long as we can keep the world away."

He let her lead him south past the Men's House, hardly aware of the grim stares that Eats Wood and Red Finger gave him as he passed. He held his wife's hand,

and wished he were someone else, someone that Power and circumstance hadn't called upon. Later, in Pine Drop's arms, he forgot even that.

The canoe bearing Yellow Spider and Bluefin arrived in late morning. Mud Stalker matched his stride with Deep Hunter's as they descended the trodden soil of the canoe landing. Squinting into the hot sunlight, he could see a small crowd already gathering. People were slapping Yellow Spider on the back, asking questions.

"Did you have trouble?"

"None," Bluefin replied, a grin breaking his normally placid face.

"Did you see any Swamp Panthers?"

"A canoe with two men," Yellow Spider replied. "We called out that we came for sandstone under Jaguar Hide's peace. They said nothing, just nodded, but they watched us the entire time. Seeing what we did, and that we did nothing more than collect sandstone."

One of the Eagle Clan men spoke. "I would be obliged for a piece of that. In fact, that piece right there on top. I'm sanding beads for a necklace."

"We are pleased to present it to you," Yellow Spider remarked with a smile as he handed over the thick piece of sandstone.

"What is this?" Clay Fat asked as he strode up to stand beside Mud Stalker and Deep Hunter.

"The first canoe load of Swamp Panther sandstone," Deep Hunter answered.

"Then it is true?" Clay Fat asked, one eyebrow raised.

"So it would seem." Mud Stalker cradled his ruined arm.

"What does it mean?" Clay Fat asked.

"Nothing!" Deep Hunter's lip curled. "An occasional canoeful of sandstone isn't going to bring Owl Clan back to prominence."

"But we must keep an eye on them," Mud Stalker mused.

"Why?" Clay Fat asked. "Wing Heart is crazy. That boy sure isn't any Speaker."

"Indeed he is not," Deep Hunter agreed. He glanced up, meeting Mud Stalker's eyes and nodding. "We must watch this Trade with the Swamp Panthers. If it becomes too popular, we must take steps to stop it."

Mud Stalker fingered the scars on his right elbow. "You and I may not agree about many things, Speaker, but we do about this."

Clay Fat looked uneasy. "It is Owl Clan's business."

"Not if we make it ours, old friend." Mud Stalker replied.

"I still haven't forgotten your obligation to my clan, Clay Fat. We prepared quite a feast. Copperhead turned down several *very profitable* offers in order to save himself for Spring Cypress." He paused, letting Clay Fat squirm.

"All it would take would be a raid. A party of warriors sent into the Swamp Panthers' lands. This Trade would end as quickly as it began," Deep Hunter said.

Clay Fat swallowed hard. "You would have to have

Council approval. This is Owl Clan's business. You cannot do this alone."

Mud Stalker considered the situation. Deep Hunter would act immediately given the slightest encouragement. But would that necessarily be good for Snapping Turtle Clan's position among the people?

"I must agree, reluctantly, with Clay Fat." Mud Stalker watched Deep Hunter's expression harden and smiled to himself. "However," he soothed, "if this sandstone becomes too irksome, Deep Hunter, I might be prevailed upon to support you."

"Indeed?" Deep Hunter muttered, sensing a trap.

"All things in time, my old friend." With that Mud Stalker turned on his heel and strode off.

# Chapter Twenty-Two

T
he fire popped and cracked, curls of thin white smoke rising from the dry wood. Pine Drop had built the rick in a hollow square, placing the cooking clays in the middle, where they would absorb the heat. The arrangement had to be made correctly so that the specially formed cooking clays heated to a white-hot glow in the center of the fire.

Normally water lotus was gathered for the great solstice feast, but the harvest had been so good this turning of the seasons that she had extra. It wouldn't keep in the midsummer heat, so she had mashed the remaining roots in the mortar to form a sweet paste. One by one she had formed the cone-shaped cooking clays, indenting the convex side to resemble the lotus's seedpods.

During the process, she sang the Harvest Song that recounted the origins of the lotus. In the beginning Mother Sun and Father Moon had both shared the Sky with equal duration and brightness. There was no night, no summer or winter, for when one dropped behind the horizon, the other waited until the first reemerged.

And then one day Father Moon glanced down and saw a beautiful woman bathing in a pond. She was the daughter of a great Clan Elder. His light shone in her long black hair and on her soft bronzed skin. He had never seen such a beauty before, and resolved to have her.

That night, when Mother Sun slipped behind the western edge of the world, Father Moon eased down from the Sky. He took the form of a young man and found the pretty young woman. She had never seen such a handsome man before, and lay with him.

Meanwhile, the night Sky had gone dark. The animals that normally were awake, bats, raccoons, flying squirrels, and crickets were all running around, bumping into things, saying, "Where is Father Moon? What is happening?"

But Father Moon was busy locking hips with the pretty young woman. He was so involved that he forgot the time. Thus it was that Mother Sun peeked over the eastern horizon to find the world in darkness, and the animals of the night running around in panic.

"Where is Father Moon?" she asked, concerned that some terrible thing might have happened to her mate.

"He is lying with a beautiful woman," opossum said. "He has left us in darkness so that he can lock hips with her."

Mother Sun sent her rays over the earth, and sure enough, there was Father Moon, lying with the pretty young woman. Rage burned in Mother Sun's heart, and in anger she fled to the south. She kept going and going, going so far that the world was plunged into darkness.

Horrified, Father Moon rose into the Sky, calling for Mother Sun to come back to him. But she refused, heading ever southward.

Father Moon chased after her, following her south across the Sky. As his light waned, Winter came roaring down from the north, cloaking the land in snow and ice. Plants died, turned different colors, and lost their leaves. Animals burrowed into the ground, desperate to save themselves from the freezing weather and the endless darkness. Birds, desperate for Mother Sun, flew south, many disappearing out in the gulf.

In the end, it was Bird Man who, seeing his world dying, flew south after the birds. There he found Mother Sun sulking at the edge of the sea, where it joined the Sky. He told her of the cold, of the dying trees, and how the animals had burrowed into the earth. He told how Father Moon was so lonely that he had hidden his face in sorrow.

"If you do not come back, the world is going to die!"

Mother Sun listened, and realized that no matter how mad she was at Father Moon, she couldn't let the rest of the world die. So it was she came back to the Sky, and the plants came alive, and people and animals were warm again. Seeing how grateful the creatures were, she shot beams of light onto the water, and a beautiful flower grew there. To this day the yellow lotus grows, its flower reflecting the face of Mother Sun. It is her promise to the world that she will always return to light the Sky.

Mother Sun never forgave Father Moon. That is why she forever moves across the Sky, always avoiding him. Father Moon still hides his face in shame and never glows as brightly as he did before the night he betrayed his mate.

Among the animals, bear, raccoon, the bats, the bees, and so many other creatures still hibernate when Mother Sun goes south with each cycle. In return, Mother Sun marks her return to the high summer Sky with the blooming of the yellow lotus. When the people harvest it for the solstice ceremony, its roots are sweet, and its flower resembles the face of Mother Sun so that people never forget her gift of life to them.

As she Sang the song, Pine Drop took damp lotus leaves from a stone bowl and wrapped balls of dough in the leaves. These she laid to one side on palmetto matting.

Her heating fire had burned down to coals, the central cluster of lotus-shaped cooking clays having taken on a white glow. She used a stick to scrape half of them onto a thin wooden platter and gingerly lowered them into the earth oven. As she poured them, she had to jerk her hand back from the searing heat.

"Hey, Cousin!"

She glanced up, seeing Eats Wood as he strode down the ridge. Sunlight shone on his muscular chest. His lightly greased skin reflected the light, and his tattoos stood out as dark blue designs on his brown skin. Several necklaces of stone and bone beads hung around his neck, and he wore a green-dyed breechcloth. A mocking smile curled his round face, and his hair had been parted down the middle and cut short to bob just above his shoulders.

"Greetings, Cousin." She shot him a polite smile

and bent down to lay the first of her wrapped lotus-root breads onto the cooking clays.

To her irritation, Eats Wood knelt beside her, asking, "Can I help?"

"No. Just a moment." She artfully laid the rest of the wraps onto the cooking clays. She couldn't help but wonder what he wanted as she scraped the last of the cooking clays from the fire and shook them from the smoldering plate into the earth oven. She had never liked Eats Wood. He let his penis dominate any good sense he might have had. The parallels between Father Moon and Cousin Eats Wood couldn't have been more clear. When she had placed the bark lid on the earth oven to seal in the steaming heat, she looked up.

"I just came to see how you were doing," Eats Wood began. He gestured around at the ramada, then at her house. "Do you need anything? Can I bring you anything? Firewood? Some palmetto for that place where the wind shredded your ramada roof?"

She picked little bits of dough from her slim brown fingers. "I appreciate your offer, but I suspect that you didn't come here because you were worried about my firewood supply."

He settled back on his butt, rubbed his sun-browned shin, and looked around at the near houses. His expression had a slightly pained look as if he were trying to find the right words.

"Is it about your mother?" she asked. Eats Wood still lived at home. He had been notoriously hard to marry off. Despite the size of Sun Town, Eats Wood's reputation preceded him. Few in the other clans considered him a likely candidate for marriage—even though

Snapping Turtle Clan's influence had grown like a north wind at winter solstice.

"She is fine, but thank you for asking." He pressed his lips together, studying her with narrowed brown eyes. "It is said that you will very likely become our Clan Elder someday."

"That day—if it comes, Eats Wood—is a long way off."

"It is said that you had a chance to divorce Speaker Salamander."

"Any woman has a chance to divorce, Cousin. That's a little fact that I hope you keep in your head when and if you do marry." She arched a challenging eyebrow.

He grinned sheepishly. "Yes, I know." Then he sobered. "Why do you stay with him?"

"I have my reasons, Cousin. Among them, because of who he is."

"He is a Speaker in name only. You could have—"

"I wasn't referring to his title."

"Most people think he is a fool, Cousin."

She considered him frankly and lowered her voice. "They are wrong, Eats Wood. I may be speaking to emptiness, but I want you to listen to me. Do not underestimate Salamander. I tell you that as a kinsman."

His round brown eyes didn't register any comprehension. "He's got that Swamp Panther woman for a wife. You could have anyone else you wanted."

"He has his reasons for marrying her."

"She was here before. She is the one his brother caught down at Ground Cherry Camp."

"So?"

"Cousin, look what we did to her and her friends!"

He leaned close. "You are part of his household, don't you hear things about her? About what she's after here?"

"You mean, does my husband trust her?"

"Yes."

"Not completely."

"She goes away every moon."

"Of course she does. Think it through, Eats Wood. Would you want her here during her moon? Hmm? Bleeding where any man, yourself included, might step in it? No, I suspect you would have her gone, far away, where her woman's blood won't make you ill."

"What's wrong with the Women's House? She can go there for her moon with all the rest."

"Put yourself in her place. Would you want to be shut up in the men's Society House in the middle of the Panther's Bones? Would you want to be surrounded by their suspicious warriors for days? Would you want to hear them snicker at your expense?"

He stared suspiciously at her. "I'll bet she meets with her Swamp Panther kin, what will you bet?"

"She has no friends here. If I were in her position, I would want to see kin, too."

He seemed perplexed. "You don't seem at all worried."

"I will worry when I have reason to." She gave him a sidelong look. "But why are you so interested in her?"

He spread his hands, trying to look casual.

"Uh-huh," she answered. "One of these days, Cousin, you are going to be like Father Moon. Some woman will possess your thoughts and lead you into a mess you can't find your way out of."

"She's dangerous," he muttered uncomfortably.

"You just watch, Cousin. She's going to get you into trouble before she's done here."

Wind howled in the thatch, poking cold fingers through the gap where the roof overhung the walls. It made a soft whistle as it blew around the house. Gusts shook the structure. cracking the wattle and daub. This wasn't a night to be out.

Salamander lay awake under the snug buffalo robe and stared up at the darkness. Anhinga cuddled next to him, her warm rump pressed against the angle of his hip and thigh. Cold air played patterns across his face, tickling loose strands of Anhinga's hair against his cheeks.

Turning his head, he could hear the soft rattle as leaves blew past. From the flapping sounds, the palmetto matting that roofed his mother's ramada was shredding and would have to be replaced.

His house shivered under a particularly hard blast. In his bones he could feel the storm's strength as it blew down from the north.

He blinked, wishing he could sleep with Anhinga's soundness. Instead, images flashed through his mind. Bits of the Dream that had awakened him replayed over and over. He had been flying, sailing across the sky on Owl wings. A black shadow had blotted the sun, and talons had ripped painfully through his back. In that instant he was falling, the ground spiraling as though rising to meet him.

Breath had frozen in his lungs, his throat locked. His stomach had lurched, weightless, falling, plummeting like a carved piece of hematite. The air rushing past had become the roar of the winter wind outside his house before he plunged headfirst into Sun Town's earthen plaza. At the last instant he had jerked awake.

"What?" Anhinga had murmured, shifting on their narrow bed.

"Nothing. A Dream. Sleep." He had patted her shoulder as she slipped her arm from across his chest and rolled onto her side facing the wall.

But he had lain there, awake, his heart pounding, the terrible image of falling still tingling in his blood, muscles, and bone. The sight of that green ground had been so real. The spreading arches of the clan grounds, the buildings casting shadows, couldn't have been imagined. Even the pathways, beaten into the grass by countless bare feet, could be seen spreading out like veins.

With great care, he slipped out from under the heavy robe. Chill washed his sweat-clammy skin as he tied his breechcloth on and found a feather cloak to wrap around him. Moving the palmetto-mat door to one side, he stepped out into the gale.

Wind whipped his hair, half blinding him. Bits of sand and debris shot pinpricks into his skin. Turning, he pulled the cloak tight and walked straight into the teeth of the storm until he reached the third ridge. Counting houses, he hunched his way to the Serpent's.

He huddled against the south wall, in the lee of the blast, and called, "Elder? It is Salamander. Are you awake?"

"I am now," the reedy voice called. "Come."

Salamander ducked into the wind, wrestled the wicker door aside, and replaced it behind him as he stepped into the cold darkness of the Serpent's house.

Here, at least, the gale was moderated to a gentler movement of air.

Wood clattered as the old man threw it atop the gleaming red-eyed coals in the central fire pit. Helped by the cool breeze, flames immediately leaped up. Their flickering yellow light showed the Serpent, sitting naked on his bed, his flesh hanging in wrinkled folds, his flat face puffy with sleep. Gray hair stuck out like winter grass in all directions.

"What is it? Salamander? What brings you here? You are not ill, are you?"

"No, Serpent. It was a Dream," he explained as the old man seated himself and pulled his elkhide blanket around his shoulders. The fire shot yellow light, and Salamander glanced about the interior. The clay walls had been engraved with designs of interlocking owls, sitting foxes, panthers, and snakes. Above the old man's bed a great bird had been carved into the daub, its wings and feet outspread, the beaked head turned sideways.

Bags of herbs hung from every rafter, their sides sooty from countless fires. A line of wooden and leather masks were propped along one bench, ritual faces that the Serpent adopted for healings and ceremonials. A pouch that Salamander knew contained stone sucking tubes, feather wands, and diamondback rattles rested by the old man's swollen feet.

Other ceramic jars and small soapstone bowls held bits of mushrooms, dried nightshade, jimsonweed, gumweed, snakemaster root, dried hemp leaves, and other medicine plants. One big bowl was filled with bear fat as a base to mix his potions.

The old man listened to Salamander's recounting of

the Dream, nodding. As he spoke, Salamander realized that the old Serpent's flesh seemed to be even thinner on his bones than it had been.

"Many Colored Crow is gaining in Power," the Serpent said after Salamander finished. He ran a hand over his flat face, the action rearranging his wrinkles.

"What does it mean? Falling like that?" Salamander extended his hands to the fire and shivered at the warmth.

"It is a sign." The Serpent pulled his elkhide close as another gust of wind shivered his house. "You are supposed to be frightened. Many Colored Crow is telling you that if you give up, go away, you will not have to be destroyed."

Salamander studied his hands, black silhouettes against the flame. "I have started to relax, Elder. As fall came to the land and the leaves changed, my world began to take form."

"And Anhinga?"

"She carries my child, but leaves with every full moon to pretend to pass her woman's bleeding in seclusion. She uses that time to plot with Jaguar Hide."

"That is very dangerous."

He bowed his head. "I know."

"Why do you not throw her out? You know she bears you no goodwill."

"Masked Owl whispers that I will need her."

"To achieve your death?"

Salamander shrugged. "I am not certain, but maybe. If I must die, Elder, to serve Masked Owl, and if Anhinga is to be the manner of it, then I accept that."

"I, too, am dying."

Salamander looked up, startled. "What?"

The old man pointed to his gaunt stomach. "I have a pain inside that only gets worse with the passing of the moon. Something evil is growing in my gut. When I squat to defecate, what comes out is half blood. It gets worse with the passing of days."

A sinking sensation left Salamander shaken. "No, not you, my old friend. I need you! Without you, I am alone. You must take something! Do something. Surely some licorice root, or..."

The old man was shaking his head. "I'm afraid the something to which you refer has already been done. It is some spirit, some evil that is eating me. When I press, I can feel it. A hardness so painful it brings tears to my eyes. Probably something I picked up from someone I cleansed. Maybe I wasn't careful enough with their vomit."

"How long has this bothered you?"

"A moon. Maybe more."

For what seemed an eternity, they sat in silence.

The Serpent asked, "What of your other wives?"

"Pine Drop missed her moon. She seems satisfied."

"Indeed. I noticed that you haven't come for more dog bane. Nor have I heard that she has been carrying on like a camp bitch anymore."

"It was Mud Stalker and Sweet Root who put her up to it."

"Umm. And Night Rain?"

"I would feed her plenty of dogbane if I could. The problem is that I can't just put a pinch into the communal food bowl without harming Pine Drop as well."

"There is talk. Deep Hunter has recalled Saw Back

from Yellow Mud Camp. It is said that he did it to favor your youngest wife. Have you heard?"

"That Night Rain is coupling with him? Yes." Salamander rubbed his hands together. "Pine Drop disapproves, but says nothing. That tells me that Night Rain has Mud Stalker's approval to lock hips with Deep Hunter and his kin." His lips tightened. "My young Night Rain has been learning new tricks. When she does share her bed with me, she isn't the same limp bundle of cloth I first married."

"Deep Hunter and Mud Stalker make a strong alliance." The Serpent bowed his head. "Moccasin Leaf seems to relish her new position as Clan Elder. I am sorry I could not bring your mother's souls back. I fear they are too tied to the souls of the Dead."

"Sometimes, Elder, we cannot win every battle. I do not understand why Power has left her demented. Perhaps it is part of the balance, part of the price I must pay." Salamander sat back, some of the warmth returning to his body. "My enemies will not act yet. They are waiting, slowly turning their attention to each other."

"Why do you not act against them?"

"Masked Owl once told me that my salvation lay in the things I knew, in being who I was. I watch, Elder. I study. It is for a reason that you named me Salamander."

"But if the fox or eagle should catch you..."

"The ways of Power are not without risk, Elder." Salamander smiled. "Since we last talked, I have watched the leaves turn and fall. The clans have returned from most of the distant camps, their bags full of acorns, walnuts, beechnuts, hazelnuts, goosefoot seeds, squash, knotweed seeds, and chinquapins. Canoe loads of fish have been dried and smoked, and the hunters have taken ducks, geese, pigeons, herons, and cranes. Deer are plentiful, and Trade has been good from the prairies, so buffalo and elk meat are plentiful. For the moment, bellies are full, and the clans are eyeing each other, trying to determine who has incurred the greatest obligation."

"The winter solstice ceremonies are barely a moon away." The Serpent rubbed his calloused hands, a dullness to his eyes. "Have you given any more thought to following me?"

"Yes. My answer is the same. Bobcat must follow you—and for many reasons. I do not know the Songs, Elder. I barely know enough of the plants and rituals. I couldn't follow you if I wanted to. I must serve Power in another way."

"As your Spirit Helper deems."

Salamander nodded, smiling. "You once asked me a question, Elder. You asked why the Great Mystery ripped the Earth from the Sky."

"Ah, yes. I remember. Have you found the answer?"

"I think so. It was because before the Creation, everything was One. Everything was the same."

"Ah!" The old man's face lit with joy, the wrinkles on his face stretching. "What was wrong with that?"

"Being One is being nothing, Elder. The world wasn't really Created until Sky and Earth were separated."

"Why is that, Salamander?"

"If you are One, you cannot see. Cannot hear. The only sensation is of yourself. There is no *Other*. The world had to be divided in order to see itself, in order to become itself. In the One, there is no beginning or end, no me or you. Only when we are separate can we inspect each other and learn the complexity and beauty of the universe. That was the lesson you were trying to teach me that night atop the Bird's Head. That is why Sun Town is so important. It is here that all things come back together. North and South. East and West. Sky and Earth."

Smiling gently, the old man nodded.

The fire popped and crackled, sending sparks toward the roof. Then the old man reached into a rabbit-hide sack and withdrew a small figurine. "Do you know what this is?" He handed it to Salamander.

The piece was smaller than his knotted fist, formed into the shape of a corpulent woman's seated torso, breasts and buttocks pronounced, arms and legs but nubbins. The head depicted the center-parted hair of a married woman, her eyes and happy mouth mere slits. The nose had been pinched out of the face, almost beaklike.

"No." Salamander turned it in the light. "I've never seen a charm like this before."

The Serpent reached into his bag, retrieving yet another one, similar to the first, and handing it over. "Men usually don't see these. Women ask for them. Take them. Bury one under Anhinga's bed when she is not present. Bury the other under Pine Drop's."

"What do they do?" Salamander studied the two figurines in his hands.

"Any evil or illness that comes to sneak up your wife's sheath to infect the infant will be fooled and will invade the clay charm instead." He pointed his finger. "Now listen. This part is important. When your children are born, the charms must be dug up. This must be done immediately. When the afterbirth is passed, it must be rubbed over the charm to cleanse it. Then, and only then, you must bring the charm back here, to this house, and snap the head off."

"Why?"

"The afterbirth feeds the evil, tricks it into thinking it is living in the baby. When you snap off the neck, you trap it inside the charm. It must be buried here because it came from here," the old man said. "From this earth, here, outside of this house. The Power must be returned to the place from which it came. Bury the pieces of the charm, Salamander, put them back where they came from. If you do not, the Earth Mother will become angry. The evil will fly back, angry at being deceived, and kill your child. Do you understand?"

"Yes, Elder."

The Serpent closed his eyes, and breath caught in his frail chest. His expression twisted, neck bending as he tenderly placed his hands against his left side.

"Elder?"

A moment later, he blinked, and tears appeared at the corners of his eyes. "I need to lie down now, Salamander. Forgive me. I cannot think when it hurts like this."

"Can I do anything for you?"

The old man nodded. "There, in the bowl with the fox on the side. That paste, it is made with ground jimsonweed seeds. Take that stick, there. That's it. Dab just a little on the end. Thank you."

The old man leaned back, taking the stick in trembling hands as he touched it to the tip of his tongue. "Things will be better now. Yes, better."

W. Michael Gear & Kathleen O'Neal Gear

Salamander placed the pale elkhide robe over the old man's bony body, ensuring it was tucked tightly. "Sleep, Elder. I'm sorry I bothered you."

"No. It's fine." He smiled wearily. "You will be the greatest of them, Salamander. If they don't kill you first. Many Colored Crow is a Powerful enemy, but he will not take you himself."

"Like he took my brother?"

The old man's eyes flashed open, brown, penetrating, as if the pain had vanished in an instant. "What makes you think that? Your brother wasn't killed by Many Colored Crow."

"Then who? Who else could control the lightning?"

"Any of the Sky Beings," the Serpent told him, voice low, as if he were sorry he'd said anything. "Now, go away. Let me sleep. Nothing else eases the pain."

# The Serpent

A Dreamer's first ascent into the Spirit World on the wings of a Spirit Helper is like a return to the womb, to a safe place filled with an awareness of the beginnings of who we are. It is a miracle of silence and beauty. A miracle that is swiftly gobbled up when we plant our feet on dirt again.

That is the heart of the Dreamer's struggle—not learning to soar, but learning to walk after you've soared.

Walking on solid ground, as though you've never sailed through blinding sunlight, is the most difficult thing any Dreamer ever does.

It is the fork in the trail.

The decision.

It may be the instant of rebirth, the moment when a man or woman is born into the Spirit World and sprouts his own glistening wings.

Or it may be the instant of accepting less, and the beginning of lifelong regret. Dreamers call this the "little death."

I cannot hope to convey to you how terrible it is. The

"little death" is like a serpent forever coiling and uncoiling inside you, forever striking, biting, and filling you with poison.

I had heard of the "little death." Somewhere along the way, every Dreamer does, but no one told me that it was everlasting. Perhaps they didn't have the courage.

I'm not sure I do either.

How can I tell this haunted boy that from the moment I decided my earthly duties to the People were more important than wings, I've never stopped dying?

Should I tell him? Would he even listen?

I wouldn't have. The People were everything to me.

But he is stronger than I was. He sees more clearly.

I pray with all my soul that he is brave enough to "abandon" his duties and fly away...

# Chapter Twenty-Three

A thick belt of clouds gave the winter day a dull cast. From the north blew a bitter wind that sucked a man's heat from his bones and sent it whimpering away toward the gulf. Mud Stalker led the way as Speaker Thunder Tail and the other hunters followed a winding trail. The way led through the depths of the forest a half day's journey north of Sun Town. The four younger men carried packs, atlatls, and darts. Their bodies were cloaked in deerskin, elkhide, and buffalo hide, giving them a thick and burly appearance as they trailed along behind the elders.

Mud Stalker squinted into the gray light. In the vacuum left by Wing Heart's insanity, Snapping Turtle Clan had grown in influence among the clans and in the Council. To his irritation leadership of the Council had gone to Thunder Tail, but that, too, would change as the seasons passed.

Now it was time to solidify his clan's position. Despite the overture of reaching out with Night Rain, Deep Hunter was playing his own games, seeking to limit Mud Stalker's growing influence. That was to be expected. In time, he would deal with Deep Hunter.

Thunder Tail was another problem. As leader of the Council, he was still uncommitted when it came to a firm alliance with Snapping Turtle Clan. Mud Stalker would need the Eagle Clan Speaker's goodwill before he moved on Salamander and the remnant of Owl Clan. Today he would begin the process. He would play on Thunder Tail's one weakness: a bear hunt.

Mud Stalker glanced up at the trees, naked and black in their winter bones. Great vines wove up the trunks, stretching from one forest giant to another. Some were as thick as a man's leg.

"There," Mud Stalker pointed as he sighted the dead tree.

The Eagle Clan hunters, Bitten Legs and Spread Thorn, pulled up grinning. The trunk was huge. Four men would have to stretch, fingertip to fingertip, to reach around the base. Rot had eaten the heart out of the dead forest giant. Then some past gale had cracked it, sheared off the top two-thirds, and sent it crashing down through the forest. Punky wood, cloaked in leaves, vines, and rising saplings marked the fallen remains.

The remaining trunk, barkless and gray from weather, stood five times the height of a tall man. At the top, jagged wood thrust up around the hollow center like stone knives.

Mud Stalker nodded, using his good arm to motion Eats Wood and Water Stinger forward. His two young kinsmen trotted ahead, each slinging a pack from his shoulder as he approached the trunk.

"He's there?" Thunder Tail asked as he fingered his finely carved atlatl. "You're sure?"

"He's there. You can see the sign." Mud Stalker stepped close, pointing to the weathered wood. Deep scars had been driven into the grain, bits and splinters crushed as if under a weight. "Those are not woodpecker holes."

"From the size and spread, I'd say he's a pretty good-size boar." Thunder Tail placed his hand over the pattern of scars. A slow smile was spreading across his broad face. "A sow wouldn't have this big a paw."

Mud Stalker bent his head back, staring up at the jagged top. "I think it's a boar, too. Too bad it's not a sow. She'd have a cub by now. I wouldn't mind taking a cub. The meat is delectable."

"A boar will do just fine."

Of all of life's treats, Thunder Tail loved bear hunting the most. He had a fascination with the animals. Their meat, hides, organs, and fat were prized throughout Sun Town. Unlike most hunters who took bears only when the opportunity arose, Thunder Tail spent full hands of time in the study of bears. He had been known to lose himself for days stalking a bruin. Not one was brought back to Sun Town but that he didn't go to see it, to measure the paws against his hand, to inspect the teeth and feel its muscles. His house was stuffed with skulls, bear bones, hides, claws, and other trophies he had taken over the turnings of the seasons.

When Water Stinger had come with news that he'd found a winter "bear tree," Mud Stalker had been jubilant. It gave him the perfect lure to draw the Speaker out of Sun Town. Mud Stalker had Thunder Tail alone for the entire day—and in a very good mood, as his smile indicated.

"By the Snakes! He's a big one if these claw marks are any indication." Thunder Tail slapped a calloused hand against the wood and grinned, his eyes shining as he shared a happy conspiratorial glance with Mud Stalker.

"I hope you find him worth your while," Mud Stalker said with a casual shrug. He and Sweet Root had begun planning the moment they had learned of the bear tree. Though they had an uneasy alliance for the moment, Deep Hunter's Alligator Clan would eventually challenge Mud Stalker's growing influence. Thunder Tail's Eagle Clan was now the unpredictable element—the clan could vote either way in Council.

"*I have worked all of my life to achieve this!*" Mud Stalker had declared to Sweet Root, his good hand clenched into a hard fist. "*I am going to leave nothing to chance. Those I cannot cow, like Thunder Tail and Clay Fat, I will seduce!*"

Sweet Root had nodded, smiling her encouragement. Night Rain, sitting to one side, had given him a curious look as she plucked feathers from a duck.

"*Green Beetle remains unmarried,*" Sweet Root had reminded. "*Eats Wood needs a wife. No one else wants him. Given his attitude toward women, he doesn't make himself particularly attractive.*"

Night Rain had said, "*I wouldn't want him for a husband, and neither would anyone else I know. If you will recall, we were warned as girls never to be alone with him. Remember? You didn't even trust him alone near his own kin.*"

Sweet Root had shaken her head. "*He talks too*

*much about that Swamp Panther woman. He's obsessed with her."*

"We need to bring Thunder Tail under our influence," Mud Stalker had insisted. *"I will have a talk with Eats Wood before we take Thunder Tail to the bear tree. If we can sway the Speaker to our perspective, Deep Hunter will have nowhere to go."*

"Eats Wood isn't the sort of man to pin many hopes on," Sweet Root reminded.

That might be true, but the young man was the closest unmarried male relative he had. Next was Water Stinger, a distant cousin whose family spent most of the turning of the seasons two days' journey to the east over at Yellow Mud Camp. So, here he was, with two eligible young hunters for Thunder Tail to inspect. At Mud Stalker's insistence, Eats Wood had been on his best behavior and doing a creditable job of entertaining Thunder Tail. To his relief, Eats Wood hadn't made a single rude comment about either Salamander or his barbarian wife.

From their packs, Eats Wood and Water Stinger had taken a fire drill, tinder, and kindling. On the other side of the tree, Bitten Legs and Spread Thorn had likewise laid their atlatls and darts to one side, producing their own fire-making kits. While Eats Wood and Spread Thorn twirled the spindle in a hardwood block, Water Stinger and Bitten Legs dragged up old branches.

In moments, puffy gray smoke rose and was blown to flame in the tinder. Mud Stalker stepped back, cradling his maimed arm as the hunters added wood, spreading the fire around the tree bottom. He enjoyed the expression on Thunder Tail's face, reading the Speaker's growing excitement.

Winter bear hunting was always exciting. Bears tended to hibernate in standing dead trees like this one. The hollow centers, soft with rotten wood, made warm nests, protected from the worst of the weather. Setting fire to the bottom of the tree awakened the bear, causing the groggy animal to emerge at the top. There, clinging to the wood as smoke billowed past, he was an easy target.

Yellow tongues of flame licked up around the wood, popping and crackling.

"We need more wood," Mud Stalker called. "Eats Wood, go drag in some of those big branches." He pointed to the wreckage left by the fallen treetop. "We want this fire a lot hotter."

"He's a good young man." Thunder Tail watched Eats Wood as he trotted off with Bitten Legs for more fuel.

"It is high time he was married. His mother, my cousin, is loath to turn him loose. He keeps her in birds, fish, and meat. When he marries, she loses that surplus. The excess in her household keeps the rest of the lineage obligated." He said it offhandedly, watching Thunder Tail's expression from the corner of his eye.

"Hmm, a young man like that is quite an asset." Thunder Tail answered, his eyes on the top of the bear tree. Smoke was curling upward along the wood.

"You have a young woman, don't you? The one who finds pearls."

"Green Beetle." Thunder Tail squinted up at the treetop as he fingered his atlatl and darts. One by one he fitted them to the spur in the back of the atlatl, testing their balance in anticipation of a cast. "The bear won't know what's happening for some time yet. The heat is still too far away, and the smoke going up the outside isn't being drawn in with this wind blowing."

"Green Beetle, that's right," Mud Stalker mused. "She's an attractive thing. I'd have thought you'd have married her by now."

"I have."

The simple pronouncement stopped Mud Stalker short. "You have?"

"Yes. It's odd that you should mention her. Deep Hunter and Stone Talon came to see my mother and me last night. To our surprise they made us a very good offer. Needs Two will marry Green Beetle."

"He will?" Mud Stalker fought to keep his voice conversational. "You got good terms?"

"Green Beetle's lineage is allowed access to those smilax-root grounds over by the sassafras grove. You know the ones I mean?"

"I do." Mud Stalker felt his heart sink. Deep Hunter guarded those grounds jealously.

"I am very fond of Green Beetle," Thunder Tail continued, apparently oblivious. He only had eyes for the treetop. "I almost married her to White Bird, you know. Good thing that I didn't. Look what happened there."

Mud Stalker studied the man through slitted eyes. "You were an old lover of Wing Heart's, weren't you?"

"Yes. It's a shame. She used be as sharp as a chert blade." Thunder Tail shot him a measuring glance, his dark eyes veiling the thoughts in his mind. "Curious, isn't it, old friend, that even the strongest of us can lose our souls?"

"Yes. Curious indeed." Mud Stalker stepped back, fingers running along the scars on his arm. How on earth had Deep Hunter managed to pull the catch out of his nets like this?

*Enjoy your bear hunt, Speaker.*

Anhinga wedged a thick branch between two closely spaced trees and threw her weight against it. She flinched at the crack as the dry wood gave. It took a well-placed kick to knock the piece loose. The process of bending over to retrieve it proved laborious. She no longer even attempted to hide the swelling of her belly. She puffed against the cold and placed the short lengths of firewood in her irregular stack. Satisfied, she bound them with a braided leather thong.

The desperate need to escape had been brewing like black drink within her. Using their need of firewood as an excuse, she had come here, deep in the forest west of Sun Town. She needed time to think. Her souls had gone to war with each other.

Salamander lay at the bottom of it. He knew she was pregnant—so obvious had it become—but indulged her in her need to get away. He hadn't said a word about her absences each moon.

She glanced up at the sky, trying to decide what sort of man he really was. Clouds rolled out of the northwest, keeping the chill in the air. During the night, fog had settled over the land. A light mist had fallen, adding to the chill. By morning, everything had been sheathed in ice.

She resettled her fox-hide cloak against the cold. A

gift from Pine Drop, it was nicely done. Tanned to soft perfection and sewn with care, the rich red fur gleamed in the light. She began knotting a leather strap to create a yoke to be used for a tumpline.

Bending down, she positioned the cord on her forehead and wrapped several lengths of furry rabbit hide around it for a cushion. She grabbed up her axe, positioned the load, and straightened. The wrap of rabbit hide pressed into her forehead as she balanced the load on her hips and leaned forward. Straightening her legs, she stood.

Looking down she could barely see over her belly.

Three moons had passed since that day his gaze had fixed on her swollen belly. She had said, "I'm pregnant."

"You have been for many moons." He had just looked at her with those fathomless brown eyes and said, "It's all right, Anhinga. Go to them. The four or five days you spend away harms nothing. But perhaps, as the child comes to term, you might not travel so far? I think your uncle would understand."

The words had struck fear into her in a way that no threat, no angry denunciation could have. Deep in her heart, she had the distinct feeling that Salamander knew her every plan. Why, then, hadn't he taken some action against her?

Logic might have led her to believe that the sandstone was worth it to him, but her worried souls knew better. No, he was playing some complex and terrible game, betting on her. How? To do what? Thinking that she wouldn't go through with her plan to kill the father of her child?

*Then you are wrong, husband. When Uncle tells me*

*the time is right, I shall strike the Sun People in a way that will shiver their hearts for ages!*

She need only remember that terrible day she had watched her friends butchered, their bodies cut to pieces and fed to the dogs. That nightmare lived and ached in her souls.

Knowing that he knew had changed something in their relationship. Salamander continued to treat her with respect and kindness. He had stopped coupling with her, fearful of damaging the child, and that, oddly, concerned her. Pine Drop was several moons behind her and just beginning to show. A worry had begun to form down in Anhinga's souls. Was he going to spend all of his nights at his first wife's house now that he could only couple with Night Rain? Not that she was any kind of a faultless wife.

*Why do you care what they say about her? You are going to kill them in the end anyway!*

It took all of her concentration to remember her uncle's warning. *"You cannot see them as people, Anhinga. That is the single greatest threat to your success."*

Some subtle reflex caused her to look up. There, perched on a high branch, a huge barred owl stared down at her. She almost missed a step. The bird's penetrating stare ate clear through her, probing like shafts of dark light. The round head bobbed slightly, accenting the facial disks. He might have been peering at her through a mask.

Unease crept up her spine. She hadn't known they could grow so big. Despite the bird's size, it triggered a memory. With its white-spotted red feathers puffed against the cold, she couldn't help but think of Salamander's carvings, of the potbellied owls he made.

"I have nothing to do with you," she called over her shoulder as she hurried away. A prickling of danger rode lightly on her nerves. She could almost feel Power crackling along the ice-shrouded branches. Hear it throbbing in the winter depths of the forest. Only after passing beyond the bird's sight did she slow down again.

Sighing with relief, she picked her way with care, watching her deerhide moccasins crush the frosted grass underfoot. Overhead, bare black branches webbed the sky. The ground, covered with ice-coated leaves, required all of her concentration. Her moccasins, while warm, made each step a tricky proposition. The smooth soles had no grip on ice-slick leaves.

She picked her way past gray vines that hung from the trees, seeking the trail she knew led the way back past the hunter's blind. Rounding the thick bole of a beech tree, she stopped short. A naked man stood in the trail, steam rising from a fresh puddle of urine.

As their eyes met, she recognized him: Saw Back. The youth who had been sent to kill her uncle. The one Salamander had tricked on the Turtle's Back. He was holding his dripping penis, naked but for a necklace made of two sections of a human jawbone. Naked? A curious state, considering the breath whitening before the young man's mouth. They stared at each other in disbelief.

"Saw Back? Are you coming back?" a familiar female voice asked from the low hunter's blind at the side of the trail.

"It's you!" Saw Back cried, finding his voice. "What

are you doing here, you barbarian bitch? Come to spy on me?"

"Anhinga?" A face appeared in the blind's shadowed doorway. "Here?"

"Night Rain?" Anhinga asked. She saw the hatred rising in Saw Back's eyes. "Slipping out to part your legs for just any camp dog?"

"Camp dog?" Saw Back cried, stepping forward, his dark skin prickling against the cold. "You call me a camp dog? You're nothing but a murdering barbarian weasel. They sent me away because of you! You *and* that skinny joke of a Speaker."

Anhinga ducked out of the tumpline, letting the firewood bundle drop with a clatter. She groped for her axe handle, quartering as she backed away, keeping it out of his sight behind her kirtle. If this turned nasty, her only hope lay in his belief that she was defenseless.

"It's me she's spying on!" Night Rain declared as she scuttled out of the blind. Her mussed black hair fell around her bare shoulders in tangles. Cold had hardened the nipples on her round breasts and coaxed a faint mist from the damp tuft of her pubic hair.

"I spy on no one," Anhinga answered hotly. "You can part your legs for every flea-infested cur in camp for all I care, fool."

"Fool? You're calling me a fool?" Night Rain thrust out a slim finger. "At least I find satisfaction with a real man."

"Look at my tattoos, barbarian bitch!" Saw Back thumped his chest. "I am a *warrior*! Not like that child who shares your bed." He stepped closer, a dangerous gleam in his eyes as he lifted the jawbone necklace.

"These I made from the Swamp Panther slime I drove a dart through at Ground Cherry Camp!"

Her vision swam for a moment. Which her friends was it? Cooter? Spider Fire? Slit Nose? From the way the bone had been ground, she couldn't be sure. The teeth gleamed whitely in the gray light.

"I could add yours," he told her, tapping the polished bone. "I could tie them under right here so they would hang under your dead kinsman's."

"You are a sneaking cur." She could feel the danger settling around her like haze, see it in his sharpened eyes, in the tensing of his muscles.

Through gritted teeth, he said, "I am a warrior. My Spirit Helpers have brought you to me." He danced a half step toward her. "My ancestors are watching, crying for your blood, and now you have stepped into my hands. After I am done with you, no one is going to find your body."

*By the Panther's Bones, he is going to kill me!* The revelation blew through her like a winter wind.

# Chapter Twenty-Four

"Saw Back?" Night Rain called, unsure for the first time. "If anyone finds out..."

"They won't," he called over his shoulder. "We'll hide her body until after dark. Bury it in the hollow under a deadfall. Once covered with leaves, she'll be rot before spring and meanwhile, her souls will wail in the lonely depths of darkness."

Anhinga swallowed hard. A vision of Spider Fire's face lingered in her memory. Somehow she knew that's whose jaw he wore.

"I thought about this the entire time I was exiled, bitch." He crouched, ready to spring. "I dreamed of my fingers choking the life from your skinny neck." He bared his teeth and leaped.

Anhinga's reaction was instinctive. She swung her axe up from behind her. To his credit, he was quick, twisting away in midair. The sharpened axe, freshly ground that morning on a slab of Panther sandstone, sliced neatly along his ribs. The impact, pain, and surprise sent him reeling, feet slipping on leaves to dump him full on his butt.

He sat there for a moment, stunned, reaching down to run fingers through the blood that began leaking out of his side.

"You witch!" Night Rain cried. "You've *killed* him!"

Anhinga stepped back just as Saw Back bunched his feet under him and leaped for her. She could have killed him. Perhaps should have. At the last instant she turned the axe and caught him full on the side of the head with the flat. The snapping smack was loud on the still air, the handle stung her hands.

The blow sent him sprawling into the frozen leaves. He lay there, gasping, fingers clenching spasmodically in the leaf mat. A look of surprise filled his face, eyes wide and glassy, mouth gaping like a dark round hole. As she watched, the damaged skin on his freshly dented cheek reddened.

*Kill him! Kill him now!* She hesitated, swallowed hard, and tightened her grip on the axe.

Something in Night Rain's horrified expression stopped her. If she killed him, she would be forced to flee—all of the moons she had spent here gone like smoke.

*Think! How do you get out of this?* Everything was changed. Her position was in peril. All because stupid Night Rain had to warm her canoe with Saw Back's worm? She stalked up to her co-wife. The young woman watched her with wide eyes, jaw hanging. Anhinga reached, twisted a fistful of Night Rain's hair, and yanked.

Night Rain came squealing as Anhinga dragged her to the tied bundle of wood. Night Rain reached out, scratching with her hands, trying to kick Anhinga. To quell her, Anhinga thumped her between the shoulders with the axe handle.

Night Rain shrieked and dropped flat beside the tied firewood. "I'll kill you! I swear! My uncle will rip your throat out!"

"Perhaps." *Panther's blood! What have you gotten yourself into here?* She had just gone for firewood, wanting time alone in the forest to think, and here she'd twisted herself into the middle of one of the Sun People's political messes.

Anhinga glanced at Saw Back. He was moaning as he tried to sit up. He had one hand to his face. Blood from where the binding on the axe head had broken the skin was leaking red behind his fingers. When he pulled his hand back to look, she could still see the dent in his cheek. Had she broken the bone?

*You can't explain this, Anhinga. Who's going to believe that he was going to kill you?* She fingered the axe. *Or you can kill them both, hide the bodies like they were going to do with yours.*

No, that was too risky. No one might have cared if Anhinga had disappeared, but people would come looking for these two. She needed a reason, something people would believe. That, or she had best smack them both in the brains and run for all she was worth, hoping to make it south before the bodies were discovered.

*And be a failure again? You'll be letting yourself, Uncle, and all of your dead friends down again. Think! You're smarter than this!*

Night Rain was blubbering and shivering, her naked body squirming as she cast a frightened glance over her shoulder. "What are you going to do with me?"

"Since it's all your fault"—Anhinga smiled as she figured a way out of her mess—"I'm taking you home."

"Saw Back!" she squalled. "Kill her! Kill her now!"

One glance showed her that Saw Back had problems of his own. He couldn't seem to get to his feet.

"Pick up that wood!" Anhinga gestured with the axe.

"My kirtle and cloak..." Night Rain glanced back at the blind.

"If you can rut naked in this weather, you can work naked!"

"You want me to walk back naked? I'll freeze!"

"The cold didn't seem to bother you before I showed up." Anhinga accented her order by whistling the axe head past Night Rain's ear. *"Move!"*

Night Rain scuttled on her hands and knees, gaping as she passed Saw Back. Blood washed his sliced side in a crimson sheet. He was dazed, eyes half-lidded at the pain in his head. Was it imagination, or were his pupils two different sizes now?

*"Pick it up!"* Anhinga ordered, pointing at the stack of wood with her axe.

Night Rain broke into sobs, her limbs shaking as she fumbled for the cord. "Why are you *doing* this? What do *I* mean to you?"

*You're my excuse, you silly, stupid bitch.* Anhinga fingered the sharp edge of her axe. It was greenstone—a fine piece traded down from somewhere far upriver. "By rutting around with scum like him, you disgrace yourself, your sister, your husband, and me."

Night Rain wailed, "Saw Back? Help!" But her lover had just bent double to throw up on his thighs.

"By the Panther's blood," Anhinga whispered, "if

you don't pick that up, I'm going to kill you both!" She took one more menacing step toward Night Rain, her face contorting.

Night Rain nearly toppled as she swung the load up, clawing to set the tumpline on her forehead. The rabbit-hide cushion had slipped so that the cord ate into the young woman's forehead. "It hurts!" Night Rain pleaded.

Anhinga slapped the axe handle across Night Rain's buttocks, leaving a red welt. Night Rain screamed.

"To hear you, I'd think someone was burning a bobcat to death."

Night Rain tottered forward, shoulders jerking with each of her sobs. "You just wait! Wait until you get hurt sometime! I'll laugh while you scream."

Anhinga fingered the scars on her shoulders, remembering, hating. "You are worthless, Night Rain. A whimpering little child. By Panther's Bones, why did he ever marry a wretch like you."

She turned, reaching down. Her fingers knotted around the necklace at Saw Back's throat. She threw her weight against it and jerked. Saw Back flopped backward and clawed at his throat. The cord parted with a snap. Stepping away from him, she inspected the two halves of human jawbone that had been polished, drilled, and strung with beads.

*It is only a small justice, my friend. I cannot kill him now. Not yet.*

She glanced over her shoulder. Saw Back just sat there, naked and cold in the leaves, looking bloody and sick.

# Chapter Twenty-Five

T he following morning, Pine Drop waved off the calls as she hurried across the southern half of the plaza. By the Sky Beings, it was the talk of every tongue!

"Pine Drop?" Eats Wood called. "Have you heard?" Her cousin came trotting toward her, breaking away from a group of his friends.

"Yes, yes." Of all the people to have to talk to, Eats Wood wasn't her favorite. Something had always been wrong with him, and she suspected that someday, as he grew older and bolder, he would finally submit to his desire for a young girl. It would fall upon her uncle to slip up behind him and cleave his head in two. The clans dealt out justice like that, taking responsibility for their own.

"What is going to happen?" Eats Wood demanded. "Elder Sweet Root has called the Council into session. She is going to demand that Swamp Panther woman pay for the insult she has paid us!"

"We don't know the details yet."

"What details! Yesterday that camp bitch drove *your* sister naked through camp! Made her work like a stinking slave! And Deep Hunter is as mad as a teased cottonmouth about Saw Back! His head is broken and swollen! You should see him. He can't stand up without weaving and falling. He may die."

"That is Alligator Clan's concern." Pine Drop frowned. "What no one has asked is what Night Rain was doing out there with him. Why were they both naked, Cousin?"

Eats Wood grinned in a manner that roiled Pine Drop's stomach. "Why do you think? I would have enjoyed seeing what happened out there." He turned away. "But for now, I have to find my weapons. If this turns as ugly as I hope it will, we might have to back Uncle with darts as well as words."

With that he was running, headed for his mother's house on the fourth ridge.

*Weapons?* She hurried forward, joining the stream of people headed toward the Council House. Tiny flakes of snow whirled past as Pine Drop pulled her blue jay-feather cloak tight about her. Snakes! This couldn't come to fighting, could it? Generations had passed since the last time blood had been spilled between the clans. Of all the People's nightmares, that was the worst. If clans began fighting with each other, they would rend the world in two.

*Blessed Sky Beings, say it isn't so.*

She didn't see him as he stepped up to match her pace. One of the curious things about Salamander was that he could be invisible if he wanted to. Overlooked, and unnoticed. She had often thought that a curious ability of his, and one that she often wished were her own. Now, however, he was the last person she wanted to see.

"I would ask a favor of you?" he began, voice muted.

"What would that be?" She couldn't keep the hostile tone from her voice.

"There is more to what happened than you know."

"What if they were out there locking hips? What of it, Salamander? Was that reason for that Swamp witch to humiliate my sister? Did she have to drive her infant-naked through the middle of Sun Town like a barbarian slave? Was that reason to half kill Saw Back?"

"No," he answered steadily, and placed a hand on her elbow, stopping her so that he could stare into her eyes. What she saw reflected there made her pause. What was it about him? That look penetrated her souls, carrying a terrible warning with it. What Power possessed him at moments like this?

"Pine Drop, you must hold your uncle back. Do you understand? If he pushes this thing, I will not be able to control it. One thing will lead to another, and there will be no way back for us. *There is more here than you know.*"

The words seemed to grow, shivering her souls. "What? What more?"

He glanced at the throng heading for the Council House, ignoring curious looks of the passersby. "I don't have time right now. I was just lucky to have found you first. We have to go. Please, you must trust me. We can't allow this to get out of hand, or our worst nightmares will become real."

He let go, a terrible fear brimming in his eyes. That look, more than anything, frightened her.

"You must trust me," he insisted as he hurried off. "Will you?"

She nodded halfheartedly, seeing relief flooding in his eyes. Then he was gone, trotting for the Council House on his thin legs.

What had she just done? What had she committed herself to?

Mud Stalker gripped his stone-headed hammer, tightening his hold until his fingers ached. Through slitted eyes he glared across the Council lodge at Salamander. The young Speaker was bundled in a warm buffalo robe. Occasional snowflakes drifted past. Wind seemed insolently to finger the thick brown hair, waving it this way and that as the cold gray day pressed down. Curse him, he had been trading one buffalo hide after another—spoils from his Trade with those Wash'ta fools who had piled all of their wealth on Owl Clan last fall. In the winter day's chill, Mud Stalker could feel everyone's envy of Salamander's buffalohide cape.

Sweet Root had arrived, a double wrap of fabric around her shoulders. Pine Drop appeared, looking worried. She wore her blue jay-feather cape pulled tightly against the chill. As she stood beside the Clan Elder, her thoughtful eyes turned to Mud Stalker. What was that measuring look? In the confusion of the Council being called, he had yet to speak to her and find out what she knew of Night Rain's humiliation. Something in her expression bothered him. Distress about her little sister, no doubt.

Thunder Tail was there, resplendent in his new

bear skin—the only person who didn't cast a covetous gaze at Salamander. He wore the glossy black pelt over his shoulder, the fur gleaming. The very sight of it made Mud Stalker's stomach twist. It seemed that embarrassment dogged him at every turn these days.

He shot a hard glance at Deep Hunter. The Alligator Clan Speaker looked as if he were about to burst like a squashed chinquapin. His expression was a hard mask, and behind him, Saw Back looked ill. The side of the young warrior's crushed face had mottled into blue-black under an angry mass of swollen scab.

Cane Frog entered Frog Clan's part of the Council circle, her thick-veined hand resting on Three Moss's shoulder.

Clay Fat and Turtle Mist were the last to take their places.

No sooner had Thunder Tail stepped out from under the awning than Deep Hunter strode out into the center by the charcoal-blackened fire pit, and shouted, "You all know why we are here by now! The Swamp Panther woman, Anhinga, has attacked a member of my clan. A young man of my lineage! She has maimed him! Crashed the side of his face! Alligator Clan demands that this matter be taken up by the Council!"

"If you will wait your turn," Thunder Tail called, "I will recognize you. You may think you are the leader of the Council, Deep Hunter, but that honor has not yet been bestowed upon you."

Deep Hunter's hands knotted as the muscles in his arms bulged. The expression on his face brought a latent smile to Mud Stalker's lips. Despite his own rage, he could enjoy Deep Hunter's rebuke.

"Very well," Thunder Tail said with simple dignity.

"Speaker Deep Hunter has brought a matter of some gravity before the Council. It seems that an altercation has resulted in one of his kinsmen receiving a serious and crippling injury."

Mud Stalker hadn't made a step to second Deep Hunter's call when Salamander leaped forward, his buffalo robe flapping. Behind him, Moccasin Leaf was a half heartbeat too slow as she tried to grab him back.

The entire Council waited in hushed silence as Salamander strode up to Deep Hunter, his small frame dwarfed by the burly Speaker. "Do you wish to pursue this, Speaker?"

"By the Snakes, I do, boy!" Deep Hunter's arm muscles bulged, his face reddening. "You hand that Swamp Panther viper over to me!"

"You may not have my wife." Salamander said it calmly, as if he were discussing a basket of prized stone blanks. His very demeanor, so thoroughly in possession of himself, left Deep Hunter off-balance.

"She attacked my warrior!"

Salamander crossed his arms, lowering his voice. Mud Stalker heard him say, "Are you sure you want to open this jar of ants, Speaker? Before it is done, we may all be bitten."

Mud Stalker stepped out into the circle. "Open it we shall! The Swamp Panther woman has made allegations! She has sullied the name of my niece. Worse, she humiliated her! Drove her naked through the middle of Sun Town like a slave!"

Salamander shot him a level glance, then looked back at Deep Hunter, saying, "This is an internal matter within my household. I will deal with my wives in my own way."

"You can't deal with anything!" Deep Hunter bellowed.

"Uncle?" the soft voice caught Mud Stalker by surprise, as did the firm hand that grasped his elbow and subtly dragged him back. Pine Drop leaned her head close, whispering, "Do not push this, or we will all regret it."

Sweet Root stepped forward, a stunned look on her face as she in turn began pulling on Pine Drop's arm.

"Please," Pine Drop urged. "Step back, or this will burn out of control like hot sparks in a dry forest."

"You would do this?" He couldn't believe the determination in her eyes as she nodded yes.

"Trust me, Uncle. Trust Salamander. There is more at stake than you know. My husband will snuff this fire before our clan is burned."

*"Him?"* Mud Stalker jerked his head back at Salamander. From the corner of his eye he could see Salamander lean close to Deep Hunter, speaking in a low, earnest voice. Even as near as he was, he couldn't make out the words.

Deep Hunter stood like a lightning-riven oak, trembling while his expression blackened. Salamander had evidently finished, for he simply stared up at Deep Hunter with calm brown eyes.

"What did he say?" Clay Fat cried. "We can't hear! Repeat what you said, Salamander."

"Speak up!" Cane Frog shouted. "This is the Council! Not some Men's House! Either we all hear, or no one speaks!"

"Speak up!" Thunder Tail and Stone Talon called in chorus. The Clan Elder leaned forward on her crutches, her toothless jaw stuck out in irritation.

"It is your decision," Salamander said loudly enough for everyone to hear. "I could repeat myself in a voice loud enough for the rest to hear."

To Mud Stalker's surprise, Deep Hunter shot him an evaluative look, hesitated, then shook his head. He stepped back, hands still balled into fists. The muscles in his arms knotted and writhed. Before he turned on his heel and stalked back to his place, he muttered, "Alligator Clan retracts its statement. This matter is up to Salamander."

"What?" Mud Stalker cried in amazement. He started forward again, only to have Pine Drop take his bad arm in a tight grip.

"Leave it, Uncle," she insisted. "It is between Salamander, me, and Night Rain. Our time will come later, when it will not make fools of us in front of everyone. More is at stake here than you know."

"How dare you?" Sweet Root exploded, struggling to keep her voice down so the others didn't hear.

"Be smart," Pine Drop whispered through gritted teeth before she let go of Mud Stalker's arm. "Figure it out yourself. I just did." Then she turned, striding purposefully out of the Council House, pushing her way through the people who had come to watch.

That, more than anything, sank through Mud Stalker's anger. He stopped short, meeting Sweet Root's eyes, seeing nothing there but baffled frustration.

Suddenly unsure, Mud Stalker stepped out into the circle, catching Salamander before he could step from the ring. "Just tell me, Speaker. What did your barbarian do out there in the forest?"

Salamander stopped short, glancing back at Saw

Back, before meeting Mud Stalker's eyes. "Exactly what she had to, Speaker. Nothing more, nothing less."

As Salamander walked past the stunned Moccasin Leaf and stepped out of the Council House, people parted to let him pass. Mud Stalker ground his teeth, his mind racing. He narrowed his eye as he shot a hard look at Deep Hunter. What bit of information could Salamander have used to back Deep Hunter down? What did they have in common?

*Night Rain! She's at the bottom of this!*

As the Council broke up, he stood in the gray center of the circle, thinking. Deep Hunter's game, he could understand. There were ways of dealing with the Speaker. But what about Salamander? Just what sort of game was he playing? Why did he care if Night Rain and Deep Hunter were dragged through the mud? What difference would it make to him if Alligator and Snapping Turtle Clans tore each other apart?

# Chapter Twenty-Six

Salamander kneaded his temples in a futile attempt to soothe his pounding headache. The idea of sneaking over to the Serpent's for some jimsonweed paste, or perhaps for a couple of puffs on the old man's pipe, was so tempting.

Now, with the Council mollified, or at least held at bay, he considered his more immediate problem. He looked at his wives, together for the first time. They sat in his house, equidistant from each other, eyes hard, brown, and fiery. Their feet rested on the burned bones of his ancestors. That thought seemed to stick sideways inside him. Was White Bird's Dream Soul watching him even now? Was he shaking his head in pity, or just laughing outright? A man with three wives deserved anything they dished out for him.

Anhinga sat defiantly, muscular arms crossed over her rounding belly, her chin high. Pine Drop shifted back and forth, fists knotting and opening as if she'd like to wrap them around Anhinga's smooth throat. Night Rain glared miserably up from the floor, a fabric wrap around her waist. Her face was swollen from tears, and a red welt marked her forehead where the tumpline had bruised it.

"The whole of Sun Town is talking about what happened!" Pine Drop cried.

"Good! Perhaps we will finally get some respect!" Anhinga shot back.

Salamander raised his arms. "Stop it!" Pain blasted through his head, reflecting on his face.

In the sudden silence, only the cracking of the fire could be heard. Then his mother's voice asked from outside, "Is everything all right in there? Do I need to send the Speaker to deal with this?"

He winced, wishing he could press the ache out of his skull. "He's here, Mother. He's already dealing with it."

"All right. Be sure and send your uncle home when he's finished. I have a stew cooking. Acorns and raccoon mixed with squash. His favorite."

"Yes, Mother." Salamander closed his eyes, fists knotting. "Snakes, if it's not one thing, it's another!"

"Husband?" He heard the first change in the timbre in Anhinga's voice. By Masked Owl, was that concern replacing the anger? "What would you have had me do? Let Saw Back break my neck and leave me under a log?"

"You did what you had to," Salamander replied, making up his mind.

Pine Drop pointed a hard finger. "Very well, Husband, I see where this is going. You just remember, I did as you asked me to today. Against my judgment I held my uncle back during the Council. You asked for a favor, and I trusted you enough to grant it—at no little risk to myself. But I'm not finished with Anhinga. She didn't have to humiliate my sister. She could have let her sneak back to camp, dressed, and with some self-respect."

"Then it would have been her word against mine!" Anhinga cried, thumping her chest between her breasts. "She and that slithering serpent she had locked hips with could have said anything about me! Who would the Sun People have believed then, first wife? Who? Night Rain? Or the barbarian bitch?"

"Enough!" Salamander cried, his souls aching in time to his head. "Night Rain, do you understand how dangerous the game is that you are playing?"

"Husband, you can't—"

He silenced Pine Drop with a slash of his hand. "She has betrayed you, too, Wife. Not just your position as first wife, but your position as the next Clan Elder." He saw the struggle inside as Pine Drop juggled the information. She was caught between loyalty and what Night Rain had done to them all.

"She is young," Salamander added in a gentle voice. "People make mistakes when they are young. We have controlled the damage."

"You *forgive* her?" Anhinga asked in disbelief.

"This stops here." Salamander squinted against the throbbing. "This is not a matter for the clans, or the Council, or the Clan Elders to work out. We barely kept our world from exploding like a mud-tempered pot out there. But for Deep Hunter's guilt, and Pine Drop's intervention, we would have Snapping Turtle and Alligator Clans at each other's throats. If it had come to blows, if some of the hotheaded young warriors had started to fight...well, you know how close we just came to the abyss."

Anhinga's cunning eyes narrowed.

"Don't even think it." Salamander turned on her. "You are part of this. Start that fire, and you will not only scorch the Sun People, but the Swamp Panthers, too. Warfare between the clans will burn its way through the Panther's Bones as surely as you broke Saw Back's head." He held her eyes. "You know I'm right."

Anhinga shrugged and turned away. Pine Drop's eyes hardened in response.

Salamander reached down and tilted Night Rain's tear-puffy face up. "Do you understand? If Deep Hunter wasn't as smart as he is, he would have forced me to tell everyone. Would you have wanted that? Wanted your uncle and mother to know you were plotting against them?"

Pine Drop's expression slacked with understanding. "Snakes, then it's true?"

"Answer me," Salamander insisted.

"No." Night Rain's voice sounded small.

He ignored Pine Drop, holding Night Rain's gaze. "He was playing with you like a toy on a cord. You are meaningless to him. A tool to be used. No more than a stone dart point. Once you lost your edge, he would have discarded you."

"No!" Night Rain blurted hotly. "He would make me Clan Elder!" Realizing what she had just admitted, she stared aghast at Pine Drop.

"I don't believe what I'm hearing." Pine Drop shook her head.

"You could only be Clan Elder if Alligator Clan could

dominate Snapping Turtle Clan," Salamander replied gently. "Think, Night Rain. They have been trying to get rid of me as Speaker for moons now, but I still speak for my clan. It isn't as easy as Deep Hunter led you to believe. The clans won't allow outsiders to meddle in their business."

"Who cares about Owl Clan? It's broken," Night Rain shot back.

"Night Rain, Saw Back tried to kill Anhinga. That's true, isn't it?" Salamander asked.

Pine Drop looked sick to her stomach as she settled back on the bedding.

Night Rain tucked her arms into her lap and leaned forward. "He didn't even have a weapon! He didn't see her axe. The camp bitch hid it behind her."

He turned to Anhinga. "Couldn't you have just walked away, ignored them?"

"Maybe you could have done something like that." Then, sensing his distress, she added in a softer voice. "He mocked me with the bones of my dead friends. He would have come after me. I could see it in his eyes."

He nodded, wondering what he would have done. Walked away probably to bide his time. It just wasn't in Anhinga's souls to react that way. He raised his eyes. "Pine Drop?"

"She is my sister." The words were wooden, pained.

"She's my wife." He lowered himself to the bench, using fingertips to massage his temples. "I remember an evening in your house when you cautioned her about behaving with responsibility. Since then she has given Deep Hunter and his warriors both her body and your clan's private dealings. I would imagine she heard a great many things discussed at Elder Sweet Root's fire."

"This is how a wife behaves? She *humiliates* us!" Anhinga cried.

"That is enough!" Salamander shot her a cautionary look. "Indignation is like sassafras root, Anhinga. Use too much of it, and the pot turns bitter." He rubbed his hands together. "The question remains: What should we do about this?"

"I *hate* you," Night Rain managed through clenched teeth. "All of you!"

Pine Drop's lips hardened. "You hate me, too?"

Night Rain nodded, lip twitching. "No one shamed you when you were bedding Three Stomachs."

Pine Drop paled.

Anhinga lifted an eyebrow. "Ah, now we see how deeply the rot runs."

"Enough!" Salamander avoided Pine Drop's stricken eyes. "What is past cannot be undone. I know of no one in this room who has not made mistakes." Going from Anhinga to Pine Drop to Night Rain, he met their eyes. "So let us start anew tonight. We have all done terrible things to each other, and to ourselves."

"I have to tell Speaker Mud Stalker," Pine Drop said listlessly. "This goes beyond this household. It's clan business."

"No!" Night Rain cried, looking stricken. "You can't tell the Speaker. He'll beat me! Cast me out! Send me off into exile!"

"You *betrayed* us!" Pine Drop cried. "Betrayed *me!*"

"Uncle arranged it! Just like he did with you and Three Stomachs!" Night Rain began to leak tears again.

"But I didn't tell him clan secrets while I..." Pine Drop winced, shaking her head. "By the Sky Beings, never mind. Our husband is right, what's done is done and can't be undone."

"There is a way for us to solve this, Night Rain," Salamander spoke wearily.

"I hope leeches drink your blood," she mumbled.

"Sister!" Pine Drop warned. "I will not hear you speak that way."

"You and your ways," Night Rain muttered. "You make me sick! So proper and correct. Over what? Him? He's a fool, Sister. You're married to a fool, carrying *his* fool child! You're a laughingstock!" She glanced up at Salamander. "And you? Are you a warrior? I see no tattoos. You are a coward. You send your barbarian bitch to do your fighting for you!"

Pine Drop paled, a hand against one of the support poles. Anhinga smiled like a fox over a nest of hatchlings. At a word, she'd have been happy to help Pine Drop thrash Night Rain into pulp.

"Your sister is a fool?" Salamander managed a bitter smile. "Strong words, Night Rain, for a woman who was marched naked through the middle of town after being routed away from her lover. Do not talk to me of fools."

"What did he promise you?" Pine Drop asked. "What did Deep Hunter say would be yours?"

"He told her that you would never be Clan Elder," Salamander supplied for her. "That's what Deep Hunter promised her. That, and Saw Back, and prestige, and status, and who knows what else. She's not as smart as you are, Wife."

"Indeed?" Night Rain asked smugly. "We'll see who's smart in the end."

"If you were," Pine Drop said wearily, "you would

know Deep Hunter is through with you. Disgraced and embarrassed, you can't serve him. Uncle is suspicious now—if he hasn't already figured it out like I told him. So is Mother. They will never speak freely in your presence. You'll be watched like a mouse in a jar. Despite the pleas of our husband, I am still tempted to tell Uncle and Mother the extent of what you've done. If I do, you *will* be destroyed, Sister."

For the first time fear glazed Night Rain's eyes.

"There is a way out, Night Rain," Salamander said carefully.

"What?" Pine Drop demanded. "Hold this over her so that she can become Owl Clan's pawn?"

"No. I would not do that. She is my wife, as you are. As Anhinga is." He paused. "Night Rain, everyone in Sun Town has heard about you. From the moment you walk out of this house, every eye is going to be on you. There are probably thirty people within a stone's throw of this house right now, their ears pricked like a dog's to hear the row."

"I could step outside," Anhinga suggested and tapped her axe. "I'll bet they'd scurry away like wood rats in a cane patch."

"Night Rain," Salamander continued, "if we forget what you've done, will you act like a proper wife?"

"Just forget?" Pine Drop asked in wonder. "Like you just said, every tongue is going to be wagging! And it's clear that she's been working with Deep Hunter!"

Salamander nodded soberly. "If she can see this thing through, learn from her shame, I would suggest that you not tell your Clan Elder, or your Speaker, about her transgressions."

Anhinga interjected, "You will be considered a fool, Salamander. People will look at you and whisper behind their hands, saying, 'Look, there's Speaker Salamander! He took his wife back after his barbarian brought her home still steaming with another man's sweat!'"

"They will, Salamander," Pine Drop agreed.

He shrugged. "I am used to it. Night Rain isn't." He took a deep breath. "Let us be honest, Wives. A great many forces are building against me. Alliances are being made in dark places, all seeking eventually to destroy me. We must ensure that the rest of you can go home and restart your lives."

Night Rain looked as if sunshine had penetrated a cloud. Pine Drop and Anhinga both looked uncomfortable. He closed his eyes for a moment, wishing the headache would pass. When he reopened them, his little world hadn't changed.

Pine Drop relented. "Night Rain, do you think you can do this? Act like a wife should to Salamander?"

She nodded.

"What if Saw Back planted a child in her?" Anhinga asked, shooting a hard glare at Night Rain.

Salamander shrugged. "That is Snapping Turtle Clan's concern, not mine. Like your people, the child belongs to the mother's clan."

Pine Drop filled her lungs and exhaled a roomful of tension. "Very well, Sister, let's take you home and clean you up."

"No." Salamander gave a brief shake of his head. "We all sleep here tonight."

All eyes turned to him, expressions ranging from

Anhinga's arched eyebrow to Night Rain's sudden horror.

He pointed at the door. "A small crowd is loitering out there in the cold. It would do them good to wait, to watch the fire's glow grow dim around the roof. Some can't wait to rush back to their clans with fresh gossip."

"Very well, for tonight," Pine Drop agreed.

"And periodically after that," Salamander amended. "If we are to survive this, we must do so together. From now on we are going to be a household."

"Yes, yes, we are agreed." Pine Drop looked at her sister, then at the crackling fire, and added with a wary chuckle, "Fortunately, someone carried in a good supply of firewood."

Anhinga smiled ironically at Night Rain.

Salamander's own smile was false, a mask to relieve his wives. His thoughts turned to Saw Back. The side of his face was crushed. He would be clawing at the walls for revenge.

Water trickled in the close darkness to explode into hissing, spitting founts of steam. Bobcat retracted the thin-walled stone bowl. The hot rocks sizzled, and invisible rolls of wet heat rose around Salamander's body. He opened his mouth, gasping, feeling the steam eat at the insides of his nostrils and his throat.

"Is that better?" Bobcat asked, his form barely visible in the red glow of the hot stones.

"Better," Salamander agreed. He used his fingers to slick sweat from his forehead, eyebrows, and nose.

The close darkness inside the sweat lodge cupped around him like hands, the rounded roof close over his head. It pressed the stinging heat into his skin, threading it through his muscles, blending it with the blood in his veins.

"You need to be cleansed every so often, Speaker." Bobcat shifted in the darkness. "Water can only wash the outside of your skin, but steaming cleanses not only the whole of the body, but the souls as well. It maintains a purity of the blood, a balance of the organs. These things go back to the beginning of the world, to a time when First Woman used fire and water to cleanse herself."

"First Woman?" Salamander smiled, feeling water dripping from his chin to spatter on the folds of his stomach.

The tops of his thighs prickled, his sides burned, and only by rubbing his hands along the outsides of his arms could he stand the steam's bite.

"So many stories are told about her," Bobcat replied. "One of the things I have learned, talking to the Traders who come from all over the world, is that they have stories about the Hero Twins, and about First Woman. About how she was there at the Creation."

"I know little about her."

Bobcat rubbed the sweat from his arms. "It is said that she lives in a cave at the center of the world. It is said that her essence is released in steam. That she was the first to teach the values of hot water to the People. She was the First Dreamer, the one who taught Wolf Dreamer the way to the One."

"Do you believe that?" Salamander asked, thinking about all the stories he had heard about First Woman.

"Do you really think she lives in a cave at the center of the Earth, and that a huge tree grows out of the cave's mouth?"

Bobcat shrugged. "I don't know, my friend. She is reclusive. Few Dreamers, Serpents, or Soul Flyers see her. It is said that while the brothers and the lesser Spirit Helpers often interact in the world of men, she prefers her cave, her Dreams slipping in and out of the One, while she mourns a long-lost love. It is said that even the Hero Twins and Sky Beings defer to her. That she is the heartbeat of the One."

"She must be very Powerful."

"I would not want to be the individual who disturbed her Dreams, I'll tell you." Bobcat shivered.

After a moment, Salamander asked, "How is the Serpent?"

"Not well. I do not know what to do for him. I have had him here, day after day. In an effort to prolong his life I have been feeding him a diet of snake meat."

"Snake meat?"

"Have you ever seen a snake that died from old age, Salamander? Snakes live forever, or until something eats them, be it a man, an eagle, a raccoon, or a weasel. Power lies in their meat."

"But it isn't helping?"

"No, my friend." Bobcat sounded weary.

"I cannot prove this, but I think that men like the Serpent hear Dream Souls, Bobcat. I think the Dead talk to them, call to them, and the Dream Soul begins to long to talk back. Think about it. So many of the Serpent's friends are dead. Perhaps he longs to join them."

313

"Perhaps. But I do not think so in his case. Have you felt the lump in his belly?"

"No."

"It is something evil, some vicious spirit that is growing inside him, eating away at his life."

"You're sure you can't kill it?"

"No, and neither can he. Snakes know, we've tried everything."

"I am sorry to hear that. He has always been good to me."

Bobcat was silent for a time. "The Serpent picks few people for his close association. He is fond of you."

"As I am of him."

"I know. It is a rare thing for him to show that kind of affection, therefore, I will have you know that I extend my own friendship, no matter what the future brings."

Salamander smiled wistfully as droplets of sweat tickled on his face. "You may wish to reconsider, Bobcat. I am caught between Masked Owl and Many Colored Crow. I don't understand my destiny yet, but I fear it will not be pleasant. Those who stand close to me should fear the lightning."

"As your brother did?"

"As my brother should have."

Salamander stared sadly at the faint glow of the hot rocks. They lay like giant red eggs in the shallow pit—cobbles imported from the source of the White Mud River. A hot fire of white ash had been burned around them for several hands of time. The heat rolling off the stones curled his skin when he reached out.

"You should know that Deep Hunter is enraged." Bobcat's voice caressed the darkness. "His nephew's face is ruined. I have done what I can for Saw Back. He will be marked for the rest of his life, and his sight is blurry in the left eye."

"You should not tell me these things. When you become the Serpent, you must favor no one."

"I have learned something from the Serpent that you have not. I must favor those who are favored by Power," he replied. "I know the responsibilities of the Serpent. I will not abuse them, Speaker. Not for you, or for anyone. But being the Serpent doesn't mean that I can't help those I think work for the common good."

Salamander steepled his fingers. "Do you think that of me?"

"I do."

"I am not so sure, Bobcat. Trouble is brewing around me like a pot of black drink. Sometimes I think it would be best if I simply left, went down to the Owl Clan holdings at Twin Circles on the gulf, or over to Yellow Mud Camp, or one of the outlying camps, and lived out my life."

"You can't, Salamander. You have responsibilities." Bobcat trickled another finger of water onto the rocks. Steam popped and billowed, the cloud suffocating in the close confines of the lodge.

Salamander leaned his head back, mouth open, and let the steam drive needles into his flesh. His skin might have been blistering, splitting from the muscle beneath. He coughed when he inhaled, and the damp fire stung his throat.

"Someone wants to kill your wife," Bobcat said softly.

"I know."

"He says she is a witch, come to kill us all. He says

she was the prisoner White Bird brought back from the Swamp Panther raid at Ground Cherry Camp."

"She was."

"He says that malevolent spirits freed her in the middle of the night."

"No malevolent spirits freed her. It wasn't magic, or anything nearly as frightening," Salamander said wearily. "I did, Bobcat. I cut her loose that night."

"Why?" An incredulous tone filled the young man's voice.

"Masked Owl told me to. He came to me in a Dream, when we were flying, and told me she would be important."

"Then she's not dangerous?"

"Oh, no, Bobcat, she is *very* dangerous. Perhaps the most dangerous person in Sun Town."

"If that is so, why do you keep her? Why don't you cast her out, send her back to the Swamp Panthers and let them suck on her poison?"

"I don't know."

"That's a crazy answer."

"Perhaps, but she's part of Masked Owl's plan. I just don't know what it is yet."

"Be very, very careful. She made a great many enemies when she wounded Saw Back." Bobcat hesitated. "I don't know how to tell you this, but I have heard that someone is following her. I have not heard who, but word is that she is stalked every time she leaves Sun Town."

Salamander took a deep breath. "I shall be careful, Bobcat. Not only is she part of Masked Owl's plan, but she carries my child within her. She is my wife. I will take care of her."

"Even if she destroys you in the process?"

"I think I will have warning before she does."

"You *think?* That doesn't sound very promising."

"No." He smiled. "I suppose not."

"Beware, Speaker Salamander. Your enemies are growing stronger by the heartbeat."

# A look At Book Three:
## The Poisoned Bride

*New York Times* **bestselling authors W. Michael Gear and Kathleen O'Neal Gear deliver an epic saga of power, betrayal, and survival in Ancient America.**

At the center of this epic story is Salamander, a man caught in a complex web of betrayal and intrigue as rival clans vie for dominance. As tensions rise between the Snapping Turtle, Alligator, and Frog Clans, Salamander must tread carefully, navigating the dangerous waters of political alliances, and fending off enemies that grow more powerful by the day. Questions about his loyalty and even his sanity begin to swirl, with some wondering whether he's still in his right mind.

But Salamander is not alone. By his side are his devoted wives, Anhinga and Pine Drop, and a mysterious Spirit Helper. Together, they face Mud Stalker, whose ambitions threaten to spark a war that could destroy everything. Accusations of witchcraft and the disappearance of Eats Wood only worsen the turmoil.

As the threads of fate tighten, Anhinga sees an opportunity to strike back at her enemies—the hated Sun People—setting in motion a series of events that could either free them all or lead to their utter destruction. Faced with impossible choices, Salamander must decide whether to pursue his own happiness and freedom or make the ultimate sacrifice to protect his people.

Rich in historical detail and brimming with complex characters, *The Poison Bride* is an unforgettable story of power, betrayal, and the enduring strength of the human spirit.

# About W. Michael Gear

**W. Michael Gear** is a *New York Times, USA Today,* and international bestselling author of sixty novels. With close to eighteen million copies of his books in print worldwide, his work has been translated into twenty-nine languages.

Gear has been inducted into the Western Writers Hall of Fame and the Colorado Authors' Hall of Fame —as well as won the Owen Wister Award, the Golden Spur Award, and the International Book Award for both Science Fiction and Action Suspense Fiction. He is also the recipient of the Frank Waters Award for life-time contributions to Western writing.

Gear's work, inspired by anthropology and archae-ology, is multilayered and has been called compelling, insidiously realistic, and masterful. Currently, he lives in northwestern Wyoming with his award-winning wife and co-author, Kathleen O'Neal Gear, and a charming sheltie named, Jake.

# About Kathleen O'Neal Gear

**Kathleen O'Neal Gear** is a *New York Times* bestselling author of fifty-seven books and a national award-winning archaeologist. The U.S. Department of the Interior has awarded her two Special Achievement awards for outstanding management of America's cultural resources.

In 2015 the United States Congress honored her with a Certificate of Special Congressional Recognition, and the California State Legislature passed Joint Member Resolution #117 saying, "The contributions of Kathleen O'Neal Gear to the fields of history, archaeology, and writing have been invaluable..."

In 2021 she received the Owen Wister Award for lifetime contributions to western literature, and in 2023 received the Frank Waters Award for "a body of work representing excellence in writing and storytelling that embodies the spirit of the American West."

# Bibliography

Alden, Peter. 1999. *National Audubon Society Field Guild to the Southeastern States.* Alfred A. Knopf. New York, New York.

Amos, William H., and Stephen H. Amos. 1985. *The Audubon Society Nature Guides Atlantic & Gulf Coasts.* Alfred A. Knopf. New York, New York.

Brecher, K. S., and W. G. Haag. 1980. "The Poverty Point Octagon: World's Largest Prehistoric Solstice Marker?" *Bulletin of the American Astronomical Society.* 12:886.

Brian, Jeffrey P. 1988. *Tunica Archaeology.* Papers of the Peabody Museum of Archaeology and Ethnology No. 78. Harvard University Press. Cambridge, Massachusetts.

Brown, Calvin S. 1992. *Archaeology of Mississippi.* Reprint of 1926 edition. University Press of Mississippi. Jackson, Mississippi.

Bruseth J. E. 1980. "Intrasite Structure at the Clairborne Site." *Louisiana Archaeology.* 6:283-318.

Byrd, Kathleen M. 1991. *The Poverty Point Culture: Local Manifestations, Subsistence Practices, and Trade Networks.* Geoscience and Man 29. Louisiana State University Press. Baton Rouge, Louisiana.

Coffey, Timothy. 1993. *The History and Folklore of North American Wild-flowers.* Facts on File. New York, New York.

Connaway, John M., Samuel O. McGahey, and Clarence Webb. 1977. *Teoc Creek, a Poverty Point Site in Carroll County, Mississippi.* Archaeological Report No. 3. Mississippi Department of Archives and History. Jackson, Mississippi.

Duncan, Wilbur H. and Marion B. Duncan. 1988. *Trees of the Southeastern United States.* University of Georgia Press. Athens, Georgia.

Fagan, Brian M. 2000. *Ancient North America,* 3rd ed. Thames and Hudson. New York, New York.

Foster, Steven, and James A. Duke. 1990. *Eastern/Central Medicinal Plants.* Peterson Field Guides. Houghton Mifflin Company. Boston, Massachusetts.

Fritz, Gayle J. 1997. "A Three-Thousand-Year-Old Cache of Crop Seeds from Marble Bluff, Arkansas." In *People, Plants, and Land-*

# Bibliography

*scapes: Studies in Paleoethnobotany,* edited by Kristen J. Gremillion, pp. 42-62. University of Alabama Press. Tuscaloosa, Alabama.

Gibson, John L. 1980. "Speculations on the Origin and Development of Poverty Point Culture." *Louisiana Archaeology.* 6: 319-348.

--. 1987. "The Poverty Point Earthworks Reconsidered." *Mississippi Archaeology.* 22(2): 14—31.

--. 1991. "Catahoula—An Amphibious Poverty Point Manifestation in Eastern Louisiana." In *The Poverty Point Culture: Local Manifestations, Subsistence Practices, and Trade Networks,* edited by Kathleen M. Byrd, pp. 61-88. Geoscience and Man No. 29. Louisiana State University Press. Baton Rouge, Louisiana.

--. 1996. "Religion of the Rings: Poverty Point Iconography and Ceremonialism." In *Mounds, Embankments, and Ceremonialism in the Midsouth,* edited by R. C. Main-fort and R. Wailing, pp. 1-6. Arkansas Archaeological Survey Research Series No. 46. Arkansas Archaeological Survey. Fayetteville, Arkansas.

--. 1998. "Broken Circles, Owl Monsters, and Black Earth Midden: Separating Sacred and Secular at Poverty Point." In *Ancient Earthen Enclosures of the Eastern Woodlands,* edited by R. C. Mainfort and L. P. Sullivan. University Press of Florida. Gainesville, Florida.

--. 1999. *Poverty Point: A Terminal Archaic Culture in the Lower Mississippi Valley.* 2nd ed. Anthropological Study 7. Department of Culture, Recreation, and Tourism. Louisiana Archaeological Survey and Antiquities Commission. Baton Rouge, Louisiana.

--. 2000. *The Ancient Mounds of Poverty Point: Place of Rings.* University Press of Florida. Gainesville, Florida.

Gibson, J. L., and J. W. Saunders. 1993. "The Death of the South Sixth Ridge at Poverty Point: What Can We Still Do?" *SAA Bulletin.* 11(5): 7-9.

Haag, W. G. 1990. "Excavations at the Poverty Point Site: 1972-1975." *Louisiana Archaeology.* 13:1-36.

Hillman, M. M. 1990. "1985 Test Excavations of the *Dock* Area of Poverty Point." *Louisiana Archaeology.* 13:1-33.

Hirth, K. G. 1978 "Interregional Trade and the Formation of Prehistoric Gateway Communities." *American Antiquity.* 43(l):35-45.

Hudson, Charles. 1976. *The Southeastern Indians.* University of Tennessee Press. Knoxville, Tennessee.

--. 1979. *Black Drink: A Native American Tea.* University of Georgia Press. Athens, Georgia.

# Bibliography

Jackson, H. E.. 1991. "Bottomland Resources and Exploitation Strategies During the Poverty Point Period: Implications of the Archaeological Record from the J. W. Copes Site." In *The Poverty Point Culture: Local Manifestations, Subsistence Practices, and Trade Networks,* edited by Kathleen M. Byrd, pp. 131-158. Geoscience and Man 29. Louisiana State University Press. Baton Rouge, Louisiana.

--. 1991. "The Trade Fair in Hunter-Gatherer Interactions: The Role of Intersocietal Trade in the Evolution of Poverty Point Culture." In *Between Bands and States,* edited by S. A. Greg, pp. 265-286. Occasional Papers 9. Center for Archaeological Investigations, Southern Illinois University at Carbondale. Carbondale, Illinois.

Kidder, Tristram. 2002. "Mapping Poverty Point." *American Antiquity.* 67: 89-101.

Lazarus, W. C. 1958. "A Poverty Point Complex in Florida." *Florida Anthropologist.* 6(1):23-32.

Mainfort, Robert C, and L. P. Sullivan. 1998 *Ancient Earthen Enclosures of the Eastern Woodlands.* University Press of Florida. Gainesville, Florida.

McEwan, Bonnie G. 2000. *Indians of the Greater Southeast.* University Press of Florida. Gainesville, Florida.

Morgan, William N. 1999. *Precolumbian Architecture in Eastern North America.* University Press of Florida. Gainesville, Florida.

Neuman, R. W., and N. W. Hawkins. 1987. *Louisiana Prehistory.* Department of Culture, Recreation, and Tourism. Louisiana Archaeological Survey and Antiquities Commission. Anthropological Study 6, 2nd ed., revised. Baton Rouge, Louisiana.

Pearson, James L. 2002. *Shamanism and the Ancient Mind.* Altamira Press. Walnut Creek, California.

Penman, John T. 1980. *Archaeological Survey in Mississippi, 1974—1975.* Archaeological Report No. 2. Mississippi Department of Archives and History. Jackson, Mississippi.

Purrington, R. D. 1983. "Superimposed Solar Alignments at Poverty Point." *American Antiquity.* 48:157-161.

Purrington, R. D., and C. A. Child, Jr. 1989. "Poverty Point Revisited: Further Consideration of Astronomical Alignments." *Journal of the History of Astronomy.* 13: 49-60.

Sassaman, Kenneth E. 1993. *Early Pottery in the Southeast.* University of Alabama Press. Tuscaloosa, Alabama.

Schlotz, Sandra C. 1975. *Prehistoric Plies: A Structural and Comparative Analysis of Cordage, Netting, Basketry, and Fabric from*

# Bibliography

*Ozark Bluff Shelters.* Arkansas Archaeological Survey No. 6. Arkansas Archaeological Survey. Fayette Ville, Arkansas.

Smith, Brent W. 1974. "A Preliminary Identification of Faunal Remains from the Clairborne Site." *Mississippi Archaeology.* 9: 1-7.

--. 1976. "The Late Archaic-Poverty Point Steatite Trade Network in the Lower Mississippi Valley." *Louisiana Archaeological Society Newsletter.* 3:6-10.

--. 1981. "The Late Archaic-Poverty Point Steatite Trade Network in the Lower Mississippi Valley: Some Preliminary Observations." *Florida Anthropologist.* 34: 120-125.

Smith, Bruce D. 1992. *Rivers of Change: Essays on Early Agriculture in Eastern North America.* Smithsonian Institution Press. Washington, DC.

Swanton, John R. 1979. *The Indians of the Southeastern United States.* Reprint of the 1946 Bureau of American Ethnography Bulletin No. 137. Smithsonian Institution Press. Washington, DC.

--. 1998. *Indian Tribes of the Lower Mississippi Valley and Adjacent Coast of the Gulf of Mexico.* Dover reprint of 1911 edition. Dover Publications. Mineola, New York.

--. 2001. *Source Material for the Social and Ceremonial Life of the Choctaw Indians.* University of Alabama Press. Tuscaloosa, Alabama.

Thomas, Cyrus. 1985. *Report on the Mound Expeditions of the Bureau of Ethnography.* Reprint of the 1894 Bureau of American Ethnography No. 12. Smithsonian Institution Press. Washington, DC.

Thomas, Prentice M., and L. J. Campbell. 1978. *The Peripheries of Poverty Point.* New World Research Report of Investigation No. 12. New World Research. Pollack, Louisiana.

Tiamat, Uni M. 1994. *Herbal Abortion Handbook.* Sage-femme! Press. Peoria, Illinois.

Vogel, Virgil H.. 1970. *American Indian Medicine.* University of Oklahoma Press. Norman, Oklahoma.

Webb, Clarence H. 1968. "The Extent and Content of Poverty Point Culture." *American Antiquity.* 33:297-321.

Webb, Clarence H., and J. L. Gibson. 1982. "Studies of the Microflint Industry at the Poverty Point Site." In *Traces of Prehistory: Papers in Honor of William G. Haag,* edited by F. H. West and R. W. Neuman, pp. 85-101. Geoscience and Man 22. School of Geoscience. Louisiana State University Press. Baton Rouge, Louisiana.

--. 1970. "Intrasite Distribution of Artifacts at the Poverty Point Site, with Special Reference to Women's and Men's Activities." *Southeastern Archaeological Conference Bulletin.* 12:21-34.

--. 1982. *The Poverty Point Culture.* Geoscience and Man 17. 2nd ed., revised. Geoscience Publications, Department of Geography and Anthropology. Louisiana State University Press. Baton Rouge, Louisiana.